D0919151

MURDER ON THE HOME FRONT

Also by Jessica Ellicott

The Beryl and Edwina mysteries

MURDER IN AN ENGLISH VILLAGE
MURDER FLIES THE COOP
MURDER CUTS THE MUSTARD
MURDER COMES TO CALL
MURDER IN AN ENGLISH GLADE
MURDER THROUGH THE ENGLISH POST
MURDER AT A LONDON FINISHING SCHOOL

The WPC Billie Harkness mysteries

DEATH IN A BLACKOUT *

* *available from Severn House*

MURDER ON THE HOME FRONT

Jessica Ellicott

**SEVERN
HOUSE**

First world edition published in Great Britain and the USA in 2023
by Severn House, an imprint of Canongate Books Ltd,
14 High Street, Edinburgh EH1 1TE.

Trade paperback edition first published in Great Britain and the USA in 2023
by Severn House, an imprint of Canongate Books Ltd.

severnhouse.com

Copyright © Quirke and Carlisle, LLC, 2023

All rights reserved including the right of
reproduction in whole or in part in any form.
The right of Jessica Ellicott to be identified
as the author of this work has been asserted
in accordance with the Copyright,
Designs & Patents Act 1988.

British Library Cataloguing-in-Publication Data
A CIP catalogue record for this title is available from the British Library.

ISBN-13: 978-1-4483-0653-4 (cased)
ISBN-13: 978-1-4483-0661-9 (trade paper)
ISBN-13: 978-1-4483-0660-2 (e-book)

This is a work of fiction. Names, characters, places and incidents
are either the product of the author's imagination or are used fictitiously.
Except where actual historical events and characters are being described
for the storyline of this novel, all situations in this publication are
fictitious and any resemblance to actual persons, living or dead,
business establishments, events or locales is purely coincidental.

All Severn House titles are printed on acid-free paper.

Typeset by Palimpsest Book Production Ltd.,
Falkirk, Stirlingshire, Scotland.
Printed and bound in Great Britain by
TJ Books, Padstow, Cornwall.

ONE
July 1940

Dear Father,

How strange it is to keep sending letters off to you without any notion of whether or not you have received the previous ones. I am torn between simply plunging on ahead as if you are up to date with all my news or writing as if there are great gaps in the story. This time round I will assume that you at least know of my relocation to Hull.

I am settled in quite comfortably with Cousin Lydia. She is far better to me than I could possibly deserve and although the city still feels like a foreign country, I have had to learn my way around in the course of my job . . .

Billie leaned away from the small writing desk tucked into the corner of the sitting room and laid down her pen. She did not wish to worry her father with her own minor troubles. He had enough troubles of his own, stuck as he was in a German POW camp. The truth was that while her cousin Lydia had made her feel very welcome in her home and in her circle, Billie had yet to make any real friends of her own.

Back in Barton St Giles she had never wanted for friends or companions, or family for that matter. Before he had volunteered to serve as a chaplain for the troops, her father's position as rector had made her family an integral part of village life and there had been no shortage of playmates or events to fill the hours and days of her childhood. Such was not the case in the city of Hull.

It was rare that she found herself with a morning off from her post. In the village she would have been grateful for a few free hours, especially since her mother surely would have found ways for her to fill them if they had chanced to appear. When her cousin Lydia invited her to make her home in the northern city of Hull after her mother's death, she gratefully accepted. Billie could never think of her mother without experiencing a raw sting of grief. Her death was still too recent for the sorrow to have transformed into a scarred-over ache. In an effort to distract herself, she spent most of her hours off with Lydia.

But today, her shift was to start in the early afternoon and she found herself alone with nothing planned and no one to plan it with. The sound of the sleek, chrome clock perched on the mantle ticking off the minutes filled Billie's ears in the silence of the house. Lydia had set off for her job at the Central Library leaving Billie facing the undeniable fact that she felt a bit lonely and adrift. Some of the newness of her circumstances had worn off and the realities of making a new life for herself were becoming more apparent by the day.

Still, there was no profit in sitting around feeling sorry for herself; she was far too much her mother's daughter for that sort of self-indulgence. She pushed back her chair and tucked the letter away unfinished into one of the pigeonholes in the desk and raised the drop front back into place.

When she was a girl, she would have given just about anything to spend a morning roaming about in a large city. There was nothing to stop her from doing so now, and better still, she had all the money from her pay packet since Lydia refused to accept her offer to help out with the household expenses. But her cousin had not forbidden her to purchase a gift for her by way of thanks.

In no time at all Billie had slipped out of her nightwear and into street clothes. She added her WPC's uniform to her shopping bag so that she could head straight to the station after her outing. If she hurried, she would be sure to find something to express her gratitude and still make it to work with time to spare.

The crowd surrounding her surged forward and swept her along beside them. Billie stepped off the curb and crossed the broad avenue into Paragon Square. A memorial statue sat at the center but the structure that caught her attention was Hammonds department store, on the corner. It ascended three stories into the Hull skyline, topped by a dome reminiscent of the one crowning the city hall. Throngs of shoppers streamed past the oversized display windows and in and out of the store's plate-glass doors.

Everything about the place seemed outsized to her as she approached the two towering columns flanking the entrance. She suddenly wished she were wearing her uniform rather than the pale-yellow frock she had chosen for her outing. It was another of her cousin Lydia's things that she had been encouraged to borrow, and while she thought it suited her well enough, she felt much more capable of facing the city with an adventurous spirit when clad in uniform.

As she stepped into the cool interior of the store, she hardly knew where to look first. It was unlike anything she had ever experienced back in Barton St Giles. Tables heaped high with yard goods for sewing one's own clothing tempted her from the right. A jewelry counter glittered off to the left. Haberdashery and household goods were listed on large placards indicating they could be found on upper floors. One of the things that surprised Billie the most about moving to a large city were the available outlets for shopping. Even though much was made in the local newspaper about shortages and long queues, Billie could not help but to be impressed by just how much the average resident of the city could obtain.

As much as she wished to feel at ease and at home in such an upscale establishment, she couldn't shake the sense that she would easily be outed as nothing more than a country rector's daughter. While Lydia had done her best to help Billie to figure out the most flattering way to dress her hair or which frocks most suited her figure, it all still felt a bit like she was playing dress-up. The only thing she truly had felt at ease in, as if it suited her down to the bones, was her new police constable's uniform.

She could not imagine what had possessed her to head into the store on her own. Perhaps she had wanted to prove to herself that she was up to such a small-scale adventure. After all, if she had spent the last several weeks facing down criminals on the streets of Hull, surely she could not be intimi-dated by the purchase of a new lipstick. Besides, she did not feel right about constantly helping herself to Lydia's things no matter how generous her cousin might be.

But she refused to be daunted. Billie had set off with a particular errand in mind. She had determined that it was high time she purchase some cosmetics of her own as well as a tube of lipstick for Lydia. While her cousin had kindly shared both her wardrobe and her beauty products, Billie felt it was time to stand on her own two feet. Although Lydia had insisted that she had more than enough for two, Billie had not felt right about using up things that might soon become in short supply.

And indeed, it seemed her fears might be justified. As she looked at a large crowd gathered round the cosmetics counter, her heart gave a lurch. Would everything be sold out before she was able to make her own purchase? Lipstick was some-thing that had not gone on the ration, but with a sudden threat of increased taxation on it as a luxury good, there had been a run on supply before the new regulations could go into effect.

Billie took a step towards the counter, hovering uncertainly near the back of the crowd of women, young and old alike. Salesgirls smiled and answered a flurry of questions from those customers pressed up against the glass cases.

She felt pushed off balance and turned her head to see where the danger had come from. Standing at her side with an apolo-getic look on her face was a young woman of about her own age, a smattering of cinnamon-colored freckles dusting her nose.

'I'm so sorry. What a crush,' the young woman said.

'It's all right. The crowd is rather surprising,' Billie said. 'I wouldn't have thought there would be so many women here at this time of day.'

The other woman shrugged. 'I suppose that I had thought it might be quieter too. I just dashed out for a quick break, but I don't know that I'm going to manage to be served before I have to get back to the office.'

'I suppose I'm fortunate that it's my morning off,' Billie said. 'Otherwise, I don't know that I would have any luck either.'

'You still might not. They may be sold out before either of us gets to the front of the queue,' the woman said. 'What do you do for work?'

Billie still could not quite believe what she was going to say. It had come as such a surprise to be recruited for the constabulary and even a few weeks into her new role it still seemed unreal, as if it might be snatched away at any moment.

'I work for the constabulary,' she said.

The woman raised a sandy-colored eyebrow. 'Are you a receptionist or a woman who serves in the canteen?' she asked.

Billie shook her head. 'Neither. I'm a WPC.'

The woman's second eyebrow shot upwards. 'A WPC. I had heard that the city council had voted to allow women to serve in the constabulary, but I hadn't had the pleasure of meeting one. Perhaps I should've committed a crime in order to do so,' she said giving Billie a broad smile complete with deep dimples. 'It sounds like a fascinating job.'

'I'm not sure that it's fascinating, but I do love it. And I'm not surprised that you haven't run into any other WPCs. So far there are only two of us,' Billie said.

'Only two?' she asked.

'For now, at least. We have openings for two additional female constables, but the positions have not yet been filled. And as for receptionists or canteen workers, we haven't any of those either. Different officers take turns at the front desk since most people want to speak with someone on the force.'

'That sounds like it might be challenging,' the woman said. 'It must be difficult to make friends if you're entirely surrounded by men.'

Billie wasn't quite sure how to answer. While what the woman standing next to her said was true, Billie was loath to cast the constabulary in a dim light. While her frequent partner, Constable Peter Upton, was always willing to go out of the way to mentor her and to do so in a remarkably pleasant manner, she wouldn't exactly classify him as a personal friend. In fact, other than her cousin Lydia, she had not really made many social contacts since she had arrived in Kingston upon Hull. The other woman's observation gave words to a feeling that had been rumbling through her mind all morning. While she

cherished the letters that she received from friends and acquaintances from back in Barton St Giles, if she were to be honest
with herself, she had been feeling ever so slightly lonely.

Even if she had not moved, so many voids had been created
on account of the war. Her lifelong friend Candace had joined
up and shipped out shortly before Billie had left the village
herself. Her mother's death and the fact that her father and
brother had been called away by the war left gaping holes in
her life that had nothing to do with her own relocation. Her
chest felt tight and her pleasure in the shopping trip dimmed
as she thought about how much it would have pleased her to
have Candace there too. Even her mother, who would have
been horrified at the notion of so many women painting their
faces, would have enjoyed perusing the stacks and bolts of
cotton, rayon and wool fabrics on display.

'It will be nice to have more women join the force one day,
but for now I am content with my lot,' Billie said.

The other woman stuck out her hand. 'I'm Trudy Beecham.
And I have a suggestion for you if you don't mind me offering
one.'

Billie thrust her own hand forward and grasped Trudy's.
'Billie Harkness. And no, I don't mind a suggestion.'

'I'm a member of the Women of Work Club and I'd love
for you to come to one of our meetings,' Trudy said.

'I think I've seen something about your organization
mentioned in the newspaper. What is it that you do exactly?'
she asked.

'We meet to discuss topics of interest to working women
such as ourselves. The age range is quite broad, but there are
many women in their twenties, mostly unmarried and looking
to make careers for themselves. I think you'd fit right in.'

Billie felt a lump swelling in her throat. She had not realized how much she would like to fit in somewhere with ease.
Back in Wiltshire as the rector's daughter her role was clearly
defined and while it had not always felt perfectly suited to her
personality and preferences, it gave her a place to belong. As
a WPC, and a new resident of the city, she still wasn't sure
of her niche.

'When do you meet? And where?' Billie asked. She felt a

flutter of excitement as she considered that she might have something to put in her diary that did not involve tagging along with Lydia or her shift with the constabulary.

'One of our meetings is at lunchtime and we hold it in a restaurant. There are several in the city we rotate through in order to spread our trade and not wear out our welcome. The other meeting is held in the evening in a meeting room at the Guildhall. That way members can attend no matter what their schedule is, at least from time to time. Many of us are on shift work in the factories or volunteer as fire watchers, so having options for when and where to meet is a necessity,' Trudy said.

'When is the next meeting?' Billie asked.

'It's tomorrow evening at the Guildhall. Seven p.m. So, will you be there?' Trudy asked.

'As long as I don't get asked to stay late on shift, I should be able to attend. I think my supervising WPC would likely be willing to give me the time off considering she's a working woman herself,' Billie said.

Trudy glanced up at a large clock mounted on the wall. 'My lunch break is going to be up before I ever make it to the front. I'll tell you what. How about if I give you some money for a tube of coral-colored lipstick and you bring it to me at the meeting? That way you'll have to come,' she said snapping open her handbag and removing a pound note. 'This ought to cover it. And any brand will do. I'm not fussy so long as it's somewhere near coral in color.' She pressed the note into Billie's hand and turned to leave.

Billie reached out and touched her arm. 'The Guildhall you say? Seven p.m.?'

'Room 203. I'll see you tomorrow evening,' she said as she waved a gloved hand and slid back through the crowd which closed around her.

It had been a bit of a scrum, but before too long Billie found herself at the front of the queue where a slim, poised woman of about Lydia's age greeted her from behind the gleaming glass counter. She wore a smart looking work smock with a badge announcing that her name was Delia.

'How may I help you today?' Delia asked.

'I would like to buy some lipstick.'

'Why don't you take a seat right here and we'll try out some shades. I'm sure there's something here that will be just exactly right for you.'

The woman gestured to a high stool and she gave Billie such a warm smile and eager expression that she settled herself gingerly on it before she could change her mind. With her handbag clutched tightly on her lap, she felt like a little old lady who had boarded a bus but was not quite certain she approved of the destination.

Delia leaned across the counter and grasped Billie's chin in her hand. 'I see that you're wearing a pale rose shade, but if you don't mind me saying so, with your dark hair and light complexion a bright red would be far more flattering. Besides, it's very fashionable since it is so patriotic. Shall I give it a try?' Delia asked.

Billie nodded. She had used bright red lipsticks from Lydia's large collection, but today had felt as though she wished to be able to blend in just a bit more for her venture into Hammonds.

Delia reached under the counter and selected a tube of scarlet lipstick in a handsome gold-tone case. She swiped the color deftly across Billie's lips and stood back to view her handiwork. 'Rub your lips together just a bit.'

Billie did as she was told and glanced about surreptitiously for a mirror. It was as if someone had deliberately kept them all out of sight. Delia reached beneath the glass case once more and seemed to be set on selecting additional cosmetics.

'That shade flatters you very well, but I'd like to go ahead and do your whole face if you have time,' Delia said. 'It's fine as it is but I think you'll be even more impressed with the results if I add a bit of blusher and some mascara.'

As she could think of no good reason to refuse, Billie nodded and sat stiffly as Delia rubbed a dampened mascara wand back and forth across the inky black cake of eye makeup. She tried not to flinch as the damp, clumpy substance brushed over her eyelashes and clung there heavily. Delia hummed under her breath and Billie could only assume that either she was well pleased with the results of her work on Billie in particular or simply enjoyed her job in general.

'You seem happy with your job,' Billie said. 'Have you been doing it for long?'

'I've been here since before the war broke out. And I am happy at it. I love knowing that I'm helping women to keep up morale here on the home front. Like the advertisements say, beauty is our duty,' she said as she leaned forward once more holding a fluffy brush aloft and touching it lightly to Billie's cheekbones.

Billie was not sure how she felt about the beauty as duty campaign. It seemed to her that there were far more important things to attend to and never enough time to do them. She also wasn't convinced that she should be obligated to look attractive for others. It ran contrary to the admonishment to modesty and to not draw attention to herself that her mother had always espoused.

But as Delia held out a hand mirror for Billie to view herself, she felt a change of heart. While the ordeal with the mascara wand had not been pleasant, there was no denying that her eyes looked brighter and larger with long dark lashes. Her cheeks had taken on a healthy glow under Delia's ministrations with the brush.

But the thing she liked the most was the dramatic Cupid's bow of scarlet lipstick. She felt much less like a country mouse as she stared at her reflection. In fact, she felt quite buoyed up by it. Perhaps that was the point of the beauty as duty campaign. Maybe it wasn't so much about the way it made others feel, but how women who managed to find a bit of time to spend on their own appearance bloomed under such attentions.

'I hardly recognize myself,' Billie said.

'I told you that you'd be impressed,' Delia said. 'Shall I wrap up the lipstick, the blusher and the mascara for you? We have a limited supply, and I am not sure when we will be restocked.'

Billie's heart hammered in her chest as she considered what all of that would cost, especially since she had entered the store with the intention to make purchases for Lydia. She looked in the mirror again and threw caution to the wind. After all, she still had most of the money from all her pay packets.

'Yes, please. While you are at it, I'd like a second shade of red and a tube of coral, too, please,' Billie said, sliding off the stool and snapping open her handbag.

TWO

Even after several weeks on the job Billie still felt a mix of elation and trepidation every time she stood in front of the door to the Central Police Station. Approaching the building in street clothes rather than her uniform required even more effort to assure herself that her position on the force was not a fanciful bit of imagining on her part. She reached for the door handle and stepped inside.

The clock on the wall above the reception desk showed that she had just five minutes to spare before the beginning of her shift. If she hurried, she could be changed into her uniform and ready for duty right on time. She turned down the corridor which led to the constables' cloakrooms. As she approached the closet that had been converted for the use of the two WPCs, the door to the male officers' cloakroom opened and Constable Drummond stepped out.

'Well, what have we here?' he said as he ran his gaze up and down Billie. 'I've never seen you out of uniform.'

Billie felt a rush of heat race up the back of her neck and into her cheeks. The confidence she had felt when she peered at herself in the mirror at Hammonds, and as she strolled along the street to the station, withered under Constable Drummond's scrutiny.

'It was my morning off and I didn't want to run my errands in uniform.' She wasn't sure why she felt as though she needed to make excuses for her appearance, but something in Constable Drummond's tone left her feeling ill at ease.

He took a step closer. 'You should run errands before work more often.' He winked at her before turning to stride back towards the main lobby.

She pushed open the door to the women's cloakroom and locked it behind her. She slipped out of her frock and into her uniform as quickly as possible. As she checked her face in the mirror, she wished she had enough time before the beginning of her shift to tone down the evidence of her visit to the cosmetics counter. Given her propensity to flush it seemed she had not needed a pot of blush to bring color to her cheeks. Still, Sergeant Skelton was a stickler for punctuality, and she doubted he would accept fixing her face as an excuse to be late. He had been in a particularly foul mood all week and she had been doing her best to avoid provoking him.

As she approached the reception desk, the sergeant waved her over. Billie felt a knot gathering in her stomach. It would take more than a few weeks for him to become accustomed to the notion of women serving on the force. In fact, he had made a point to let her know that it was unlikely he would ever become pleased with the idea of women doing men's jobs and that one of the happy outcomes of winning the peace would be sending women back to their traditional roles as wives and mothers.

The scowl on his face did nothing to drive her concerns from her mind. Nevertheless, it would do no good to drag her feet. It would only serve to fuel bad feeling towards her.

'WPC Harkness, I'm putting you on the desk today. It's about time you got to know what it's like to deal with a steady stream of complaints from the public,' he said.

Billie's heart sank. She vastly preferred to be out on the beat doing something she perceived to be far more useful. Staffing the desk didn't feel like police work so much as it felt like being a sort of receptionist. She had never wanted to be someone's secretary or the like and had been pleasantly surprised when she had been allowed to spend so much time out in the field for the police department.

Still, WPC Avis Crane, her superior, had told her that she should be prepared to turn her hand to whatever form of work was required of her. The point of allowing women in the service was to pick up the slack and fill in the holes left by the male officers who had abandoned their jobs in order to join the armed forces. She silently chided herself for her attitude. It was likely that most of the men on the front would have preferred to be doing other jobs as well.

'Certainly, sir. I'm happy to do my best,' Billie said stepping through the swing door that separated the public space from the reception counter.

Sergeant Skelton loomed over her, a towering bulk of a man. He slapped a memo pad down in front of her and tapped a blunt forefinger on the top page.

'If someone comes in with a complaint or to make a report that you feel is necessary to document, use this pad. Make sure that your scrawny little girly arms are up to the task because the forms need to be filled out in triplicate.' He gave a slight tug to a piece of carbon paper overhanging the edge of the pad. 'Do you think you can handle that?'

Billie nodded. She felt her uniform cap shift slightly as she tipped her head up to look at him. She reminded herself to ask Lydia if she had any spare bobby pins with which to fasten it more securely. It had been difficult to find a hat from among the inventory small enough to fit her head properly and it wouldn't do to end up disgracing herself by losing the only one that did.

'I'm sure that I will manage to fill out the forms. But how will I know which complaints or reports warrant documenting in the first place?' Billie asked.

'Now, that's just one of many reasons that I didn't advocate for women joining the department. I'm not sure that it's possible to teach you lot common sense. I guess you'll just have to muddle through somehow,' he said. 'If you think it's beyond you, you can always resign your post.'

Billie felt her cheeks burn for the second time since entering the station. Out of the corner of her eye she could see other officers sneaking glances towards her. None of them were looks of reassurance. None of them came from her frequent partner, Peter Upton, as he wasn't there. She was on her own, at least for the time being.

'I am sure I will figure it out, sir.' She slid the memo pad closer to her, then adjusted her uniform cap. Sergeant Skelton cocked an eyebrow and then looked over at the officers milling about the station.

'The rest of you get back to work, too,' he said before step-ping out from behind the counter without giving her another glance.

She took a look around at the piles of paperwork, telephone messages and a number of dirty teacups left cluttering the space. She wondered if Sergeant Skelton always left the desk looking like such a disaster area, or if he had wanted her to know how little he respected her by leaving so much for her to clean up. Did he think of women constables as nothing more than a maid service?

But before she was able to carry the teacups to the small room at the back of the station where the officers had set up a sort of canteen, a member of the public walked through the door and made a beeline for the reception desk.

By the time Billie had been at the desk for an hour she had fielded complaints of a bewildering variety. Four different people had attempted to convince her to dismiss a summons to the police court for blackout violations. Another two wanted to complain about violations of the same blackout regulations committed by their neighbors. She took down the particulars concerning a lost dog and another from a man who wished to report a conversation he had overheard on the bus. The city had embarked on an effort to quell gossip and the man railed against the many people inclined to ignore that suggestion while using public transport.

Billie found herself channeling some of the memories she had of her mother fielding similar sorts of concerns from members of the parish in Wiltshire where her father had served for so many years as the rector. How effortless her mother had made it seem as she acknowledged the concerns of others without adding fuel to the fire. Billie was surprised to discover that she had a similar ability to acknowledge without inciting. Although, truth be told, those members of the public who wished to convince her to forget about their lighting violations did not leave feeling better than they had when they arrived. All in all, however, she felt as though she had acquitted herself creditably.

She did wonder how many of the complaints about fellow citizens were based on real concern for enemy activity and how many of them were the result of petty grievances and spite. Sadly, that was something that was often at the heart of parishioner complaints in Barton St Giles too. Her mother had been a master at navigating those tensions as well and Billie found herself reminded of her again and again throughout the afternoon.

She wondered how long it would be before she could think of her mother without such heaviness in her heart. A lump rose in her throat that was unbecoming of an officer. She was almost grateful to see another member of the public stepping up to the reception desk with a scowl on her face.

'How may help you?' Billie said feeling the lump dissolve.

'I am here to file a complaint,' the woman said. The woman placed her handbag on the counter and clutched it towards her chest. From her appearance Billie would have judged her to be in her fifties and unused to dealing with the police. She gave off the impression that she was both nervous and determined. Billie knew just how she felt. She nodded reassuringly.

'You have come to the right place. What is it that you would like me to help you with?' she said.

'Are you a constable?' The woman's eyebrows lifted slightly as she posed the question.

'I am. Now, what is this all about?'

'It's my son,' the woman said.

'Is he missing?' Billie asked.

So many people came in to report loved ones missing since the bombing raids had started. So far, most of those reported missing were simply delayed by air raids and had sought safety in one of the city's many shelters. Other times they had changed their address without letting friends and family know where they had gone. The police station coordinated with the local information bureau hosted by the public library to keep a running list of address changes and hospital inmates, but even with their best efforts people sometimes fell through the cracks.

'No, nothing like that. It's about a job. Or rather, about the promise of a job,' she said.

'If you are hoping for a job for him in the police department you might want to speak with my sergeant,' Billie said looking around the room in search of him.

'I see that I am not being clear.' The woman took a deep breath and exhaled slowly. 'An acquaintance of my son's offered to help him secure a job with the Ministry of Supply but so far he has failed to do so.'

'I'm not sure that that's the purview of the constabulary. We have no authority to influence the hiring practices of any agency other than our own,' Billie said. This seemed to be exactly the sort of complaint that did not require the use of the triplicate form.

'Of course I don't expect the police to have influence with the Ministry of Supply. I express myself so badly.' The woman drummed her fingers on the surface of the counter. 'My son gave an acquaintance quite a large sum of money for travel expenses to pay his way to London in order to recommend him to a connection he has at the requisitioning department. When I asked my son about the job, he said that there was no decision yet made and that I should stop bothering him about it.'

Billie could see how the son might be frustrated with the woman standing before her. Everything seemed to take longer now that war had broken out, but since the Battle of Britain had begun things were all the more chaotic.

'I'm still not quite certain what it is that you think the police can do for you,' Billie said.

'You could get the money back, of course,' the woman said her voice raising a notch. Billie felt a few pairs of eyes turned in her direction once more.

'I'm not sure that's possible. Did the man forcibly help himself to the money? Are you suggesting that your son was robbed?'

'No. I saw Melvin hand the notes over quite willingly. There's no question of robbery.'

'I'm afraid it's not a crime to give another party a sum of money willingly unless it is to pay for something illegal,' Billie said. 'It doesn't sound as though that's the case.'

'It was rather a large sum. It seems as though something ought to be able to be done. After all, if he handed over that much money, Melvin must have been quite confident in his acquaintance's ability to procure the job for him.'

'Perhaps it simply is a matter of a bit more time. After all, most things are not running quite as smoothly as they did before the war.'

The woman made a noise down in her throat that sounded like disgruntled acquiescence. She slid her handbag off the counter and hooked the handles over her forearm.

'So, I suppose there will be no satisfaction to be had?' the woman said. 'Is that what you're telling me?'

Billie pulled the memo pad towards herself. 'I'm happy to take down the name of your son and the man who he gave the money to. I can file an official report of your suspicions and that way there will be a paper trail in case you have any other concerns in this matter. I'm afraid that's the most I can do. If your son would like to come in and lodge a complaint himself, we might be able to take things a bit further.'

'I suppose I shall have to content myself with that. Not that Melvin seems to have been as concerned about this as I have. Children just don't seem to understand the value of money these days,' she said shaking her head.

'I've heard that mentioned from time to time,' Billie said. 'What's your son's name?' She held her pen poised above the pad hoping that she looked official.

'Melvin Hayes. Our address is 153 Polk Street,' she said.

'And your name?' Billie asked.

'Mrs Geraldine Hayes. I live at the same address.'

'And the name of the man to whom your son gave money?' Billie asked.

'Donald Sumner. I'm not sure of his address,' Mrs Hayes said.

'Do you have any details about this Donald Sumner?' Billie asked. While she didn't expect there would be a need to follow up on the complaint it would be best to have any pertinent information at hand if she were proven wrong.

'He works for the gas company. He first came to the house because of a report of structural damage on our street. He was going door-to-door inspecting the houses in the area for gas leaks. When he said that everything checked out at our house, I thought that was the end of it.'

'But it wasn't?' Billie asked.

'No. A day later I returned home from the grocer to see Melvin handing him a wad of notes. When I asked what was going on Mr Sumner said that there had been a call about the smell of gas on our block and he was following up. Melvin told me that the two of them had got to talking and that Mr Sumner had offered to help him to procure a job with the Ministry of Supply.'

Billie still wasn't sure how the police were supposed to get involved in what appeared to be a perfectly legal personal transaction.

'I think that's enough for us to begin with. I'll put this in our files and if Melvin wants to come in and make a complaint as well, we will at least have a notation of your concerns when he arrives. I wouldn't be surprised if this will straighten itself out before too long,' Billie said. She laid her pen down hoping it would serve as a signal that there was little more that she could do.

Mrs Hayes gave a curt bob of her head, turned on her heel and strode out the door.

THREE

Special Constable Upton's Police Notebook

Peter hadn't awakened feeling well rested since war had been declared. Not that he expected anyone else had either. Between working a second job as a special constable in addition to his role as a dock inspector, there just wasn't much time left over for sleep. Still, there was no sense in grumbling about any of it. It wasn't as though he was the only one pitching in for the war effort.

He rolled out of bed and walked to the window. He pulled back the blackout curtain and looked out at the street below. Here and there people picked their way along the street side-stepping piles of rubble created by the bombing raids. A long queue had formed at the corner shop opposite the boarding-house in which he lived. In the months since ration books had been issued, there never seemed to be a time when the shops were open and the queues were not stretched along the pavement. The assembled shoppers appeared cheerful enough as they stood chatting with their neighbors while they waited. A clutch of small boys squatted nearby; heads bent intently over a game of marbles.

Peter turned to the washstand and began soaping his shaving brush. As he gazed into the mirror hanging over the washstand and raised his razor to his face, the effects of his lack of sleep were easy to see. The man staring back at him appeared to have aged by a decade in only a few months. Deep pouches hung below his eyes and his mother's concern that he had lost weight was something he could no longer dispute.

While he had been upset to discover that his occupation as a dock inspector was one of those reserved by the government, he had been more than happy for the opportunity to join the constabulary, albeit as a special constable. Even though the extra job was often a thankless one, and entirely without pay, he found it to be rewarding. The notion that other men were facing danger on the front lines, while he stayed at home to inspect cargo and ships coming into the port at Hull, left him with a bad taste in his mouth. He knew that his duties were vital to keeping the country's shipping lanes working as efficiently as possible under arduous conditions, but it still rankled when he thought of the sacrifices made by so many other men.

Working as a special police constable had helped him to feel as though he were doing his bit in a way that really made a difference. While handing out summonses for blackout violations might not be heroic, he knew that every little bit that contributed to the war effort helped. In an important port city like Hull the temptation for the enemy to rain down incendiary bombs had proven too much to resist. The blackout regulations were important all over the nation, but in important port cities like Hull, the stakes were even higher.

While no one really liked to think about such things, the very landscape features that had been the source of the city's wealth, the rivers Hull and Humber, aided enemy pilots in navigating the terrain from hundreds of feet above. Even with strict adherence to blackout regulations the city was vulnerable from its position between the two easily spotted rivers.

Despite his exhaustion Peter felt a thrum of energy begin to course through him. He hummed to himself just slightly under his breath as he dragged the straight razor across his cheeks leaving them smooth and presentable. While he did not entirely wish to consider why it was that he was hurrying through his morning ablutions, a small quiet voice in the back of his head reminded him that his work with the constabulary had become that much more enjoyable since a certain WPC had joined the ranks.

He reached for his uniform shirt, slipped his arms through the sleeves, and quickly buttoned it up. As he glanced in the mirror once more, he could hear his mother's voice chiding him for the wrinkles on his shirt. She never would have allowed him to leave the house without giving his clothing a moment's attention beneath an iron.

But his landlady Mrs Cummins had no such scruples. Although she was a good-humored woman, she could not be accused of fastidiousness. Her boardinghouse always sported a fine layer of dust on those surfaces not in continual use, and her own attention to appearance, while not slovenly, was certainly not a point of pride for her. She provided laundry services for her lodgers but did not make more effort on their behalf than she did on her own.

It could not be said that Mrs Cummins was a dab hand in the cookery department either. Her meager ability to turn out appetizing meals had only been hampered further by the advent of rationing. Some women seemed to rise to the challenge of constraint and had found ways to produce ingeniously delicious meals despite the shortages of butter, bacon and sugar. Mrs Cummins only seemed to find such things baffling. Perhaps his weight loss was due more to a lack of appetite than to overwork.

He reached for his uniform jacket and slipped it on. He patted his breast pocket and felt for his badge. It wasn't there. Quickly checking all of his other pockets and finding them empty, he glanced about the room while asking himself where he might have left it since his last shift with the constabulary. A search of the top of the bureau, the drawer of the small writing desk and the floor of the walnut wardrobe yielded nothing. He pulled back the coverlet spread over the narrow bed and felt along the iron frame where it pressed against the wall. A quick inspection of the space beneath the bed was no more fruitful.

Now what was he going to do? He had fallen into a fairly easy rapport with his sergeant, but it had taken quite a lot of time to gain his superior's respect and trust. The loss of his badge was the sort of mistake that was unworthy of any officer, but certainly not one with his months of experience. He tried to think of where he had been when last he had needed to show someone his credentials.

Over and over in the course of a shift walking the beat he found himself confronting a variety of residents about chinks of light showing through their blackout curtains or allowing their headlights to shine too brightly as their motorcars crawled along the darkened streets. He used it when approaching young couples canoodling in alleyways taking advantage of dense pools of darkness. No single incident stood out in his mind as the last time he had used it.

Perhaps it had fallen out in his locker at the police station. There was no need to mention that it was missing to the sergeant until he had checked every possibility. And maybe Mrs Cummins had seen it. He grabbed his uniform hat and adjusted it on his head before glancing around the room a final time. Assuring himself that his badge was nowhere to be seen, he headed out into the faintly grubby corridor on the second floor of the boardinghouse.

He could hear his landlady singing to herself somewhere on the first floor. He followed the sound and discovered her standing over a pot bubbling on the cooker. From the scorched smell wafting from it, he fervently hoped it was not what was for lunch. She glanced up and gave him a warm smile as he stepped into the kitchen.

'Just the man I was hoping to see,' she said pointing at him with a wooden spoon covered in something sticky.

'What is it that I can do for you?' Peter asked.

'There was a man round yesterday while you were at the docks. He was a billeting officer with the RAF, and he was here to determine how many servicemen we might be able to put up in the boardinghouse. I know your room is small, but he told me it was likely that we would need to squeeze another boarder in with you,' she said.

Peter felt his heart sink even lower than it would have done if she had offered him a bowl of whatever god-awful mess was boiling away on the cooker. If he was already having trouble getting enough sleep alone in the room he couldn't imagine how much more difficult it would be if he was forced to put up with the noise of someone else rolling over or snoring.

Not only that but having been an only child he was not one who had ever learned the art of sharing personal space with another. While his mother had by no means been a well-to-do woman, there had always been a space carved out for his own private use in the small home they occupied throughout his childhood. But, under the current conditions, everyone needed to make sacrifices and he certainly wasn't going to shirk his duty.

'If it comes to that I'm sure I will make it work somehow,' Peter said.

'Must we accommodate him?' Mrs Cummins asked. 'After all, if you ask me the house is full to the scuppers as it is. I really don't know how we would manage if we were required to add more members to the household. Not to be indelicate, but there's already a line to the washroom almost around-the-clock.'

Peter hadn't even considered how additional members of the household might impact access to the most popular room in the house.

'Did he indicate how many additional boarders he expected you to be required to take on?'

'He said that I should be prepared to make room for at least one additional person per bedroom, not including my own,' Mrs Cummins said.

Although her husband had died many years before, he was sure she would consider it unseemly to be sharing her bedchamber with another. Framed photographs of Mr Cummins cluttered many of the horizontal surfaces throughout the board-inghouse. The gaunt, bewhiskered man gazed down at them as they sat around the dining-room table forcing down Mrs Cummins culinary offerings or as they congregated in the sitting room in the evening to play cards or to read. Peter had often wondered if he had kept in trim as a result of his wife's cooking.

'I'm afraid we will have to accommodate him and anyone he decides to billet here. No one seems to have very much say in such matters and I'm sure that none of us wish to be accused of being unwilling to do our part for the cause,' Peter said.

'I'm sure you're right but it does seem as though it will prove likely to make us all miserable. Do you want me to make you a sandwich to take with you to work?' She pointed at him with the spoon once again and a shudder ran up the nape of his neck.

'I'll just pick something up at one of the mobile canteens on my way,' he said taking a step backwards. 'I actually came looking for you to ask if you had seen my badge anywhere.'

'You haven't gone and lost it, have you?' she said.

'I'm sure it's simply mislaid. So, you haven't seen it?'

'I'm sorry, I haven't.' She inhaled quickly as a puff of smoke rose up out of the kettle. She slid the pot to the back of the cooker and gave him her full attention. 'I hate to think of you wasting your money at the mobile canteen. After all, you pay for both room and board. Are you sure you don't want me to fix you a little something?'

'Please don't trouble yourself. The canteen food will do me just fine,' Peter said raising his fingers to the brim of his cap before turning and starting out the door.

While he had no pleasure in the idea of sharing his room with another, perhaps an increased number of boarders would divert Mrs Cummins's attention from her constant insistence on feeding him. As he pulled the front door closed behind him, his attention returned to his shift at the station. His steps quickened ever so slightly as he thought about the fact that he might just be sent to walk the beat with the station's newest recruit.

FOUR

B illie felt her stomach rumble and realized that she had spent lunchtime at the cosmetics counter. Since she had not thought to pack anything before she set out that morning she would have to content herself with a cup of tea until she left for the day. Lydia had invited her to attend a charity fundraising event with her that evening and there would surely be plenty of refreshments served there. She gathered up the teacups scattered over the surface of the counter, careful to keep the stack from tumbling to the floor.

'I'll take a cup since you are going in that direction already,' Constable Drummond called out to her.

'I'll have one, too,' his partner, Constable Thompson said. 'Why don't you make a pot for everyone? After all, what good are women on the force if they don't make the tea?'

With a rising feeling of irritation, she headed for the hallway leading to the canteen. Not that one could really call it a canteen per se. It was hardly more than a closet-sized space. There was room for a gas ring, a small sink for filling the kettle and washing crockery and a small rolling cart which served as a work surface. Two shelves were mounted on the wall to hold clean cups and plates.

The sink already held a quantity of filthy crockery and sticky spoons. It seemed that it had not occurred to the other officers on duty to clean up after themselves. She wondered what the constables had done before she and Avis had been hired. Had they decided that they no longer had to do any of the tasks they considered women's work now that there were two female constables? Billie considered simply adding the dirty cups in her hands to the others in the sink and leaving them, but somehow, she couldn't make herself do it. Being a good sport was one way to build relationships and she definitely could use allies.

She turned on the tap and filled the kettle before she reached for the dishcloth. In only a couple of moment's time the crockery was cleaned, rinsed and dried. As she reached up to place a cup on the shelf she heard a sound behind her. Before she turned her head to see who was approaching, she felt a pair of large hands reach around her from behind and pull her backwards. Startled, she dropped the cup and watched as it smashed into pieces in the sink below. Her mind went blank as the grip around her waist tightened and she felt a blast of warm breath against her ear.

The hands moved higher, and her brain seemed to be moving more slowly than usual. She felt a wave of shock roll through her, made stronger by the realization that the sleeve on the arms entrapping her were covered by a police uniform jacket. She tried to protest but her voice had completely abandoned her. Instinctually, she lowered her arms and folded them across her chest in an effort to protect herself. She glanced down as one of the hands reached up and pulled at her arm in an effort to paw at her without a barrier. Suddenly her brain sprang back into action, and she tried to twist away. The grip on her waist only tightened further. She felt her breakfast roil in her stomach as her assailant let out a low chuckle, then said, 'I like it when girls play hard to get.'

'Constables, I don't much care what you do on your own time, but I don't appreciate you messing about during work hours,' Sergeant Skelton said.

Billie felt the hands drop and her assailant take a step back. Relief flooded over her, and her legs began to shake. She dropped her arms and gripped the side of the sink to keep from collapsing. Gathering all her courage she turned to see who had put her in such a compromising position. Constable Drummond winked at her before turning to face Sergeant Skelton.

'I'm sorry sir. You can't fault a man for being tempted,' Constable Drummond said.

'Get back to your desk, Constable,' Sergeant Skelton said to his male colleague. 'WPC Harkness, I would have expected better from you. I suggest you finish making the tea and then get back to the front desk.'

He turned on his heel and strode back down the corridor before she could explain. The tea kettle began to whistle but as she reached for it her hand still trembled too much to be trustworthy. She forced herself to draw in a few deep breaths as she switched off the flame. As the shriek of the whistle died down the sound of laughter from the station floated down the corridor towards her.

An image of her mother's face flashed into her brain. Before her death, she had forbidden Billie to join any of the women's auxiliary forces. She had not come right out and said it, but she had implied that such organizations were not suitable places for women, especially those who were as young and unworldly as her daughter. Her mother's way of dealing with any unwanted attention was to simply avoid placing herself in situations where such unpleasantness might occur. She had shared no wisdom whatsoever on how to deal with them once they had.

Her appetite had completely abandoned her and as much as a nice cup of tea would have been her general preference for treating the sort of shock she had just experienced, the very notion of facing her fellow constables made her feel vaguely panicky. Still, she told herself, there was nothing for it. She could not remain in the canteen for the rest of her shift, nor could she imagine simply disobeying Sergeant Skelton's direct order. She had no desire to be relieved of her position.

She willed her hands to stop shaking and lifted the kettle from the ring. She reached a teapot down from the shelf and filled it with boiling water. She placed it on the cart along with several cups and maneuvered the cart out into the hallway. One of the wheels made a squeaking noise as she pushed it along and she forced herself to concentrate on that rather than the faces of her fellow officers as she entered the main lobby of the station.

She stopped short of the desk area and left the tea cart several steps from where the officers had gathered. The sergeant had ordered her to finish preparing tea. He had not indicated she was required to serve it. Without a word she headed back to the reception desk and felt a sense of safety as she slipped behind the counter. She could feel the gazes of the officers lingering on her as she busied herself making stacks out of bits of paper and hastily scribbled messages.

She glanced up at the clock on the wall once more. It hardly seemed possible that in just ten minutes she had gone from feeling like a competent professional to feeling like a victim. She forced herself to focus on the task at hand as a middle-aged man entered the station and hovered uncertainly near the door. He was accompanied by a woman who took him by the arm and practically dragged him towards the desk.

'My husband would like to speak with a police constable,' the woman said as she stopped in front of the reception desk.

It looked to Billie as though the man standing in front of her had no desire whatsoever to be there, let alone to speak with an officer. His wife elbowed him in the ribs and he nodded his head grudgingly.

The man looked her up and down, then looked over at the male constables clustered around the tea cart.

'I suppose as you seem to be the only one working at present you will have to do. We are here about a missing person.'

People turned up missing every day. Since the commencement of the air raids more and more citizens were fleeing the city. In fact, relocations were so frequent that the library had set up an information bureau as a place where lists of address changes were kept in order for those left behind to be able to discover where their loved ones had gone. Many people who had lived in the city for most of their lives had packed up their families and headed off to stay with acquaintances in more rural areas. While she was not loath to spend effort on a missing persons report, she thought it was far more likely that the person was not missing at all.

'Who is it that you would like to file the report about?' Billie asked.

'It's a lodger in our home. I didn't think we ought to trouble the police about it for a few more days at least, but my wife was insistent. So here we are.' He shrugged his shoulders slightly in resignation.

'Tell her, George,' the woman said. 'Tell her how he just up and vanished.'

'Let's start with your names and address,' Billie said reaching for a pen and her memo pad.

'George and Phyllis Sanford. 21 Amberly Crescent,' Mrs Sanford said before her husband could answer.

'And the name of your lodger?' Billie asked.

'Dennis Partridge,' Mrs Sanford said.

'And how long has he been missing?' Billie asked.

'Since yesterday,' Mrs Sanford said.

Billie looked up in surprise. Even people whose closest loved ones had disappeared after a bombing raid did not usually report their absence so quickly.

'That doesn't seem to be a particularly long time for him to have been gone. Is there a reason that you are especially concerned about him? After all, if he is a capable adult man, he may have just spent the night away with friends or over-indulged at a local pub and wandered off somewhere to sleep off the ill effects of it,' Billie said.

'See Phyllis, that's what I told you they'd say,' Mr Sanford said. 'A bloody waste of time this is. I was due at work an hour ago.'

'I don't care what anyone says. He was a week late paying his rent and now he's gone missing. I wish to be paid what's owed us and if he's done a bunk, it's the constabulary's job to find him.' Mrs Sanford stared at Billie as if daring her to disagree.

'I'm afraid it is not the duty of the police force to track down debtors. Is there any reason that you feel he is likely to have gone missing as opposed to simply stolen away without paying his rent?' Billie asked. 'Were there any signs of disturbance in his room? Has he ever done anything like this before?'

'Well, he hasn't actually been with us all that long so it's not as though we have years of experience to draw upon,' Mr Sanford said.

'He's only lived with us about six weeks,' Mrs Sanford said. 'And no there were no signs of disturbance. His room is just as it's been all along.'

'He hasn't removed any of his belongings from his room?' Billie asked.

'No, everything seems to be just as I would expect it,' Mrs Sanford said.

'I would say that strengthens the theory that he is more likely to have simply stayed away overnight than that he intends to leave without paying his rent. I should have thought that he would have taken his belongings with him if he intended to abscond while still owing you money,' Billie said.

'I suppose that makes a sort of sense,' Mrs Sanford said. 'Perhaps he will come back after all.'

'Has he ever been late with his rent before?' Billie asked.

'He is not always the most prompt with his payments, but he always comes through in the end,' Mr Sanford said. 'I know that he is one for the occasional card game so it's possible he was simply caught a little short this week. Maybe he's a bit embarrassed and is staying away until he can come up with the extra money.'

'I'll tell you what I'll do,' Billie said. 'I'll fill out a report that you have expressed concerns about his whereabouts. If he still has not returned in the next two or three days, why don't you come on back and we will make some enquiries as to his whereabouts?'

'Is there really nothing you can do before that?' Mrs Sanford said. 'We have bills of our own to pay.'

'Now my dear, that's more than a fair offer. The police have much bigger things on their mind than our financial worries,' Mr Sanford said taking his wife by the arm and stepping back from the counter. 'And we will have more worries to contend with if I don't get to work.'

Billie watched as the pair of them hustled towards the door. It was not the first time she had taken a missing persons report from a concerned citizen, and she was certain it would not be the last. And she was far more concerned about the strange glances she was continuing to receive from the assembled group of fellow officers around the tea cart than she was about a missing lodger.

Before the door swung shut behind Mrs Sanford, Avis Crane called her name from the hallway leading down to her office.

When Billie glanced towards her, her superior officer waved her over. Billie slipped out from behind the reception desk and hurried to the older WPC's side.

'If you can spare a few moments, I have something I wish to discuss with you in my office,' Avis said.

She turned and headed back towards her office without waiting to see if Billie would follow. Billie looked back over her shoulder wondering if Sergeant Skelton would appear out of nowhere to scold her for abandoning her post. Since the sergeant wasn't in sight, she hurried to catch up with Avis.

Avis took her place behind her scarred wooden desk and gestured for Billie to take a seat in a metal folding chair squeezed between the desk and a supply closet. A narrow shaft of light filtered through the only tiny window in the room and highlighted a spot on the desk where Avis drummed her fingers against the battered wooden top.

Billie's stomach lurched. Had the sergeant told Avis that he had caught her behaving in a manner unbecoming of a constable? She had little doubt that such a thing could lead to her dismissal. Avis was not one to comport herself with anything less than the strictest level of professionalism. Billie had no reason to believe that she expected any less of her subordinates.

If Avis taxed her with inappropriate behavior, she did not know what she would do. Being sacked for something she did not do was not something she wished to accept. But the alternative of staying on the force after carrying tales about one of her male colleagues did not hold much appeal either.

'There's no need for you to look as though you were going to your own execution,' Avis said. 'I've had a request from the chief constable for a job he wants you to do.'

Whatever she had thought Avis would say, an opportunity from the chief had not crossed her mind.

'I'm happy to help in any way that I can,' Billie said. She hoped that whatever Avis had to say would not make those words a lie. She had worked with the chief previously to close a case, but the matter had been heartbreaking. It seemed to her that if he stooped to be involved it would likely be something more complicated than handing out blackout violations or staffing the reception desk.

'That's the spirit,' Avis said. She riffled through a stack of correspondence piled up on her desk in a neat pile and drew out an envelope. She pulled a letter from inside and unfolded it. 'I've received a written request from the chief constable for you to appear with him at an upcoming meeting. He wants you to give a brief overview of your role as a WPC and to be prepared to answer questions from the councilors.'

Billie's heart hammered in her chest. Public speaking was not something she had ever been called upon to do. Certainly, she had attended meetings in her small village back in Wiltshire and on occasion had spoken in front of a group, but it was always made up of friends and neighbors. It had also never been anything formal. She had filled in for her mother at rectory events from time to time, but the role of speaker at the club had never been hers. She would not know where to begin. And besides, why would the city council care to hear what she had to say?

'I'm not sure that I am at all suited for such a task,' Billie said. 'Surely they must be expecting someone with a great deal more experience than me to speak to the city council.'

'What matters is that you are what the chief constable is looking for. You are a young modern woman making her way in a predominantly male job. Your success here so far and the support of the chief would serve as proof that adding women to the constabulary is an asset to the city. I think you do a great disservice to yourself in assuming that you are not up to the assignment,' Avis said giving her a hard stare.

Billie's heart gave another loud thump. 'Don't you think you would be a better choice to speak to them? After all, you've been on the police force quite a while longer than me. I'm sure that you have much more knowledge of what it takes to be a woman on the job.'

'It's not just a matter of experience, WPC Harkness. We could really use someone as young, energetic and likable as you serving as an example of the sort of woman who has proven adept at taking on the role of police constable. With tensions rising I'm afraid we will have greater demand than ever before for officers to help secure our community and fewer men every day to do it.'

As much as Avis's words sent a chill down her spine, Billie could not disagree with her reasoning. July had brought on increased hostilities with Germany and not a day went by without reports streaming in from all over the country about bombing raids on airbases and armament factories. Conflicting reports flooded the newspapers concerning how to prepare for invasion. Every single person needed to do their bit to hold the line against an advancing enemy.

Should the Germans achieve an assault on land, the police force would be vital in keeping order on the home front and to provide an authority to whom people could turn with their questions. Billie knew that women were the key to winning the war, even if the men with whom she worked did not always seem to feel that way. What was a little fear of public speaking in the face of fear of the enemy?

'Is there a particular topic the chief would like to hear me speak upon?' Billie asked.

Avis glanced down at the letter in her hand. 'Women and the home front constabulary,' she said.

'Doesn't he give any more details?' Billie said. 'Is there no more guidance than that?'

'None whatsoever. My guess is that he trusts you to be well informed enough about your own role as to not need a great deal of direction from him.'

'When is the meeting scheduled to be held?' Billie asked.

'Wednesday next, at one o'clock in the afternoon,' Avis said consulting the letter once more.

A warm rush of relief flooded through Billie. 'I'm always scheduled to work at midday on Wednesdays so I'm not sure I will be available.'

'Don't trouble yourself about that. I am the one who makes the schedule for the WPCs, such as we are. And I am sure that it would be in the best interest of the force for me to schedule you to attend the council meeting that day.' Avis slid the letter across the desk towards Billie and nodded. 'Go on and read it for yourself. I'm sure that you will agree that it will be an excellent use of your time. It cannot be any worse than fielding requests and complaints from the general public. Speaking of which, you had best head back out to the front desk before Sergeant Skelton notices that you are missing.'

FIVE

Peter strode through the station door and headed straight for the cloakroom. He was relieved to note no other constables were present as he made for his locker and unfastened the lock. The missing badge wasn't visible at a glance and so he began a methodical search of the small space from top to bottom with rapidly fading hopes of finding it. Convinced that the badge was not lurking anywhere in its depths, he shut the door and replaced the lock. There was nothing for it but to notify the sergeant that he had managed to lose it sometime since his last shift.

As he stepped out into the corridor, he spotted WPC Harkness exiting the closet that served as the women's cloakroom. She did not return his smile as he raised a hand in greeting. He wondered if he had done something to offend her as she scurried past him and headed for the reception desk. He thought back to the last shift that they had worked together but could not think of any reason she would have had for a grievance with him. In fact, as he cast his mind back a few days he only remembered how easily they seemed to work together and that he had finished the shift with a sense that they had made a good team.

When Sergeant Skelton had first assigned him to train the new WPC, he had not readily warmed to the idea of taking her under his wing. She was young, green and not even street savvy. Her upbringing in a rural village had not seemed equal to the task of urban policing. Added to that, she had not been particularly concerned with how she might ruffle the feathers of important members of the community by her insistence on asking uncomfortable questions. But, as he had got to know her better, she had proven far more astute and engaged than any of the War Reserve Constables serving on the force.

He told himself that as soon as he made a clean breast of things with the sergeant, he would do his best to get to the bottom of whatever ailed WPC Harkness. Peter struck off towards Sergeant Skelton's office and rapped on the door.

'Do you have a moment, Sergeant?' he asked as he stepped into his superior's private space.

The sergeant gestured for him to take a seat opposite. 'I am glad you came knocking. It's saved me the effort of coming to find you. There's a bit of trouble brewing here in the station, and I want you to help me with it.'

'Whatever you need from me, Sergeant,' Peter said.

'It's WPC Harkness. She seems to have got herself into a bit of trouble.'

So that was it. She'd had another run-in with the sergeant. Although Sergeant Skelton did not seem all that interested in having women serving on the force, Peter had been surprised that he proved more protective of their newest recruit than he would have expected him to be. Still, the sergeant wasn't above giving her a hard time whenever the opportunity arose. His criticism must have been particularly savage for her to have taken it so much to heart after all these weeks. He had seen her shrug off, at least by all appearances, a public dressing-down on more than one occasion.

'What sort of trouble, sir?' Peter asked.

'The kind that was bound to come up with women being added to our ranks. I walked in on her and Constable Drummond locked in an embrace in the canteen,' the sergeant said.

'Are you sure?' Peter said.

WPC Harkness had never done anything to indicate that she was the least bit interested in any of the men in the department. She was pleasant and even friendly with most of her fellow constables, but he had never seen her engage in any behavior that could be considered the least bit flirtatious. There was no denying that she was an attractive girl in an unsophisticated sort of a way, but she did not use it to her advantage like so many other young women. In fact, if he had to venture an opinion, he would say that she went out of her way to behave in a strictly professional manner at all times. The notion of her indulging in a spot of hanky-panky on the job was completely out of character with anything he had ever observed of her.

'The only thing I'm sure of is that when I walked into the canteen, Constable Drummond had his arms wrapped around her and seemed to be whispering sweet nothings into her ear. I'd like to see the two of them kept apart and since I don't worry that you will get up to any such antics while on the job I want you to keep her out of the station as much as possible for the rest of the week.'

Peter wasn't sure whether he had been complimented or not. But it made no difference one way or the other. He most certainly would not try to get up to anything with his female colleague, at least not during working hours.

'Do you want me to take her on the beat with me?' Peter asked. They had often walked the streets of Hull together during a shift.

'No. Actually, I have a specific matter that requires attention. I just received a phone call from an air-raid patrol warden who is all worked up about something involving some of the public air-raid shelters. I want you to take WPC Harkness with you out to interview him and see if you can get to the bottom of it,' the sergeant said. 'The sooner you get her out of here the better.'

WPC Harkness's Police Notebook

Billie looked up as a woman stepped away from the desk and Peter took their place.

'Skelton is sending us out on a complaint call phoned in by a Mr James,' Peter said. Billie forced herself to meet his gaze and could not quite make out the expression she saw there. Was she imagining things or was he looking at her with a look that was more wary than usual? Even if he had lost his unguarded friendliness, she could only be relieved to find herself with an excuse to leave the station.

As they reached the door Peter stepped through it before her rather than holding it open for her to pass. She wasn't sure if she was pleased to be treated as an equal or if it was some sort of commentary about what had happened in the canteen. Did he no longer consider her to be a proper sort of woman? Her thoughts ran back to the chief's request that she speak at the city council. Somehow the idea of encouraging them to consider adding other women to the police seemed even less appealing after what had happened in the canteen.

Could she really look herself in the mirror if she was to place other women in the sort of situation she had found herself in? On the other hand, if more women entered the workforce would such things become less common? Was the best strategy to remain separated by inhabiting the sphere traditionally occupied by women? Or would it be better to engage in new frontiers en masse?

As they strode along the streets of Hull her mind could not settle on any one particular line of thought. The farther they went from the police station the more the strangeness of what had happened sunk in. As a rector's daughter in a small village, she had never encountered the sort of unwanted advance that had occurred that afternoon. In fact, even if she had wished for someone to behave in such a manner, she doubted she would have found any takers. The rector's daughter had been strictly off limits in the eyes of the local men and boys and Billie had had no real experience in some of the more ordinary rites of passage described to her by her girl chums.

Nor had her mother ever spoken with her on such subjects. Perhaps she had believed Billie would pass her entire life in one place. Her mother had hoped she would settle down with a nice young man from the local area, ideally a man of the cloth like her father, where one would never expect to encounter such vulgarities. Billie had of course read of such things obliquely referred to in novels borrowed from the Barton St Giles reading room, but there was a vast difference in reading about it in a book and experiencing such an outrage first-hand.

She kept turning over and over in her mind what she had done to encourage Constable Drummond's overtures. She had resolved upon nothing as Peter came to a stop in front of a small brick house in the middle of a narrow side street. If he had noticed her silence on the walk, he gave no indication. He consulted his police constable's notebook, then tucked it back into his pocket and mounted the steps. She followed behind him as he rapped loudly upon the door.

A small trim man with an outsized mustache opened it as if he had been waiting with his hand on the knob.

'May I see some identification, please?' the man said in a surprisingly deep voice.

Billie was taken aback when Peter stepped to the side and beckoned her forward. She reached into her uniform jacket pocket and pulled out her badge. She wasn't sure she felt as proud of it as she had when she placed it in her pocket that morning. The man leaned forward and peered at it closely before bobbing his head and waving them inside. Peter followed closely behind him appearing to take notice of the furnishings and the photographs and artwork hung on the walls on either side of the narrow hallway.

To Billie's eyes the space appeared neat and tidy and reminded her a great deal of a retired military man she had known back in her village in Wiltshire. Their host led them into a small but comfortable sitting room and indicated they should make themselves comfortable in a pair of chairs opposite a sofa where he seated himself.

'What I'm about to tell you must remain confidential. I trust you can do that,' he said, raising an eyebrow and looking at each of them in turn. Billie nodded and out of the corner of her eye she saw Peter do the same.

'It's not the policy of the police to gossip about investigations and concerns brought to them by members of the public,' Peter said.

'My concerns extend beyond my own personal desire for privacy. I'm not sure if your superiors mentioned this to you, but I am an air-raid patrol warden for this district and thus entrusted with public safety as concerns the war effort.'

'Yes, sir, he did. He told me that you were concerned about some trouble with one of the shelters,' Peter said. He reached into his pocket and pulled his notebook out once more.

Mr James eyed it and spoke again. 'I have concerns that if

what I'm about to tell you became a matter of public record it could significantly damage the public trust in the air-raid patrol as an organization. It might also give ideas to the sorts of people who see the conditions of the war as an opportunity to enrich themselves and get up to all sorts of mischief,' Mr James said.

'I can only repeat my assurance that the police do not indulge in idle gossip,' Peter said.

Billie felt Mr James's eyes on her. 'All members of the constabulary uphold the same standard, sir,' she said.

'It's not just gossip I'm concerned about. Should you get to the bottom of this difficulty it might become a matter for the police courts. I would like to have your assurance that whatever you discover will not end up in the newspapers. I've seen the police report printed in the *Hull Daily Mail*. It could do irreparable damage to the public trust for such a thing to occur.'

It was not the first time Billie had heard such worries. In fact, the first case she had worked on with the police had led to just such a complication. She felt certain that if something as egregious as murder could be dealt with in a way that brought no damaging details in front of the public, the same could be accomplished for a simple matter of disturbances in an air-raid shelter.

'These are unusual times and there are many ways to uphold the law and keep people accountable for their actions without endangering the common good,' she said.

Mr James looked at her for a long moment and then leaned back against the sofa as if satisfied with her answer. He then explained what had taken place.

'Yesterday morning a man dressed in a coverall and carrying a toolbox knocked upon my door. He claimed to have been sent by the council to verify that the air-raid shelters in my quadrant were still in good working order, and providing the level of safety the public would expect. Naturally as someone who encourages members of the public to seek shelter during the course of an air raid, I was pleased to hear that the council was taking the integrity of the shelters so seriously. I accompanied him to the first shelter on his list and watched as he performed his inspection. He was thorough to the point of being pedantic, but I was gratified to see that he was so committed to the task at hand.'

'I assume you did not contact the constabulary because you were so satisfied with his job performance,' Peter said.

'Certainly not. As he had several shelters on his list and his pace was so slow, I expressed concern that I could not remain with him throughout his inspections. After all, it was a workday, and I had a job to get to. As it was, I knew I would be late and so I handed him the keys for the shelters with the understanding that he would return them to my home as soon he was finished,' Mr James continued.

'But he didn't?' Peter asked.

'No, he did not. Furthermore, when I returned home to discover he had not done so, I took it upon myself to use a second set of keys to check another two shelters from the list.'

'Was that where some sort of a mischief had occurred?' Peter asked.

'I should say there was. Not only had he not simply inspected the shelters, both places had been stripped of anything portable of value. Any bits of metal, oil lamps, any furniture left by citizens for their own comfort like folding chairs or bedding. All of it was gone.' Mr James leaned forward and began gesticulating wildly.

Billie was grateful for the distance between them. 'How can you be certain he was the one who was responsible for removing the items?' she asked. 'Had you been in those shelters recently?'

'Who else could it have been? The shelters are kept under lock and key, and he was the only person besides me with keys. Don't they teach you anything when you enlist in the police force?' he said, jabbing his finger in Billie's direction.

'Constable Harkness is a more than competent officer. And she raises a valid point. While it's easiest to enter a locked building when one possesses the key, ample experience with the police has taught me that it's not the only way. Was there anything about this inspector that caused you to believe that he might take advantage of your trust?' Peter asked.

Peter slipped a glance at Billie and she felt just a little of the day's tension seeping from her body. Perhaps Peter didn't think so very ill of her after all. Or maybe he simply didn't want someone from outside of the police force casting aspersions on the organization.

From what she could tell, the constabulary operated a bit like a large family. While members within could give each other a hard time and apparently even try to take advantage of each other when no one was looking, they tended to close ranks and become quite prickly if criticism was lobbed at them from the outside. It was possible that Peter was simply reacting out of reflex.

'If he's so innocent, why didn't he return the keyring?' Mr James asked. 'That seems highly suspicious to me.' This time his jabbing finger pointed at Peter.

'Are you married, sir?' Billie asked.

She had noticed indications that a woman shared the home with Mr James. A basket of knitting rested on the floor near a comfortable chair. Photographs of Mr James standing with a woman approximately his own age were displayed about the room. The sorts of bric-a-brac that she generally associated with women took pride of place on the mantle and hand-tatted doilies were spread out under the lamps and served as anti-macassars on the backs of the wingback chairs.

'I am, but my wife is away at present. Why should that matter in the least?'

'Perhaps when the workman tried to return the keys there was no answer at the door. You had said you needed to go to work and it's possible that he completed the task before you returned home,' she said.

'That might be possible,' he said. 'But why has he not come by today? I told him at the time that I would need the keys returned promptly.'

'Did he say that he would return the keyring that day or did he say he would return it when he had completed the job?' Peter asked.

'I can't quite recall. I believe he said he would return it that day but perhaps I had simply assumed it would not take him longer than a few hours,' Mr James said. 'It's a good job that

I have three sets of keys instead of just one. You never know when there will be an air raid after all.'

'You said that he was very meticulous. Maybe he was unable to complete the task in one shift. For all you know he is also a firefighter or a firewatcher overnight as are so many men these days,' Peter said.

'Did you inspect every shelter that was on the list?' Billie asked. 'Did you verify that there were things missing in each of them?'

'No. When I went out this morning to check I discovered the thefts in the first shelter and hurried home to ring the police.'

'I'll tell you what we'll do,' Peter said. 'If you will trust me with one of your remaining sets of keys, WPC Harkness and I will check on the other shelters. Do you happen to have the workman's name?' he asked.

Mr James stood and crossed the room. He opened a drop-front desk and retrieved a ring of keys. As he held them out to Peter he said, 'David Phillips.'

'Could you describe Mr Phillips to us please, sir?' Billie asked.

'He was of about medium height and build with dark blond hair. I'd say he had light-colored eyes, but I cannot say for certain. As I said he was wearing coveralls and carrying a toolbox. There was nothing particularly distinctive about him.'

'That's enough to get us started. That is if you'll provide us with the addresses of the shelters on his list,' Peter said.

'Even if he's not the one who stripped any valuables from the shelter, somebody did. It's just the sort of thing that demoralizes the public and that we can't allow hooligans to get away with. No matter whether or not this David Phillips is responsible, I want you to get to the bottom of this,' Mr James said as he gestured towards the doorway.

'Rest assured we are taking this very seriously. The constabulary agrees wholeheartedly that an increase in crime is no way to keep up the spirits of those on the home front. We will keep you abreast of our investigation,' Peter said. He touched his uniform cap and held the door for Billie to exit before him.

* * *

Peter consulted the first address on the list Mr James had provided and turned along the narrow street heading back towards the main thoroughfare. He tended towards long strides and Billie found herself hurrying to keep in step with him. As they rushed past piles of debris and buildings with visible signs of fire damage, she felt a trickle of perspiration slither down her back. But she was determined not to show her discomfort or to ask him to slow down. If she wanted to be treated as an equal, she needed not to ask for any sort of preferential treatment.

When they stopped at the corner to wait for a traffic light she caught her breath enough to ask a question that had been on her mind since they first arrived at Mr James's house.

'Why did you ask me to be the one to show my identification?' Billie asked. 'Isn't that usually the job of a senior officer?'

'Not necessarily. As long as someone provides identification usually members of the public are satisfied. Besides, it seems to me that you've been on the job long enough that you should feel comfortable putting yourself forward a bit more often.'

'I don't feel as though I've been on the job very long and it seems strange to think about taking a leading role so early on,' Billie said.

'If there's anything I've learned since war broke out it's that timelines have shortened considerably. Do you think the pilots who are doing their best to keep the Germans from bombing the hell out of us have had as much time as they would like to get ready to take the controls and head for the skies?' he said.

Billie felt as though she'd been slapped. There were so many young men who were shot down from the sky every day that certainly Peter's words must be true. Her friend Candace worked for the RAF and had sent oblique hints that the death toll was terrifying. With the Battle of Britain raging in the skies overhead Billie could well believe any reports that made their way to the average member of the public.

And maybe it was Peter's way of giving her a little more authority as an officer. After all, she couldn't expect to be treated with respect if she couldn't even see herself as being on equal footing with a fellow constable when it came to showing identification. The fact that she felt so disinclined to push herself forward with her badge made her wonder if she was having difficulty believing that she truly was worthy of carrying it. Did she feel like an impostor? With a cold feeling gathering in her stomach, she realized that's exactly how she felt.

It was something she had often felt when she really gave it some thought. As a rector's daughter there was an expected role for her to play and one that she had not always felt that she was aligned with on the inside. It wasn't so much a lack of faith, but rather a disinclination to simply accept what she had been told without questioning it. She found little comfort in the rituals associated with the liturgical calendar or value in the good works women of the church were expected to fill their days with from the time they were old enough to contribute needlework or fund-raising efforts to their community.

She had not always felt like the dutiful daughter many members of her community had praised her for being. She had often argued with her mother on matters both large and small. She read books in the reading room that made her question the small circle in which her life had been scribed and felt the demands of it chafe. As she had gone about her daily business attending meetings of the Women's Institute, the knitting circle, or the housebound helpers, it was often as if someone else was going through the motions and the real Billie Harkness could not break free of her.

Was it any wonder the role of police constable also felt as though it were not truly who she was? Matters weren't helped by the fact that she was new to the city of Hull and the force was new to having women on it. She did not feel adequately trained in investigatory techniques, protocol or even how to find her way around the city. Truth be told, she still found it nerve-wracking to be among so many strangers as well as to be confronted by the interminable buzz and clang of traffic on the streets.

That said, as she imagined the pilots with only a few weeks training under their belts taking to the skies bravely attempting to protect their fellow countrymen from invasion, she had to believe that they found a way to get up to speed with their new identities very quickly. How could they perform their duties if they had not? And how could she perform hers if she refused to step fully into the role she claimed to inhabit? She looked at Peter with new eyes. Since she had known him, he had not been one to sugarcoat his thinking or to dissemble. If he thought that she was ready to take the lead from time to time it seemed to her that she could trust that.

'I appreciate you sticking up for me back there with Mr James. He didn't appear to feel all that comfortable with a WPC being sent out.' Billie looked up at Peter hoping to see the earlier wariness gone from his face. Instead, her colleague kept his expression stiff and inscrutable.

'If you plan to remain on the force you're going to have to learn to stick up for yourself,' Peter said coming to a stop. He turned towards her and looked down from above. 'There is not always going to be someone there to help you out of an uncomfortable situation, whatever sort that may be. If you don't learn how to advocate for yourself and show your own strength you're going to come to grief.'

His gaze remained riveted on her face as if willing her to understand him. Billie couldn't tell if he was referring only to what had happened with Mr James or if he was intending for his remarks to include anything he might have heard from their fellow officers about herself and Constable Drummond. She told herself she ought to speak with him about it directly, but somehow she couldn't make the words come out. Instead, she simply bobbed her head and turned back towards the road in front of them.

SIX

As they crossed the street and came to a stop in front of the first shelter on Mr James's list, Peter wondered if WPC Harkness had understood him. He couldn't come out and say to her what was on his mind without feeling like he had crossed a line. Being a mentor to a fellow officer was one thing: chiding her on her comportment and possible lack of propriety was another matter entirely. Perhaps he would have felt more comfortable doing so if he were more experienced with such matters in general.

But as an only child he had not been raised with any sisters with whom he might have developed a bantering sort of knack with women. Not that he wanted to think of Constable Harkness as a woman. It would be far easier if he could completely forget that she was not simply an officer like any of the other colleagues with whom he walked a beat or stopped in after a shift for a pint at the local. Peter had heard that WPC Harkness had moved in with her cousin, a woman who was well known in the city for being an outspoken modern sort of woman. Perhaps she would be able to provide her with just the sort of guidance she needed about such things.

He retrieved the brass ring of keys lent to them by Mr James from his pocket and tried two or three before he found one that fitted the lock on the air-raid shelter door. He pushed it open, hearing a loud creak of the hinges and peered into the gloom, finding the sunlight that penetrated the space somewhat inadequate for the task.

But even in the low slanting light filtering through the doorway it was possible to see that the space was denuded. In the shelters in which Peter had spent time during the air raids that had rained down on the city, he had taken the presence of oil lamps for granted. Sometimes there were other comforts available as well. Some shelters had benches built all along the sides for people to sit upon. Other times the city's inhabitants had transported folding cots or chairs with them when they hurriedly made their way into the shelters as the sirens blared above their heads.

'It's just as bare as he said it was,' WPC Harkness said peering around his shoulder. 'I can see why he was concerned.' She pointed at several empty nails driven into the walls of the shelter. Peter had to assume that was where the oil lanterns had hung.

'I suppose he was lucky they didn't pull the nails and take them too,' Peter said. 'There's no sign here of who did this, however. We'd better check the next one on the list.'

WPC Harkness's Police Notebook

After relocking the shelter door, they made their way towards the next building on the list a few blocks away. It seemed like little distance as they made their way along the streets, but Billie knew from hard-won experience how far away a shelter could seem when planes flew overhead, and the sound of the air-raid sirens split the night with their blaring. The back of her neck grew hot as she remembered that first night in Hull crouching in a darkened cinema with her cousin Lydia, hearing the rumble of the bombs dropping overhead and then the horror of exiting the building after the all-clear signal to see the devastation in the street. Under those circumstances, the distance between shelters could seem very great indeed.

She waited as Peter fitted a key into the lock and pushed open the door. Once again, the shelter appeared utterly stripped. Not a lamp, not any sign whatsoever of human occupation.

'This isn't looking good no matter what alternate explanations you might have thought up for David Phillips's delay in returning Mr James's keys,' Peter said pulling the door shut behind him and locking it once more. 'We'd best check the next one.'

They turned right at the end of the block and sped along the pavement. Billie was grateful for the leafy canopy covering them with welcome shade as they rushed along. To her, the trees also provided a little bit of the countryside right there in the heart of the city. She hadn't realized how much she had taken the lush greenery of Wiltshire for granted until it was not constantly in her line of sight.

The third shelter on the list had been placed in a public park and was nestled beneath a small copse of trees. She wondered at the wisdom of placing a public safety building in a location more hidden from view than the ones she had often seen dotted about the city. Perhaps that was part of a grander design, to have even the shelters not particularly visible from above. There had been talk of underground shelters being built should the war continue, or the bombings increase, but she had not heard of any such plans actually coming to fruition. Perhaps using natural cover to simply obscure the shelters from view, much like the function of the barrage balloons, was a step in the right direction.

Peter handed her the keyring and nodded as if she should give it a go. It held a bewildering assortment of keys and it took her several tries to find the one that fitted the lock. But when she inserted it, the handle turned smoothly enough, and she gave the door a push. But unlike the doors to the first two shelters this one did not swing open entirely. She gave it another try, pressing her shoulder into the door, but could not make it yield to her efforts. Peter stepped up behind her and placed his large square palms on the door giving it a mighty shove.

Billie thought she could see something beyond the door and as she slipped through the small space their efforts had created, she could not quite make out the details before her. Her eyes slowly adjusted to the gloom, but still the scene made no sense. The shelter appeared to have been the site of a struggle. The smell of lamp oil rose up from the concrete floor and filled her nostrils. Shattered glass littered the concrete floor and the base of the lamp sat abandoned nearby. A long wooden bench lay overturned and partially dragged away from the wall. But most unexpected of all was the form of a medium-sized man sprawled out across the floor by her feet. She bent down to touch his shoulder and to give him a little shake, but his body flopped away from her. As she went to reach her fingers to his neck to feel for a pulse, she noticed a length of cord tied round his neck.

It wasn't the first time that Billie had encountered a dead body, but that didn't make the discovery any easier. The contents of her stomach asserted themselves as she stared down at the bulging eyes and parted lips on the body displayed at her feet.

'What's the holdup in there?' Peter asked. 'Is something blocking the door?'

Billie stuck her head back through the gap in the doorway. 'There's a body blocking our entrance. I'm quite sure he's been murdered.'

Peter's face registered shock as her words reached him. 'Have you touched anything?' he asked.

'I only checked for a pulse. I haven't touched anything else. Should I move him so that you can enter and look for yourself?' she asked.

While he had not been serving as a special police constable for many months longer than Billie had been on the force, he still knew a great deal more about procedure than she did. Besides, he seemed to have developed a far better relationship with Sergeant Skelton than had she. She didn't like to imagine the consequences if the sergeant were to feel that she had violated protocol in some way that compromised a crime scene.

'Step away from the door and let me see if I can squeeze in far enough to take a look,' he said.

She felt a surge of relief as she made room for her partner. He poked his head through the gap between the doorjamb and the door and squeezed his shoulders through as far as they would go. While Peter was not an overly large man, he was slightly above average height. He was, however, quite trim and he managed to slide more of the upper half of his body through the gap than she would have expected. She kept her eyes firmly on his face as he swept his gaze over the scene in front of him. It took him a moment, as it had for her, for his vision to adjust to the gloom, but a quick inhalation on his part told her he had done so.

'Is that a cord round his neck?' he asked.

'As far as I can tell it is. It looks like ordinary clothesline to me,' Billie said. 'Although in these dim conditions I can't say for certain.'

'Would you say that he's wearing a coverall?' Peter asked.

She forced herself to look back at the body and noticed another detail that had eluded her before. 'That's how I would describe it. And if you are able to see just beyond him, that appears to be a toolbox on the ground by his body.'

'I think we might've found our missing air-raid shelter inspector,' he said. 'Do you see any keys like the ones Mr James reported missing?'

Billie looked out into the far reaches of the darkened shelter. The light from the partially opened door had barely managed to illuminate any details as it was, and now that her partner was blocking the little light there was, it became even more difficult to see.

'I don't see them but that doesn't mean they aren't here somewhere. Should we take a closer look ourselves?'

There was no reason to think a ring of keys would have been in his hands when he died. Once an inspection of his pockets and of the toolbox could be conducted, she thought it more likely they would turn up tucked away.

Peter shook his head. 'I'll stand guard here at the door while you run to the nearest police call box to request additional officers. There's one at the other end of the park.'

He slid out from the gap in the door making room for Billie to pass. As she ran towards the far edge of the park people walking their dogs or strolling arm in arm turned and stared as she rushed past them. Was it because she was a WPC or because she was a police officer who appeared to be on an urgent mission that drew their attention? By the time she reached the call box she was breathless and sweating. Her hat had shifted so precariously on her head she had removed it and held it clutched under her arm as she lifted the call box receiver to her lips. Relief flooded through her as the voice of one of the boys in the police telephone office answered her call.

She explained briefly what they had discovered and gave a location. She requested that officers with crime scene experience be sent immediately to the scene. The telephone operator assured her that help was on the way and with a sense of relief she replaced the receiver and headed back towards her partner and the dead body.

As much as she usually would have preferred to stay until the crime scene investigation had concluded, the arrival of Constables Thompson and Drummond made it easier to be dismissed from the crime scene at the end of her shift. Constable Drummond had offered to be the one to take her statement and she had found herself backing away again and again from him as he pressed uncomfortably close. She jumped at the chance to leave when Constable Thompson announced she and Peter were not required to stay on.

In her haste, she barely noticed when she parted ways with Peter as she turned down the main thoroughfare leading towards Linden Crescent. A slight breeze had picked up through the course of the afternoon and she was grateful for the way that it cooled her as she hurried along. There certainly would be no time for a bath before she needed to leave for the event she had promised to attend with her cousin that evening.

SEVEN

Her footsteps dragged as she turned to mount the steps to number seventeen. Even though Lydia had done everything within her power to make Billie feel welcome in her home, she still felt out of place from time to time. After the troubles of the day, she was hit by a wave of homesickness for the comfortable, but undeniably shabby rectory that until so recently she had called home. As much as she admired the luxurious furnishings of Lydia's house, they still left her feeling slightly surprised every time she entered it.

With its clean lines and Art Deco style it was unlike any other building she had ever seen in real life. But it suited her cousin right down to the shoes. Billie had never met a woman more inclined towards a modern outlook than Lydia. Her cousin was an outspoken advocate for modern policies, technologies and attitudes. She had no interest in cooking, housekeeping, or behaving in a way calculated to attract a husband.

Lydia had managed to ruffle a few feathers in her tenure as the city librarian, but she had attracted her share of admirers too. Unless Billie missed her guess, the chief constable was among them. The fact that he esteemed her cousin did not leave Billie feeling any more secure in her own position on the police force, however. She was loath to mix her personal life with her professional one.

As she entered the light-filled hallway and pushed the door closed behind her, Lydia's voice called out to her from the sitting room. Billie removed her uniform cap and placed it on the hall table. She glanced at her reflection in the mirror and smoothed her brown hair. A strand or two had come loose from the pins she used to keep it tucked up and out of the way in an effort to appear more professional, and if she were to be honest with herself, perhaps a bit older too. She could not help but feel that her age did not give her an advantage in the constabulary. Perhaps if she were a decade older, she might have proved a less vulnerable target for the attention of Constable Drummond, or at the very least would have developed ways of deflecting his unwanted interest.

She removed the lipstick she had purchased for Lydia from her handbag and carried it to the sitting room where her cousin lay stretched out on a chaise longue, her favorite perch in the house. She sat up as Billie entered the room and smiled in greeting.

'This is for you,' Billie said, handing her the lipstick before taking a seat on the sofa opposite.

Lydia uncapped the gold-tone tube and twisted the bottom to reveal the color. 'What an unexpected pleasure. You shouldn't have.'

'I certainly should have, and long before now,' Billie said. 'I don't think you already have that exact color.'

Lydia turned the tube over and squinted at the label stuck to the bottom of it. 'I definitely do not. It is just lovely. Still, I wish you wouldn't spend your hard-earned wages on things for me.'

'It is the least I could do considering all that you have done for me. With the government planning to tax cosmetics, I was afraid lipstick might become difficult to obtain and I hated to think of you running out because you had been so generous in sharing with me.'

Lydia leaned forward and patted Billie on the knee. 'Thank you for the gift. It is a delicious shade of red.' She let her gaze rest on Billie's face for a moment. 'You look as though you made good use of the cosmetics counter where you purchased it.'

Billie wasn't sure after what happened with Constable Drummond that she would describe allowing the saleswoman to do her whole face up as good in any way. Still, Lydia meant it as a compliment.

'I went to Hammonds before I headed into the station and the woman there offered to try a few things out on me. I liked them well enough that I purchased some cosmetics of my own so that I won't be raiding yours all the time,' Billie said.

Lydia squinted at her. 'You don't look as though you were entirely pleased with your purchase.'

The temptation to unburden herself about the incident with Constable Drummond washed over Billie like a tidal wave. But as she parted her lips to give voice to her concerns she hesitated. After all, didn't her mother always say that the least said, the soonest mended? Maybe if she were lucky nothing like it would happen again and she would regret saying anything to anyone.

No, holding her tongue seemed by far the best course of action. She would need a plausible explanation that would not make things more difficult. The one she came up with was not exactly a lie even if it were not the sole reason for her unease.

'It isn't the purchase that is on my mind. It's just that the chief constable has requested that I give a talk at an upcoming city council meeting on my role with the constabulary. I tried to convince Avis to do it instead, but she said the task had fallen to me.'

Lydia tipped her head to one side. 'Are the councilors considering eliminating women from the force?' Lydia's lips pressed into a thin line and her eyebrows drew closer together.

Billie knew that her cousin had played an important part in opening up the Hull Constabulary to women and she took a keen interest in the success of both of the city's WPCs.

'No, it's nothing like that. In fact, it is quite the opposite. Apparently, the chief wants the city council to authorize positions for more women and he hopes that a good report from me will help with that.'

A broad smile spread across Lydia's face. 'I am certain you will convince them to authorize as many WPCs as the chief sees fit,' she said. 'As far as I'm concerned trying to limit women's roles in any sector of the workplace, especially during a time of war, is utter nonsense.'

While Billie wasn't sure she believed that her words would have quite so much weight with the council, Lydia's comment reminded her of something else that had happened that day.

'Speaking of women in the workplace, I met someone

named Trudy while waiting in line at Hammonds who invited me to a meeting of the Women of Work Club. Have you heard of it?'

'I certainly have. In fact, I've been to a few of their meetings over the years. I should have thought to suggest it to you as a way to meet some other women of about your age,' Lydia said. 'I hope you accepted the invitation.'

Billie nodded. 'I agreed to attend the meeting they are having this week at the Guildhall.'

Lydia glanced over at the mantle clock and got to her feet. 'The Guildhall is where we are due in just over an hour. If we are to arrive on time, we had best get ready.'

Billie followed Lydia up the stairs and soon stood in her bedroom exchanging her police uniform for a white sleeveless dress and matching cropped jacket with navy piping. As she sat at the dressing table positioned in the corner of the large room and leaned towards the mirror, she felt the worries of the day begin to fade.

She pulled out her hairpins one by one to let her dark hair fall to her shoulders in loose waves. A few strokes with a hairbrush and a swipe of Victory Red applied to her lips completed her look. She emerged from her room to find Lydia standing in the hall dressed to the nines in a smart navy-blue ensemble in a severe cut that flattered her lean figure. Her cousin smiled in approval as she took her by the arm.

When they arrived at the Guildhall the event was already in full swing.

'Shall we head straight for the punch bowl?' Lydia asked.

'I'm nearly parched to death. I never took time for lunch. Do you think there's any chance of something to eat?' Billie asked. She heard a voice behind her.

'It sounds as though I should speak with WPC Crane about your working conditions.'

Billie recognized the chief constable's voice even over the sound of the crowd. She turned. 'Good evening, sir. My lack of a lunch break wasn't Avis's fault in the least. I simply was so caught up with a case that I didn't stop to think about eating.'

'It seems that you're taking your duties very seriously,' he said.

'I am making every effort to do so,' Billie replied.

'You know I never would have recommended her for the position if I didn't think that she would do it credit,' Lydia said. She gave the chief constable a broad smile and Billie thought she saw a bit of color warm the chief's cheeks.

'I would expect nothing but excellence from the women in your family, Lydia,' he said.

The chief constable had a habit of showing up at events Lydia attended. Billie thought it was more than mere coincidence. He also tended to compliment her with a degree of regularity that suggested high regard. She wondered if Lydia had noticed too.

'She tells me that you have asked her to speak in front of the city council,' Lydia said.

The chief looked at Billie. 'That's right, I did. Avis telephoned me this afternoon to tell me that you have accepted the invitation. I am most grateful since we are more in need of good officers than ever before.'

'Are you concerned about our numbers, sir?' Billie asked.

She wondered if perhaps she was being too forward, but several more members of the force based at her own station house had announced that they were being shipped out within a fortnight. There was definitely a need for fresh recruits.

'It's not something that I would like to broadcast to the public in general, but I feel the two of you could be trusted with what I'm about to say,' the chief said looking from Lydia's face to Billie's own before proceeding. Both women nodded. 'There have been some alarming statistics about the rise in crime coming across my desk of late and I am very eager to make sure that we do not come up short as far as available officers go. If we could add to our numbers, I would feel greatly relieved.'

'Do you really think they will authorize more women for the constabulary? It was like pulling teeth to get them to approve the four original slots for female officers,' Lydia said.

'I think Billie will manage to convince them, especially in

light of what transpired as a result of her first case,' the chief said.

Billie wasn't sure how to reply. While she had been eager to work on the case he spoke of she was not aware that it had raised her in the esteem of the city councilors. In fact, if she had to guess, she would have been inclined to believe it had done exactly the opposite. The chief was in a position to be much better informed than was she on such a subject. If he thought it likely that more women would be approved to be appointed to the constabulary, then who was she to second-guess him?

She was encouraged by the attitude the chief displayed. If he was eager to add more women into their ranks maybe he would not look favorably on the way that Constable Drummond had behaved. Perhaps she would not be encouraging other women to enter into a hostile environment after all. Between what he had to say, and the comments made by Peter earlier in the day, she wondered if things were not quite so bad as they had seemed earlier. But something else he said left her feeling less optimistic.

'Perhaps it's not my place to ask, but what sorts of statistics are you talking about?' she asked.

'It's good for morale to put out the message that everyone on the home front is eager to do their bit and that we are all pulling together to fight the enemy, but the sad fact of the matter is that is not entirely the case,' he said.

'Avis said something similar about a case I'm working on right now,' Billie said. 'She said that there were always those people who looked to take advantage in any circumstance.'

'I'm afraid that's it exactly. As much as I understand the need for increased regulations, the reality is that such things create opportunities where none previously existed.'

'Are you talking about black-market sales?' Lydia asked.

'That's one part of it. Any time you restrict availability or sales of any sort of goods the demand for them increases. So does an eagerness to make a profit from selling them by those not authorized to do so. But it's more than that, I'm afraid,' he said.

'The blackout helps people who wish to do things without being noticed, doesn't it?' Billie asked.

'That has been a real problem. Smash and grabs at jewelry stores and other high-value retail establishments has gone through the roof. Traffic accidents, street crime and if you don't mind me speaking so frankly, indecent assaults on women in darkened buses and air-raid shelters have increased at an alarming rate,' he said. 'We could use all the help that we can get if we are to maintain the peace on the home front.'

'But that's just monstrous,' Lydia said. 'What sort of person would take advantage of wartime circumstances? I thought that holding items under the counter for preferred customers was a distasteful enough practice, but the idea that there are people who are using the blackout to take advantage of their neighbors is disgusting.'

'I would agree wholeheartedly, but I'm afraid that might just be human nature. Just because we have a common outside enemy doesn't mean that we don't have real enemies within our own borders. Some of those doing the most damage are the sort of people you would pass on the street with a nod and a smile.'

Billie's stomach gave a squeeze. The chief could be describing Constable Drummond.

The chief turned to Lydia and smiled. He held out his hand. 'I believe that the band is about to start a new number. Lydia, may I have this dance?'

As Billie watched them head off for the polished parquet floor in the center of the room, she thought back to Mr James, the air-raid patrol warden and how very ordinary he had seemed when he lodged the complaint about the shelter inspector. If ordinary men and women were behaving criminally every day of the week, she had to ask herself if he might be responsible for the murder. After all, he was quite possibly the last one to see the inspector alive.

EIGHT

It had been a hell of a day. By the time Drummond and Thompson had arrived at the air-raid shelter and finished interviewing both Peter and WPC Harkness, it was well past the end of his regularly scheduled shift.

All the way back to his boardinghouse he puzzled over how WPC Harkness had kept a distance from Constable Drummond. If there was any truth to Sergeant Skelton's suspicion of a romantic relationship between them, it looked as though they had had a lovers' tiff. For his part he could see no sign that she was the least inclined to be within an arm's reach of him. In fact, he thought she had gone out of her way to give him a wide berth. Still, it could be that she had heeded the sergeant's admonishment not to mix business and pleasure and was trying her best to do so.

When he had arrived back at his boardinghouse Mrs Cummins offered to heat him up something to eat but he found he had no appetite and only had interest in stretching out on his bed and falling into a deep sleep. He tumbled into bed gratefully, not even pausing to completely undress. But slumber eluded him. Every time he began to drift off, he could see WPC Harkness's face, her dark eyebrows drawn together, and her lips parted in shock. Then, the scene shifted to a man not much older than he sprawled out on a cold concrete slab, his eyes bulging from his head. Peter managed to drift off after what felt like hours, but he awoke again and again chased through the night by bad dreams.

When he awoke the next morning, his stomach felt as empty as the burgled air-raid shelters had been the day before. He changed into his dock inspector's uniform to the sound of his stomach rumbling. As he bent down to tie his boot laces, he was surprised he was actually looking forward to whatever was on offer for breakfast. He hurried down the stairs without bothering to make his bed and arrived in the dining room where his landlady and one of the other boarders sat tucking into toast and porridge. His stomach growled again at the sight of the food. Truly he must be half starved to feel so much anticipation for something as unappetizing as Mrs Cummins's cooking.

'Peter, you haven't seen my change purse lying around anywhere, have you?' Mary Parker, a young woman engaged in war work at a nearby armaments factory, asked as he stood at the sideboard ladling porridge into a waiting bowl. It might have been made more palatable by the addition of a generous splash of cream or a heavy-handed application of sugar. Sadly, the wartime rationing had cut back such luxuries to the bone and the only addition to the oatmeal that he could expect was a sprinkling of salt.

'What does it look like?' Peter asked as he carried his steaming bowl to the table and took a seat. He reached for a slice of toast noting that it had already been meanly dressed with the thinnest of scrapings of butter. At least there was a small pot of jam in the center of the table. While Mrs Cummins was not a good cook, she had a sister who lived in the country and often sent delicious things made of preserved produce.

'It's made of green Moroccan leather. One of those that snaps with a clasp at the top.' Mary reached for a piece of toast of her own and smiled at him.

While Peter did not think of himself as a ladies' man it had become clear to him over the last few weeks that his fellow lodger was determined to snare his attentions. While he had no interest in such a connection, it could not be said he did not enjoy a bit of harmless flirtation. It would never do to take up romantically with one of his fellow lodgers, however. If things took a turn for the worse life in the boardinghouse would become exceedingly awkward.

Besides, Mary was not the sort of girl he could see himself really falling for. She was good looking to be sure, but he had never found that he enjoyed being pursued, at least not quite so overtly. Mary had made her intentions clear from the moment he had arrived at the boardinghouse. A small part of him wondered if her claims about a missing change purse had more to do with an excuse to converse with him than it did from any real loss.

'I'm sorry, I haven't. When did you last see it?' he asked. He hoped his question sounded sincere. He would hate for her to feel offended. After all, that would make life in the boardinghouse awkward too.

'I last remember having it a few days ago when I went to the post office to purchase some stamps. I can't say for sure when it went missing in the intervening time, but I can't find it anywhere,' she said.

'Did it contain quite a bit of money?' Peter asked.

'Just a few shillings and pence I would say. I don't tend to keep much cash on hand because you never do know what might become of it,' Mary said sending a sideways glance at her landlady.

Peter noticed Mrs Cummins stiffen. While his landlady might not have enjoyed a particularly positive reputation as a cook, she was known for running a perfectly respectable boardinghouse. She needed to do so considering it was her only source of income, a fact she had remarked upon to Peter on many occasions when she stopped by to collect his rent.

'While I'm sure it's good practice to keep the majority of your money safely locked away in your post office account, I'm sure there is no real risk on these premises,' Peter said trying to smooth things over between the two women.

Mary finished chewing her bite of toast and carefully wiped the corners of her mouth with her serviette. 'You might just be mistaken there,' she said. 'When I asked Thomas Maren if he had seen my coin purse, he told me that he was missing a pair of cufflinks from his bureau drawer. I would have thought with a police constable living on site we would be less likely to be the sort of place a thief would strike, but perhaps I was mistaken.'

Mary pushed back her chair and swept out of the room without another word. Peter glanced over at Mrs Cummins whose face had drained of color. In fact, she resembled to a remarkable degree the contents of his porridge bowl.

'What do you think her game is? Do you think she's trying

to wriggle out of paying her rent for the week?' Mrs Cummins asked Peter.

'Has she ever made such accusations before? Or ever tried to get out of paying her rent?' Peter asked.

'No one has made such accusations before. I pride myself in running a very respectable boardinghouse and I vet my tenants exceedingly carefully. I should be absolutely shocked to discover that someone living among us had a tendency towards pilfering,' she said.

Peter thought back to his missing badge. Was it possible that there was a thief living in the boardinghouse? Three objects of value going missing in a relatively short span of time seemed to indicate that was the case. Was it likely that all three of them had simply mislaid their items? He thought probably not. As far as he could tell his badge had simply up and vanished. It sounded as though Mary and Thomas had experienced the same sort of inexplicable loss.

'You haven't taken on any new boarders that I don't know about, have you?' Peter asked.

Mrs Cummins shook her head slowly. 'No, I haven't. It's the same group we've had for weeks without any sort of trouble whatsoever.'

'Do you know if anyone who lives here has had some sort of change of circumstance? Has anyone lost their position with their employer? Or has anyone indicated any need for additional funds?' he asked.

'Not to my knowledge, but I try to make it a habit not to pry. Unless someone had come forward with that information voluntarily, I would have had no idea about it.'

Peter would have to agree with Mrs Cummins's opinion of herself. He had never known her to be one to stick her nose into her tenants' business. In fact, she kept her curiosity to herself to a remarkable degree. She had never asked prying questions of him in any way and the temptation to do so must have been very great, especially once the air raids commenced a few weeks earlier.

As a member of the constabulary, he was in a position to access information not available to the public. He had appreciated the way she had held her tongue whenever he came home late and tired and covered with sooty bits of debris. Still, had her lack of curiosity indicated a general lack of imagination? Would she have been the sort to even recognize if there was something unsavory about one of her lodgers?

Peter himself could not imagine any of his fellow tenants helping themselves to the possessions of others. Even with his time on the police force and the way that such a job tended to foster suspicion of others, he could not truly say that any suspects from among his fellow lodgers sprang to mind

'Perhaps it will all die down without any intervention if you just give it a bit of time,' Peter said.

'But what if it doesn't? What if I gain the reputation as the landlady of the house where one cannot trust the safety of their possessions?' she said. 'After all, who would be in a better position to rob the tenants than I would be?'

'I'm sure no one thinks that way about you,' Peter said. 'If it makes you feel any better, I could look into it as soon as I have a bit of extra time.'

'If you're sure it would be no trouble I would appreciate it,' she said reaching out a plump hand to grasp his own and give it a firm squeeze. 'After all, my reputation is the only thing I have of value and malicious gossip will rob me of it.'

Peter couldn't help but think there was nothing to be done to quell rumors should they start. Gossip was so rife in the city that the city councilors had enthusiastically jumped on the suggestion from the national government to institute a no gossip week during July. The newspapers had admonished the local residents to hold their tongues when it came to any sort of rumor. Despite such efforts, the city roiled with talk about invasion, fifth columnists and rising prices for necessities. There was real fear among officials that the wrong sort of information might reach enemy ears and be used against them all. The port was an active one and much of the business of the war came through it. From supplies coming in to equipment going out, Hull was an important point in the home front efforts.

And even as he tried to assure his landlady that things would certainly turn out in the end, he couldn't push from his mind the truth that his badge was missing. He would not be able to put off alerting Sergeant Skelton much longer. Perhaps an investigation into the other missing items might turn up his badge before he needed to do so.

NINE

B illie had trouble sleeping. She had not passed such a difficult night since her very first in the city of Hull. On that occasion the vision of a dead woman had filled her mind every time she closed her eyes. This time it was a man who stared up at her as she began to dream. As she pushed her way into the police station the following morning, she felt less ready for a long shift than she ever had before. Not only was she exhausted, but she also found herself bracing for a confrontation with Constable Drummond or a chorus of laughter and derisive glances from her fellow constables.

Truth be told, she had considered feigning a stomach ache and calling in sick. Or perhaps feigning was the wrong word. As she walked down the empty corridor towards the women's cloakroom, her guts squeezed with pain. She kept glancing back over her shoulder worried that Constable Drummond would appear out of nowhere, his unwelcomed, grasping hands reaching out for her. With relief she reached the door of the women's cloakroom and stepped inside, shutting it firmly behind herself and locking it. She sagged against it and chided herself for her hammering heart and queasy stomach.

Surely, she must be overreacting. Had what Constable Drummond done really been so frightening? She was a police constable after all and as such ought to be able to handle herself in difficult situations. If she could stare down a dead body in the darkened air-raid shelter, couldn't she face her colleagues right there in the station?

By the time she had gathered her courage and headed into the lobby of the station once more, Sergeant Skelton was standing behind the reception desk drumming his fingers on the countertop. He scowled down at her and then glanced at the clock on the wall above the door.

'It's nice of you to join us. Weren't you supposed to be here ten minutes ago?' he asked.

'I'm sorry, sir. I was here, but I was in the cloakroom,' she said. She could feel the eyes of the constables in the room turning towards her and she heard a stifled snigger.

'If you want to spend time fixing your face and applying your patriotic lipstick, make sure to do so before you leave home for your shift. I expect you to be on time and ready to work. Personal matters do not belong at the constabulary. Do I make myself clear?' he said leaning over her.

There was an undercurrent weaving below his words that Billie did not quite like. She had worried at the time that Sergeant Skelton had misinterpreted what he had seen in the canteen. From the look he gave her and the tone of his words she felt convinced of it. A flash of heat rose in her cheeks made worse by another snigger coming to her from the clutch of constables at the far end of the room. Mortified she bobbed her head.

'It won't happen again, sir,' she said.

'See that it doesn't. I have an assignment for you that needs dealing with immediately. You are to type up the notes from the crime scene from yesterday's investigation. I've asked the constables involved to leave the notes on your desk. They may be hard to decipher, but I'm sure you'll be able to figure it out,' he said.

With that he turned his attention to a woman who had entered the station with a small boy in tow. Wordlessly Billie made for her desk and pulled out her chair. She turned her attention to the task at hand trying to block out the whispers and guffaws emanating from the other occupied desks. She rolled a piece of typing paper under the bar of her typewriter and pulled out one of the memo pads.

She worked her way through the chronicled information until she reached a list of the contents of the victim's pockets. An identification card had been found in his toolbox and another was tucked into the pocket of his coverall. The identification in his coverall matched the name that the supposed shelter inspector had given to the air-raid warden. The one tucked into the toolbox did not.

Not wishing to engage with Sergeant Skelton in front of her colleagues once more, she finished typing up her notes and then jotted down the names and identification numbers from the national registry cards in her police constable's notebook. Without a glance at the other constables, she made her way towards Avis's office. She knocked on the door and was relieved when she heard her superior officer's voice beckoning her inside.

'Do you have a moment, Avis?' Billie asked.

'Certainly. What can I do for you?' she asked.

'I know that I am not one of the investigators for the body that Peter and I found yesterday, but I did have a question about something those officers discovered at the scene,' she said.

'What is it?' Avis asked.

'There were two identification cards found with the body. One of them matches the name of the man Peter and I were sent out to find. The other does not.'

'How do you know this?' Avis asked.

'Sergeant Skelton assigned me to type up the notes on the investigation from the constables' notebooks,' Billie said.

'Sergeant Skelton is having you act as a secretary without speaking to me about it first?' Avis leaned forward in her chair.

Billie knew that Avis and the sergeant did not always see eye to eye on matters at the station. Avis had made it clear that Billie reported to her rather than to the sergeant. That didn't mean that the sergeant didn't take it upon himself to overstep his authority whenever the chance arose. Billie had not thought much of it since Avis had explained when hiring her that the addition of women police constables to the force would involve both walking the beat and administrative tasks.

The only reason women had been permitted to join the organization was to help fill in any gaps left by male members of the constabulary who had joined the armed forces. As tedious as transcribing information jotted down in notebooks tended to be, it had seemed to Billie to be a valid part of a police investigation.

'I had no idea you had not been consulted. I should have spoken to you first, but it can be difficult to refuse the sergeant, especially in front of the rest of the constables. He doesn't seem to be the sort of man who would take being questioned in front of his subordinates very well.'

'You're right about that.' Avis leaned back and let out a deep sigh. 'So, what is the concern that you have?'

'I didn't see any indication that anyone followed up on the discrepancy. I wondered if perhaps the investigators simply assumed that one of the identification cards belongs to someone else. After all, the note said that it was tucked into the victim's toolbox. Perhaps he thought the victim had found it just lying about in the shelter and had picked it up for safekeeping,' Billie said.

'That's one way to look at it. But there are at least two others,' Avis said lifting two fingers in the air.

'Do you think they simply didn't bother to investigate? It was very late last night by the time they finished up,' Billie said.

'That thought had crossed my mind. Not every constable is as thorough as we might like for him or her to be. I don't like to cast aspersions over whole groups of our colleagues, but I have not been entirely impressed with the war reserve constables working out of this station. They strike me as an unapologetically entitled lot and I have little use for them,' Avis said.

'What was the second possibility?' Billie asked.

'I think that it would be wrong to assume that the second identification card was something that the victim picked up along the way. Has it occurred to you that perhaps he was carrying two separate cards of his own?' Avis said.

'Why would he do a thing like that?' Billie asked.

'For a good many reasons. Firstly, if he has two different identities, he could apply for two sets of ration cards. There are any number of people who are interested in gaining access to more food for a variety of reasons.'

'Like what?' Billie asked.

Billie felt shocked to her marrow. While she wasn't entirely naïve, she did like to think the best of people and to her mind observing the ration regulations was the duty of everyone on the home front. After all, it only seemed right to ensure that everyone received their fair share, especially if it meant the difference between feeding the troops adequately or not.

'There are people who tend to be hungrier than others and would like to be able to supplement the quantity of food they are entitled to. There are those who have an extra sweet tooth and find the sugar ration to be desperately punitive. And there are those who would be delighted to collect a second week's worth of supplies which they could then sell on the black market with no reduction in their own ability to eat,' Avis said.

'I suppose that it's possible, especially since he ended up dead,' Billie said. 'Do you think that the discrepancy in identity cards could have some bearing on his murder?'

'I think it would be well worth looking into. Do you know how to read the identity cards?' Avis asked.

Billie nodded. It was one of the first things she had learned since joining the force. In fact, she had had a vague notion of how the identification numbers and letters printed in each of the cards had worked even before she had joined the constabulary. The creation of a national registry was a novelty, but one that had taken root as soon as war was declared. With so many people moving about the country in unprecedented numbers, it must have been a massive undertaking to create such a database.

Each identification number was in fact a series of numbers and letters created from both the name of the individual and the household address at which they lived. At a glance police officers could make a swift assessment as to whether or not the person whose papers they were inspecting was anywhere near their own home. Any large discrepancy between their permanent address and their location was bound to prompt questions.

It had become an even more often used piece of information since the shoreline defense zone had been implemented. No one without legitimate business within five miles of the sea could be permitted to enter such zones. Billie had participated in a number of roundups of individuals and inspections of identity cards. It had never sat well with her, but she could not quite bring herself to speak out against it.

'I do know how to read them. I'm sure that I would be able to locate this address and to make some enquiries. I could easily give a description of the victim to the householder there,' Billie said.

'I think that Sergeant Skelton can relieve you of your typing duties for the rest of the afternoon, especially considering he had no authority to assign them to you in the first place. Head out and confirm the addresses in question and then report back to me with what you find. Will you be all right doing that on your own?' Avis asked. 'Or would you rather that I asked for one of your fellow constables to be assigned to accompany you?'

Billie shook her head vigorously. 'I'm more than happy to go on my own.' She tucked her notebook into her uniform jacket pocket and headed for the door.

TEN

As she consulted her memo pad and deciphered the location the listed address, she strode off confidently towards the south west of the city. Her heart lifted as she made her way along the busy pavement, dodging piles of debris from the air raids as well as long queues forming in front of almost every one of the grocers, butchers and corner stores between the police station and the address she sought.

Perhaps it was the chance to get out of the station and out from under the watchful eye of Sergeant Skelton and the scornful sniggers of her colleagues that improved her mood. Or maybe it was simply the fact that despite all the chaos in the world around her, the sky was blue and birds still flitted across the sky, landing on rooftops, and settling along the leafy branches lining the broad avenues of the city.

The warm summer sun reached down and touched the back of her neck. The smell of ripe fruit wafted towards her, carried on a soft breeze from a greengrocer stand further up the block. On the opposite side of the street a gang of small boys raced off on some sort of adventure known only to themselves, a shaggy brown dog capering at their heels.

Despite the world situation and the nature of her errand, Billie felt like whistling. Her mother had always chided her for her inclination to such an unladylike show of good cheer and for a flicker her elation dampened. Thoughts of her recently deceased mother were still too painful to pass without notice. But dwelling on such things would not change them and wallowing in gloom was not the way to best honor her mother's memory.

She drove thoughts of what she had lost out of her mind as she ran through her mental map of the city. Unless she had misremembered, she was only two or three blocks from the address she sought. Some of the points of interest along the way made it easy for her to maintain her bearings. The

River Humber with its salty breeze served as a constant by which to navigate. It would not matter how many bombs were dropped on the city when it came to using the river to navigate. The very thing that had made it so much easier for the Germans to find Hull even in blackout conditions also made it easier for a newcomer like herself to find her way around.

At the corner she cut through Victoria Square and turned left to skirt Prince's Dock. She was tempted to linger as she passed the window of the art gallery standing on the corner. Promising herself she would come back when she had the time, she hurried along Osborne Street. Cinemas and churches dotted the route. More and more housing sprang up the further she walked from the city center.

But as she came to lower Union Street, she slowed her steps. She turned down the side street and began searching the fronts of the buildings for numbers. Carefully she made her way to the end of the street and then consulted her police constable's notebook again. The address listed on the identity card found in the victim's toolbox was for 67 Lower Union Street. But as she made her way along, she realized the final address on the street was number 63. And as she turned her attention to the street signs, she realized that Lower Union Street terminated abruptly into Great Passage Street.

She looked at the notes once more and wondered if somehow she had misunderstood the system that the national registry used to assign identification numbers. She turned right and entered Upper Union Street wondering if perhaps the numbering simply continued from one street to the next. But no, there was no number 67 to be found on that street either. She doubled back and rechecked to be certain she had not simply missed the address somehow.

But try as she might she could not seem to see number 67. As she stood on the pavement looking up and down, she spotted an older woman laden down with bags. The woman turned towards a building a few houses away and began to mount the stairs. Billie hurried towards her hoping perhaps a local might be able to point her in the right direction.

'Excuse me, ma'am, I wonder if you could help me with some directions,' Billie asked as she approached.

The woman looked her up and down in surprise. 'Are you a constable?' the woman asked as she pointed at Billie's uniform. She still regularly drew stares from passersby as a woman in a police constable's uniform, but she had grown accustomed to attracting notice simply by fulfilling her duties.

'That's right. My name is WPC Harkness, and I am looking for number 67. You wouldn't happen to know where I might find it, would you?'

'I live at number 61 and next door is the last on the street. There isn't a 67,' the woman said. 'But I suppose until recently there weren't any WPCs in the city either. What's it like doing your job?'

From the tone of her voice, the woman sounded like she was genuinely interested in her answer. Although Billie had been growing more and more accustomed to drawing curious glances from members of the public and even the occasional outright criticism, she had far less experience with appreciative commentary or genuine curiosity about her role. It felt strange but not unpleasant to be asked about her job by someone who seemed intrigued rather than repelled by her unorthodox occupation.

'I suppose it's much like doing any other job that is usually performed by men. There are a lot of aspects to the role that are challenging, but for the most part I find it rewarding. I like being able to help people and the constabulary provides me with that opportunity. Are you interested in working with the police?' Billie asked. If the need for WPCs was as dire as the chief had made out it wouldn't do any harm to do a bit of advertising.

'Me? Certainly not. I can't imagine what my husband would say if he found out. But it does seem as though it might be an exciting experience,' the woman said as she leaned forward and scrutinized Billie's uniform more closely. 'Do they provide you with the uniform?'

'Absolutely. I'm not to go out walking the beat without it. And you might be surprised at your husband. A lot of roles that women were discouraged from taking on have opened up in light of the war. Would you have ever thought that so many women would work in armaments factories or even be allowed to enlist in one of the services?' Billie said.

'I suppose not. I've heard rumors that women are going to be required to sign up for some form of war work before much longer. I suppose that I might enjoy working for the police at least as much as I would working in a factory in some part of the country where I'd never been before,' the woman said. 'Are they hiring more women for the constabulary now?'

'I believe that we are looking to hire at least two more women at present. If you're interested in the role stop in at the Central Police Station and ask for Avis Crane. She's the one who hired me,' Billie said.

'I'll keep that in mind. I'm sorry I wasn't able to help you find the address you are looking for. Was it connected with some sort of a crime?' the woman asked.

'Now that I realize it doesn't exist, I'm not exactly sure what it's connected to.'

'It sounds as though your job can be frustrating.'

'I suppose that's one way of looking at it. But for me, anytime I run up against something that can't be explained I'm inclined to be curious rather than frustrated. I'll just need to look into this from another angle,' Billie said. 'Please do stop by the Central Police Station if you want to learn more about the job.'

She touched her uniform cap and took her leave. She looked back when she reached the end of the block and noticed that the woman still stood on her front steps staring at her. Billie raised her hand to wave and the woman returned the salutation before disappearing into her home. Perhaps she would be good at speaking convincingly in front of the city council after all.

She consulted her notebook once more and wondered if the entry in the identity card was a mistake or if it had been purposefully deceitful. With so many cards needing to be produced at such a rapid rate it seemed likely that mistakes would occur. But the fact of the matter was that a card with such an egregious error on it had been found at the scene of a crime. Did that mean it was more likely that there had been a deliberate attempt to falsify the document? As she thought about it, she felt a fool. She should have asked the neighbor if she recognized the names from the identity cards. While speaking with her she had been so focused on trying to recruit her for the constabulary that she had forgotten her purpose for being there in the first place.

She considered returning to ask the woman more questions, but thought better of it. She did not wish to give the woman a poor impression of the only WPC she had met. Besides, perhaps the identity card did not belong to the victim, but rather was something he had simply come across during his inspection of the shelter? If so, the woman would not know him, which begged a question: had anyone verified the address on the identity card he had tucked into his coverall pocket? She had simply assumed that Constables Thompson and Drummond had taken it upon themselves to inform other members of his household what had befallen the victim. She quickened her pace and hurried back to the police station far more eager to return to it than she had thought possible earlier.

ELEVEN

T he station house was relatively quiet when she returned to the building. It was something she had been surprised to notice in her time with the constabulary. Inexplicably there would be a sudden surge of people swarming about the lobby. It was as if there was some sort of mysterious force prompting people to appear to lodge complaints about neighbors or to report missing dogs all at the same time. There were days or parts of days when it could be said that there was standing room only in the lobby of the station. But then, just as suddenly, the entire place would empty out and there would be little else to hear besides the clacking of typewriter keys as constables took advantage of the available time to type up long-overdue reports.

She made her way back to her own desk where she hoped to find those memo books from the crime scene investigators still stacked, awaiting her prowess with a typewriter. But they were nowhere to be seen. Perhaps it was too much to ask that the investigation would have waited for her to return from her errand before someone came to claim their notebook. There was nothing for it but to bring herself to ask Sergeant Skelton if the other address on the second identity card had been verified. She thought it likely he would chide her for sticking her nose in where it didn't belong, but she knew she would not be able to let it go unless she asked.

Sergeant Skelton was not standing behind the reception desk as was his habit and she cast a glance down the corridor leading to the canteen wondering if he might be there. Her stomach knotted up at the thought of returning to a place that had been far enough removed from public view as to make her vulnerable to Constable Drummond's unwanted advances. She couldn't bring herself to move down the corridor to seek out Sergeant Skelton. Before she could convince herself that she was overreacting, the sergeant came into view in the corridor leading from the cloakrooms. She turned on her heel and headed straight for him. If he was going to criticize her for involving herself in the investigation without his permission, it would be better for him to do so away from the lobby.

'So, you've bothered to return to the station, WPC Harkness,' the sergeant said as she stopped directly in front of him. 'I thought perhaps you were off having a picnic, possibly with a gentleman friend, considering the weather is so beautiful.'

She winced at the implication. Did the sergeant really think so little of her professionalism? Matters would likely not be helped by neglecting to consult him before making enquiries behind his back. Still, there was nothing for it but to report her findings.

'Actually, sir, I was following a line of investigation authorized by Avis,' she said.

'What sort of investigation? I thought I told you to type up the notes Thompson and Drummond took yesterday,' he said.

'I did just that and as I completed the task, I came across the information that the victim was found in possession of two identity cards. I took it upon myself to verify one of the addresses. The assumption of the investigators was likely that the victim had simply located someone else's lost card and had placed it in his toolbox. I thought it would be in the public interest for me to return it to whoever had mislaid it,' Billie said.

'Avis authorized this jaunt out into the city on a fine summer day?' he asked.

Every time the sergeant criticized her Billie could not help but notice how much taller than she the man stood. His physical size was intimidating, and it seemed to her that he used it to his advantage whenever he interacted with his subordinates. Her father was a tall man too, but somehow he had never seemed to loom over her the way the sergeant did. She had discovered over the past weeks that if she cowered, it encouraged him to press her harder. Showing a bit of backbone seemed to take some of the wind out of his sails.

'Indeed, she did, sir. And it appears as though there is

something amiss with the identity card,' she said. Before he could mock her for making mountains out of molehills, she hurried on. 'The address listed on the card simply does not exist.'

'That doesn't seem likely. I expect you just missed it since you are a newcomer to the city. And everyone knows that women are no good with directions,' the sergeant said crossing his long arms over his broad chest and scowling down at her.

'I had considered it possible that I had simply missed something, so after pacing back and forth along the street as well as the next one, scouring the buildings for the right number, I approached a resident there and she told me that there has never been a number 67 Lower Union Street,' Billie said.

The sergeant loosened one of his arms and reached up to scratch at the stubble on his chin. 'You're certain about that?' he asked.

'I am,' Billie said. To her surprise she realized that she felt as confident as she sounded to her own ears.

The sergeant nodded slowly. 'Come with me.' He strode past her and made his way into the warren of desks at the far side of the lobby. He stopped at those occupied by Constables Thompson and Drummond. The two men looked up as they approached, and Billie's stomach lurched as Constable Drummond made a show of glancing up and down the length of her. Constable Thompson didn't seem to share his partner's enthusiasm for her presence. In fact, the sneer on his face left little doubt of his attitude towards women on the force. A man in his fifties, Constable Thompson had been on the force ever since he returned from the Great War. As one of the more senior officers in the constabulary it had only seemed sensible that he had been assigned to evaluate the scene of the crime.

Billie was glad she had never had much reason to interact with him during her time with the police. After all, she took every opportunity offered to her to walk the beat, usually with Peter. Constable Thompson spent most of his time at his desk. She was not entirely sure what he did while he sat there, but it was not her place to question him in any way.

'Constable Thompson, have you identified the victim found yesterday?' the sergeant asked.

Constable Thompson's gaze moved between the sergeant and Billie. Constable Drummond's leer remained fixed upon her. She had an almost overwhelming desire to duck behind the sergeant to remove herself from his sight.

'Not yet. Why do you ask? Has someone been complaining about me?' He glanced at Billie once more before clamping his lips together in a thin, bloodless line.

'I'm complaining about you. Identifying the victim should have been at the top of your priority list. Why haven't you bothered yet?' the sergeant asked.

'It took time to document the crime scene and to have the body transported. My shift was long over by the time the coroner collected the body so I figured it could wait until today. He's not about to get any less dead by a few hours delay, is he?' Constable Thompson said with a shrug.

Billie felt the sergeant stiffen and draw himself up to his full height. She noticed that she was holding her breath and forced herself to exhale slowly and silently.

The sergeant turned his head to include Constable Drummond. 'Have either of you verified the victim's address?' he asked.

'What do you mean verified it? His address was written down in his identity card like everyone else's,' Constable Drummond said.

'It's come to my attention that there were two identity cards found at the scene in the victim's possession. Is that how your memory serves?' the sergeant said.

'That's right. There was one identity card in the victim's pocket and another stashed in his toolbox. What of it?'

'WPC Harkness attempted to return the second identity card to the address listed on it and discovered that there was no such address. Now why that might be, I'm sure I cannot yet say. But it seems to me that someone needs to get to the bottom of this man's identity straightaway,' Sergeant Skelton said. 'We don't really know if either of those identity cards belonged to the victim.'

'You're the boss,' Constable Thompson said. 'We'll head over there right now.'

'Don't trouble yourself. I wouldn't want to disrupt your

important work of sorting paperclips and consuming a cup of tea as you ease into your shift. You just stay right here and I'll get someone else to take care of it,' the sergeant said pointing at a steaming cup of tea positioned on Constable Thompson's desk. 'WPC Harkness, you're with me.'

Sergeant Skelton wheeled on his heel and strode towards the station door. Billie could feel the other constables' scowls boring into her back as she hurried after him.

Sergeant Skelton was even more difficult for Billie to keep up with than was Peter. He strode along like an angry giant. Pedestrians veered off their course to avoid being in his oncoming path. As Billie broke into an undignified trot in order to keep up, she could not quite believe that he had asked her to accompany him.

As part of a previous investigation, she had tagged along at Sergeant Skelton's request once before. But that situation was one in which he had relied upon her involvement because he felt that the task at hand was no more than women's work. But this seemed to be a different sort of something. It almost felt as though it were a silent acknowledgment of capability.

The sergeant wove through the streets like the native-born resident she knew him to be. A group of young boys scurried towards them galloping along the pavement and as they approached, she noticed one of them towered over the others. A smile flitted across her face as she imagined Sergeant Skelton running the streets as the tallest member of his own childhood gang years earlier.

The sergeant hurried along the length of Prospect Street and then turned on to Marlborough Terrace. For the first time since they left the station he turned and addressed her.

'What was the number again?' he asked. She flipped open her police notebook and consulted what she had written.

'Number 21,' she said.

He nodded, strode halfway up the block, and took the steps up to a brick three-story building two at a time. She followed behind him as quickly as she could and stood on the top step as he grasped the heavy brass door knocker in his large hand and rapped firmly.

After a moment Billie could hear the sound of footsteps

beyond the door. It creaked open with a loud groan of the hinges and standing in front of them was a young woman with a baby held on her hip. Her hair was covered with a headscarf and a faded floral pinny covered her dress. If Billie had to guess she would have said that they had caught the woman in the midst of some housekeeping duties.

The baby stared at them with large blue eyes and slipped its small thumb into its mouth. Billie's heart gave a squeeze as she wondered if the woman standing before them was about to hear her baby was fatherless. As the woman seemed to realize that a pair of constables in uniform stood on her step her face took on a guarded expression.

'May I help you, Officer?' she asked as she wrapped her arm a bit more tightly around the baby.

Sergeant Skelton removed his hat and tucked it under his arm. 'Would a Mr David Phillips be a resident here?' he asked.

The woman gave her head a slight shake. 'No. No one by the name of David lives here. Are you sure you have the right address?' she asked.

'Is this number 21 Marlborough Terrace?' the sergeant asked.

'Yes, that's right,' the woman said. 'But there's no one named David here.'

The sergeant turned to Billie. 'Are you sure you have that address down correctly?'

'Absolutely, sir.' She turned to the woman. 'Are you new to this residence?' she asked.

'Not particularly. I grew up in the flat on the second floor and when my husband enlisted, I gave up my place across the city and moved in here. My parents still live in the flat above and are helping me out with the baby. In all the years that I have lived in this building there's never been a David Phillips in residence, at least not to my knowledge.'

'The man that we are looking for is approximately six feet tall with sandy blond hair and blue eyes. He has a medium build and works as an inspector for the city. Does that ring any bells?' Sergeant Skelton asked.

'No, I can't say that it does. There are only three flats in this building and besides my parents and me the only other resident is an elderly woman and her daughter who live on the third floor.'

'Could this David Phillips have simply been staying with your elderly neighbor or her daughter? Could he have been family or a friend?' Sergeant Skelton asked.

'I shouldn't have thought so. I'm home most of the time with the baby and I've never seen anyone matching that description entering the building. The residents of the third floor keep to themselves mostly and their flat is tiny. I don't think there would have been room for another person to have moved in,' she said.

'Thank you very much for your time. I'm sorry if we worried you,' Sergeant Skelton said.

'You did rather. I thought maybe you were bringing me terrible news about my husband,' she said shifting the baby to her other hip.

'I apologize for that. But if you remember anything about someone matching that description or you happen to hear something from your neighbors, would you get a message to the Central Station?' he asked.

'I don't expect I shall, but I'll do so if I remember anything,' she said stepping back into her hallway and pushing the door shut.

'Well, WPC Harkness, what do you make of that?' the sergeant said as he made his way back down the steps and on to the pavement below.

'I think it seems as though perhaps this murder is more complicated than it might have looked like at first sight,' she said.

'I'm inclined to agree. What would you do next if you were the one leading this investigation?' he asked.

Billie glanced up at him in surprise. Was he mocking her? The look on his face appeared sincere and she wondered if perhaps she had been attributing thoughts to the sergeant that he was not actually having. As she considered it, she concluded that his gruff demeanor did not only include her. His treatment of Constable Thompson had certainly not been friendly. She turned her thoughts to his question.

'I think that while I awaited the coroner's report, I would

do my best to identify the victim. It seems to me that it would be impossible to solve the crime if we didn't at least know that much,' she said.

'Very commendable. And how would you go about identifying this man?'

'I suppose I would contact the national registry and ask for all the listings for the name David Phillips in the city.'

'Is that all you would do?' he asked.

'No. As we now have proof that he was discovered with two identity cards containing false information, there is no reason to believe either of the names on the identity card were legitimate. I think that it would be unwise to assume that even if the national registry could provide a list of David Phillipses in the city, we would be any closer to identifying him for certain.'

'So, what would be your course of action after that?' he asked keeping his gaze trained on her face.

'The air-raid patrol warden who called with the original complaint told Peter and me that when the victim appeared at his door he claimed to work for the council. I would verify whether or not someone named David Phillips is in fact employed by the council as a shelter inspector,' she said.

'That seems like a very sound course of action. Let's head back to the station and have you start making some calls,' he said brushing past her and striding quickly down the street.

As she raced to catch up with him, she felt a glow of pride at his unexpected praise. Could it be that the sergeant was simply tough on all new recruits? Did it have very little to do with her gender and more to do with the fact that she was a complete novice?

And what did it mean that he was trusting her to contribute to the investigation? Not only that, would his show of confidence put her even more on the back foot with her colleagues? She couldn't imagine that Constable Thompson would be particularly happy to have his investigation hijacked by the newest member of the constabulary, and a woman at that.

TWELVE

Her first call was to City Hall. It took some time to be connected with the person in charge of public air-raid shelters, but once she did, she hit another dead end. According to the man in charge, no person named David Phillips was on the staff as a city inspector in any capacity. Undaunted, she asked to be transferred to the person in charge of payroll.

By the time a quarter of an hour had passed, she was able to ascertain that no one by that name was employed in any capacity by the city council. She then contacted the national registry and made enquiries about persons by the name of David Phillips in the city. While the woman with whom she spoke was pleasant enough, she indicated it would be some time before her request could be processed. The registry was constantly overwhelmed by requests for information and were far too short-staffed to meet their regular demands to be able to quickly find an answer to her question. The woman promised to get back to her as soon as she could, but as Billie disconnected, she couldn't help but feel stymied.

As she made her way to the front desk to report her lack of success to Sergeant Skelton, a bulletin board mounted on the wall across from the reception desk caught her eye. She paused and looked it over carefully. There pinned to the wall were sketches of several wanted persons. She turned and stepped towards the desk with considerably more enthusiasm.

'Have you discovered a name for the victim yet?' Sergeant Skelton asked leaning towards her.

'Not quite yet. Truthfully, I've had very little success with the city council or the national registry. I've been able to ascertain that he was not an inspector, at least not as far as the city knew. It will be some time before the national registry will be able to get back to me,' Billie said.

'So not a particularly desirable result for your efforts,' he said.

'I would agree, sir, but I did have another possible avenue to pursue. Could we have a police sketch artist create a rendering of his likeness to put up throughout the city? I could even go door-to-door and make enquiries in the general area in which he was found,' Billie said.

The sergeant drummed his long fingers on the countertop then nodded. 'I'll make some calls and have a sketch artist sent over to the morgue right away. As soon as a couple of copies of the sketch can be made, I'll send you and Peter out to canvass the neighborhood where he was found. We'll start with house-to-house in light of the paper ration, but if you don't turn up anything soon we will make flyers to post up around the city.'

'Perhaps you might make one additional copy to be put up at the information bureau at the library. I could ask my cousin Lydia to have the staff there direct patrons' attention to it as they come in on other information bureau business,' Billie said.

'Not bad, WPC Harkness. Not bad at all,' Sergeant Skelton said, his voice lifted a little above a comfortable speaking tone. Billie could feel Constable Thompson's gaze lingering on her. As proud as she was of the sergeant's praise, she was certain she was going to pay for it with her colleagues.

It took far less time for a sketch to be produced than Billie would have expected. There was something to be said about having the sergeant's backing if one wanted to get things done in a hurry. Rather than wait for copies to be produced, Billie suggested that she take the original sketch and begin the door-to-door search. Sergeant Skelton agreed that she could head out on her own and suggested that it would be expeditious if she met Peter at his boardinghouse to begin his shift rather than waiting for her partner to come to the station.

Billie couldn't be sure, but she wondered if perhaps the sergeant was trying to get her out of the station. It wasn't like him to be so interested in allowing her to walk the beat rather than performing administrative duties in the station house. In fact, until recently, he had seemed to be against the idea of women serving out on patrol and it had taken Avis forcing the issue for her to be allowed out on the beat in the first place. Could it be that the incident with Constable Drummond was on the sergeant's mind and that was why he seemed so eager to get her out of the way? Or was it possible that he was starting to consider she might be a capable officer and that he actually trusted her to perform her duties?

Regardless of his motivation, she was glad to be out on the street once more. Peter's boardinghouse was situated in the general area in which the body had been found. It made sense to begin in the victim's last known location and to fan out from there. She had never been to Peter's residence before, but she knew approximately where he lived and was pleased to see that it was a leisurely ten-minute walk from the police station.

The sun had grown high in the sky and despite the fact that temperatures in the north were so much cooler than those she was used to in the south, she was becoming a bit warm in her uniform jacket. Perhaps she was acclimatizing to the temperatures as well as the other things about the environment that had been so alien to her only weeks before. Her first few days in Hull had felt absolutely icy, especially considering she had arrived in June. Even though the city was many miles inland from the sea, it lay against the River Humber which was in fact a tidal waterway. Cool damp winds from the North Sea made their way straight through the city, funneling between buildings like cold, salty knife blades.

She had not been prepared for how pervasive the presence of the sea could be even miles inland. Her village in Wiltshire had no such conditions. In fact, the nearest body of water was a mill pond in the village green. The sea was another sort of beast entirely. From the constant tickle of the wind to the way that the damp air turned bread and biscuits stale in less time than she could have thought possible, the sea made its presence known.

As she made her way along, she stopped now and again to inquire of people hurrying along the street if they recognized the man in the sketch. Person after person paused briefly, squinted at the paper outstretched in her hands, and shook their heads before hurrying along on their own business. She thought it likely that they would need to make copies and pin them up throughout the city if they were to make any progress in identifying him. After all, the city was large, and it was easy for a single person to get lost in the crowd. Surely someone must know who he was, but finding that person in among the thousands of other residents felt a daunting task.

She wondered too if the possibility of posting up leaflets would actually yield a result. If there was an air raid there was no guarantee that there would be any leaflets left when all was said and done. The incendiary bombs placed so many things one would have taken for granted only months earlier in doubt. With paper shortages being what they were, she hated to embark on a course of action that would simply be counted a waste.

She consulted her police constable's notebook and double checked the address Sergeant Skelton had provided. Just a little further along the street her partner's lodgings reared up from the pavement. The house was built of dull, buff brick and was completely without ornamentation. No shutters, gingerbread or iron scrollwork clung to the façade in an attempt to soften the blunt edges of the building. But it looked well-kept and the street was filled with similarly respectable buildings.

She felt a nervous flutter in her stomach as if somehow lines were being crossed. She believed that she had developed a good working relationship with Peter, but she would not have described them as friends. It occurred to her that arriving unexpectedly at his home might be perceived as overly familiar.

She mounted the steps and rapped upon the door with what she hoped sounded like more confidence than she felt. The door opened almost as soon as the second blow landed upon the heavy wooden plank and Peter stood before her, a quiz-zical look on his face.

'WPC Harkness, what are you doing here?' he asked.

'Sergeant Skelton sent me to meet you here for the begin-ning of your shift. He wants us to conduct a house-to-house enquiry to discover the identity of the man we found in the air-raid shelter,' she said.

'He still hasn't been identified yet?' Peter said stepping

backwards and beckoning her into the hallway. She followed him into the cool narrow space.

'No, he hasn't.'

'I thought there were identity cards found with the body,' he said.

'There were two, but neither of them seems to actually have been valid and there was a certain lack of urgency on Constable Thompson's part about looking into the matter in the first place,' Billie said wondering if Peter would share her views on their colleague.

'I wondered what kind of result would be had by Constable Thompson being in charge of the scene of the crime. He never struck me as a particularly dedicated officer,' Peter said.

'I think Sergeant Skelton is inclined to agree with you. He gave him quite a dressing down at the station. I think that may come back to haunt me,' Billie said.

'Why should Constable Thompson blame you for something that the sergeant did?'

'Because I was the one who brought to his attention that the identification had not yet been made. The sergeant asked me to type up notes from the crime scene and when I investigated further it turned out that he simply hadn't bothered to follow through,' Billie said.

'I'll bet that didn't sit well with him,' Peter said. 'Was Drummond raked over the coals, too?'

'The sergeant reprimanded them both. It was awkward to say the least.'

Peter raised an eyebrow and Billie wondered if she had said something that surprised him. She couldn't imagine that he would have found it comfortable to witness a pair of their colleagues receiving a dressing-down. Could it be that Peter thought she found the situation uncomfortable because he was under the impression that she held Constable Drummond in any special regard? She felt a flash of heat to her cheeks. She wished she felt she could tell him what had actually taken place in the station's kitchenette. Instead, she changed the subject.

'So, because the victim is still unidentified, you and I are doing a house-to-house.'

Billie held out the sketch and Peter took a close look at it before handing it back. She followed him to the end of the hallway to the kitchen where a woman of approximately her mother's age stood stirring something on the cooker. The woman turned around and gave Billie a welcoming smile.

'You must be the WPC that Peter has mentioned from time to time,' the woman said.

Billie stepped forward and held out her hand. 'That's right. I'm Billie Harkness. It's a pleasure to meet you,' she said.

'This is my landlady Mrs Cummins,' he said.

'It's about time you brought her round. Can I interest you in a cup of tea, young lady?' Mrs Cummins asked.

'Thank you for the offer, but Peter and I have to head out on our shift. We're making house-to-house enquiries about an unidentified man,' Billie said.

'Surely you must have time for just a bit of something. I've got a cake that I've made for tea and since Peter won't be here again this evening, I could slice a piece off now to tide you over before you go out. I'm sure it's hungry work walking about the city, especially in this heat,' Mrs Cummins said fanning herself slightly with her pinny.

Peter reached his hand out behind Billie's back and tugged on her jacket, a gesture she interpreted to be one suggesting that she refuse the offer once again.

'I'm sure it wouldn't do for us to be taking a break while on duty. Besides, the matter is one of some urgency and I don't believe the task will prove easy. I suspect that we will need all the time available to us. Perhaps another time,' Billie said smiling at Mrs Cummins in an effort to soften her words.

The landlady took a step forward and glanced down at the sketch that Billie held. 'Let me take a look at that,' she said reaching out and plucking it from Billie's hands. She held the sketch up in front of her then turned to Peter. 'It doesn't look exactly the same, but this man looks remarkably like the billeting officer that was here a few days ago from the RAF.'

'Are you sure?' Peter asked.

'Well, I cannot say for absolute certain, but it looks remarkably like him. Has something happened to the poor man?' she asked as she handed the sketch back to Billie.

'I'm sorry we really can't give out any information about an ongoing investigation. Do you remember what he said his name was?' Peter said.

'Dermot maybe, or Delwin. I can't remember for certain,' she said.

'Do you remember anything else about him? Did he show you any identification when you answered the door?' Peter asked.

'I don't believe so. You know it wouldn't have occurred to me to ask him for something like that. He was in a uniform after all,' Mrs Cummins said with a shrug. 'If you can't trust an officer in uniform, who can you trust?'

Billie turned to Peter. 'We could check with the local outpost of the RAF to ask if they had an officer answering to this description who has gone missing.'

Peter nodded. 'You've been a really great help, Mrs Cummins,' Peter said. 'I'll see you tonight.'

'You be sure to bring your young lady back for tea sometime. It's nice to see you making friends on the job, Peter,' Mrs Cummins said turning her attention to Billie once more. 'I worry about him, you know I do. Constantly run off his feet, he has no time for a social life and never one to be seen with the young ladies. You're a bright spot.'

Billie wasn't sure where to look. She felt heat rising on the back of her neck. The notion that her connection with Peter could be interpreted as a social one left her feeling awkward and uncomfortable. It was one thing to behave as friendly colleagues, but another to be labeled as a girl he spent time with. Perhaps that was the reason he had tugged on her jacket. Maybe he wanted to let her know that a collision of professional and personal would not do. She doubted very much she would be returning to Peter's boardinghouse for cozy cups of tea in the sitting room.

'It's kind of you to say, Mrs Cummins. Thanks again for your help.' She lifted her hand and touched the brim of her uniform cap.

Peter made his goodbyes and turned towards the hallway. She followed him out of the house and down on to the pavement. Out of the corner of her eye she was certain she noticed a curtain pulling ever so slightly sideways. Had Mrs Cummins scurried to the front window to watch them walk away? No wonder Peter had been eager to minimize their time in her presence.

'Rather than spending all afternoon walking the beat, it seems to me our time might be better spent heading back to the station and contacting the RAF base,' he said.

'That would certainly save us a lot of time and effort if he did work for the RAF. But considering he also said that he worked for the council and that turned out to be an untruth, I'm not sure I'm holding out much hope,' Billie said.

'What you mean he didn't work for the council?' he asked.

'That was one of the other things I followed up on. I placed a call to the council using the identity card found on his body. There was no employee of the city in any department under either of the names found on the cards.'

'Let's stop at the next police call box and have one of the telephone operators place the call for us. That way if it comes to nought we can head straight back out on to the house-to-house again,' he said.

Billie nodded and struck off in the direction of the call box she had passed on her way to Peter's boardinghouse. The system was remarkably efficient and something she had not given a lot of thought to before joining the constabulary. Police call boxes were placed at even intervals throughout the city and made communication smooth and surprisingly easy. It was even possible to have calls patched through to other locations from the telephone office within the police station. Not that the boys who served as telephone operators were always the most focused, but given the times, she thought they were more useful than having no one to do the job at all.

Upon reaching the call box Peter connected with the station house and requested that the closest RAF base be contacted. After agreeing to check back by the time they reached the next call box, he hung up and turned to Billie once more.

'We could try all the houses between here and the next call box. Perhaps we'll get lucky,' he said.

'That would make for a pleasant change,' Billie said.

As they approached building after building fewer than half

of the residences appeared to have anyone at home. But of those residents who answered the door, several of them confirmed Mrs Cummins's story. They too had received a visit from a man in an RAF uniform on the same day Peter's landlady had. None of them could seem to recall the man's name nor had they made any sort of thorough examination of credentials. Each of them had admitted they had simply trusted him at his word based on the mere fact that he wore a uniform. Many of them recognized the man in the sketch. By the time they reached the next call box it had become clear that their victim had spent at least some time in the neighborhood before he died.

Billie rang the station from the call box and asked to be connected with the operator making enquiries at the base.

'They were quite certain that there was no one who had been sent to make billeting enquiries on their behalf this week?' Billie asked. She turned and looked at Peter as she listened to the rest of the message.

'According to the spokesperson at the RAF base, they haven't had anyone making billeting enquiries in the last couple of months.'

'I suppose it was too much to hope we had found him considering the lie he told to Mr James,' Peter said.

'Who in the world was he?' Billie asked.

THIRTEEN

Special Constable Upton's Police Notebook

As they continued on their task he surreptitiously glanced over at his partner. He couldn't be sure, but he thought there was a new guardedness in her demeanor. Was it his imagination or had she left a bit more distance between them than was her habit as they made their way along the pavement? Her usual running stream of chatter comprised of questions about the job at hand was completely absent. As much as it surprised him to notice it, he rather missed being peppered by her many questions, most of which were surprisingly astute.

No, whatever had transpired between WPC Harkness and Constable Drummond, it had cast a shadow over her. He hoped, not only for the sake of the case, but for the way it would give her something different to think about, that they would discover the victim's identity very soon. The summer sun beat down on his shoulders and before they had knocked on a dozen doors, he wished that his uniform jacket were made of lighter fabric. Still, he was lucky to have a uniform at all. The special constables had not been provided with any sort of uniform until an inspector for the king had arrived in the city and had lodged a complaint with the city council.

The inspector had railed against the city councilors for neglecting to provide them with such necessary equipment. With the cost of shoes being what they were, and the fact that more and more items were becoming difficult to procure, it had been quite a hardship to walk off good shoe leather in the course of their duties. Added to that was the fact that war reserve constables, like Constable Drummond and Constable Thompson, were not only paid for their time on the job, but were given uniforms from the very beginning of war being declared. It had done a great deal for the morale of volunteers like himself to be provided with uniforms and a pair of sturdy leather boots.

Despite any envy about the other man being paid, Peter knew that the tightness in his chest came from imagining Constable Drummond putting his paws all over WPC Harkness, whether he was invited to or not. Peter tried to push such images from his mind and refused to examine closely why he would be so bothered by them. He told himself that if there was one thing he hated to see it was men taking advantage of women.

He had had more than enough of that when his mother had remarried, and the true nature of her new husband's character had come to light. Despite his mother's efforts to hide them, Peter had discovered the bruises that his stepfather had left on her not long after their marriage. He had taken it upon himself to sort his stepfather out decisively. But this seemed to be another matter entirely. Who was he to say that WPC Harkness didn't fancy Constable Drummond? She didn't seem to be the sort of girl who would mix her professional and personal lives, but what did he know of how such things were done down south? Maybe the rules of society were far more lax in communities where everyone seemed to know each other.

His thoughts were brought back to the task at hand when he heard her call out to him from a house across the street from where he stood. Peter crossed the broad avenue to join her.

'I've just spoken with a woman living here who said she thinks she recognized the victim as someone who lives three houses down. She said she couldn't be absolutely certain, but he looked extremely familiar,' Billie said.

'In which direction?' Peter asked.

Billie pointed up the street, an eager look on her face. 'She said it's that one.'

They hurried up the pavement and climbed the stairs to the indicated multistory building. It looked remarkably like Peter's own boardinghouse with its utilitarian design and slightly shabby appearance. He knocked upon the door with more force than strictly necessary, a fact he realized when the door opened, and a startled looking woman stood in the doorway. Behind him, he heard WPC Harkness sharply draw in her breath.

'May I help you, Constable?' she said looking Peter up and down while clutching the side of the door until her knuckles turned white. 'We haven't violated any blackout ordinances, have we?'

'Not that I know of. I'm actually here to ask if you recognize the man in this sketch?' he said.

He held out his copy of the victim's likeness for her to see. Her eyes widened even further. She looked up and seemed to spot WPC Harkness for the first time.

'That's him. That's our lodger, the one that I came to the station to report missing,' she said. 'You're the constable I spoke with at the front desk.' She pointed towards WPC Harkness.

'Are you saying that the man in this sketch lived here?' he asked.

'Lived here? Are you saying something happened to him?' she said gripping the door even more tightly.

'Perhaps it would be better if we came in,' WPC Harkness said taking a step forward. 'This might not be the sort of conversation to be had in front of all the neighbors.'

The woman took a step back and pulled the door open widely. 'You'd best follow me.'

She led them down a short hallway to a small sitting room where heaps of magazines and a basket of mending filled two of the chairs. He and WPC Harkness stood awkwardly as the woman sank into the only available spot on the sofa as if she did not have the strength to stand.

'It's Mrs Sanford, is it not?' WPC Harkness asked.

'Yes, that's me, Phyllis Sanford.'

'Could you please remind me of the name of your lodger?' WPC Harkness asked.

'Dennis Partridge. Are you going to tell me what's happened to him?' Mrs Sanford asked.

'I'm sorry to say he was found dead in an air-raid shelter,' Peter said.

'I wasn't aware that anyone had been killed during any of the air raids lately,' Mrs Sanford said looking up.

'I'm afraid he wasn't killed during enemy action. It's just that his body was found in one of the air-raid shelters,' Peter said.

Mrs Sanford looked at Billie. 'When was he found?'

'The day before yesterday,' WPC Harkness said.

'Why did it take you so long to inform me?' Mrs Sanford said.

'We had rather a lot of trouble identifying him,' WPC Harkness said.

Mrs Sanford sank further back against the sofa. Her hand reached up and clutched at the base of her throat. 'Was he disfigured in some way?'

'No, it was nothing like that. It was just that there were some irregularities with his identification card,' WPC Harkness said.

'Would it be possible for us to take a look at his room?' Peter asked.

'Why would you need to do that? Didn't he die in some sort of an accident?'

'We're still trying to determine exactly what happened. It would help if we had more information about Mr Partridge. Do you know anything about his family? For instance, was he a local man?' Peter asked.

'No, he had come to Hull recently from somewhere further south. His accent wasn't from around here. A bit posh, if you know what I mean,' Mrs Sanford said.

'It really would help us if we could take a look at his room,' WPC Harkness said.

'I'm afraid that my husband insisted we box up all of his possessions and let the room to someone new. I didn't want to since I hoped that Mr Partridge would return, but George said that we had already lost enough money on him since his rent was past due. He had no patience with waiting any longer to turn a profit on the room,' Mrs Sanford said. 'We didn't do anything illegal, did we?'

'I don't believe so. Do you have the boxes here on the premises?' Peter said.

Mrs Sanford got to her feet and motioned for them to follow her. She led them to a cupboard under the stairs and yanked on a string dangling from the ceiling. The small space filled with light and Peter could see two cartons stacked on the floor before them.

'I really don't think there's anything else I can tell you and I have a lot of work to do here at the house before I head out for my shift at the mobile fire canteen. If there's nothing else, I'd like to get back to it,' Mrs Sanford said.

'We should like to have your permission to remove these items and take them with us to the station until his next of kin can be contacted to collect them.' Peter gestured towards the boxes and Mrs Sanford gave a bob to her head in consent.

'Before you go could you tell us where Mr Partridge worked?' WPC Harkness asked.

Peter chided himself for not thinking to ask that question himself. Although, to be fair, they had been told two lies about his employer already. Perhaps Mrs Sanford was no more knowledgeable about his actual employer than the air-raid patrol warden or his very own landlady had been.

'He worked as a lorry driver for one of the armaments factories on the west side. He was already working for them when he came to lodge with us. Perhaps his colleagues will be able to tell you more about his personal life than I can. He was rarely here and while he was a very pleasant man he did not speak about himself very often.'

Peter handed the smaller of the two boxes to WPC Harkness and lifted the larger himself. As soon as Mrs Sanford closed the door of the boardinghouse behind them, he turned to his partner.

'What do you think the chances are that he will actually be employed as a lorry driver?' he asked.

'I think our best course of action given his track record would be to take these boxes back to the station house and go through them. We could always place a telephone call from the station to his supposed employer to verify whether or not he worked there,' WPC Harkness said.

Peter thought about Sergeant Skelton's admonition to keep

WPC Harkness well away from the station house as often as possible. Heading back with the boxes straightaway would not accomplish that task. Still, there was nothing else to be done. As they made their way down the street Peter thought of how sad it was that all that was left of a man's life could be contained in just two cartons.

FOURTEEN

I f Billie had thought that the day had grown warm on her way to Dennis Partridge's boardinghouse, it was nothing compared to the walk back to the station heavily laden by a box of his possessions. While she did want to be treated as an equal, she was grateful that Peter had taken the larger box himself. It even seemed to her that he had slowed his usual rapid strides to a more sedate pace in order to give her the opportunity to keep up.

By the time they reached the station house she was desperate for something to drink but was determined not to return to the station canteen. After placing the box on Peter's desk she excused herself to the women's cloakroom and using her cupped hands slaked her thirst under the tap.

She removed her uniform hat and smoothed her hair into place as she gazed into the mirror hung above the sink. She opened her locker and retrieved her new lipstick from her handbag and turned back to the mirror to touch up her face. She could hardly believe how accustomed she had grown to the ritual of applying makeup. She still did not feel like any sort of expert at the process, but she had come to view it as part of her daily routine.

As she touched the crimson lipstick to her lower lip she felt a sudden pang of anxiety. Her mother had always discouraged the use of cosmetics and had claimed that wanton use of them would destroy a woman's reputation. Could it be that her use of lipstick was part of the reason Constable Drummond felt emboldened to make such unwanted gestures towards her?

But if that were the case, why would the government be so encouraging to take special care with one's looks? Hadn't every woman in the country been urged to keep up appearances and that it was a sign of morale as opposed to loose morals if a woman wore lipstick on a daily basis? Surely the prime minister had not intended for rosy lips to serve as a welcome mat for those who might wish to take advantage. She told herself to stop wasting so much energy by rehashing the whole sordid incident in her mind and to second-guess her every move. She swiped a fresh coat of Victory Red over her lips before returning the tube to her handbag and stepping out into the hallway with her head held high.

Peter had prized the lid off his carton and had begun spreading items from within it over the surface of his desk. Billie was surprised to see what appeared to be an RAF jacket, an ARP armband as well as a pair of coveralls.

'What was this man involved with?' Billie asked. 'It seems as though he had an iron in every fire.'

Peter nodded and reached back into the carton. 'Take a look at these,' he said pointing down into the box. Billie stepped closer and peered into its depths. Along with a few shirts, pairs of socks and underthings the box held an assortment of hats that would easily suggest that he was working in a number of different occupations. She reached in and pulled out a fireman's helmet that had clearly seen good use.

'I wish that thing meant that he at least served as a volunteer firefighter, but I have my doubts,' Peter said. 'For all we know nothing about this man was as it seems.'

'Maybe there will be something in this box that will be of use,' Billie said lifting the lid of the second box and peering inside it.

She pushed aside a tatty pack of playing cards, a cigarette lighter and a dog-eared paperback detective novel; something more promising caught her eye. Several pay envelopes were held together with a paperclip. Each of the envelopes listed Dennis Partridge as the payee. She felt a flutter of excitement as she considered that they might actually be discovering the victim's real identity.

'Mrs Sanford was right about his name and his place of employment from the looks of things. These are from the East Riding Armaments Factory.' She pushed her box aside and held out the envelopes to Peter who looked at them and nodded.

'I think our next move would be to go on over to the factory and see what we can find out about Dennis Partridge,' Peter said as he tucked the bundle of envelopes into his uniform jacket pocket. She followed Peter's lead and hurriedly returned the items to the box before her.

'Are you sure we shouldn't simply telephone the factory first? After all it seems as though we have been running all over the city looking for this man,' Billie said.

'Would you rather stay here at the station house?' Peter asked.

He gave her such an intense glance that she wondered again if he understood how uncomfortable she was to be near Constable Drummond. Was it possible that he was trying to give her the opportunity to avoid him? If so, it raised him in her esteem. Not that he had needed any raising. After all, he had been a good mentor to her since she had arrived.

Out of the corner of her eye she could see Constable Drummond making halfhearted efforts to type up something. The only reason she might wish to stay around the station was to report what she and Peter had discovered about the victim to Avis. There was something about the case that worried her.

The rumors of fifth columnists in the country and in the city itself could not be easily dismissed. In fact, they could not be dismissed at all. There were no real numbers to be had of how many ordinary subjects of the Crown were sympathetic to the Nazi cause, but what was known was that they existed and that they were not easy to spot as they went about their ordinary lives. Billie glanced at the variety of clothing items on Peter's desk with the growing feeling of concern.

It was possible that the victim had simply used those items for some sort of personal gain. But it was also possible that he had used them in aid of the enemy and that was the sort of thing Avis would want to hear about. Not only was her superior concerned with the more run-of-the-mill crimes that occurred in the city, but also with those with far greater stakes for them all than petty thefts or even something as egregious as an individual murder.

It was not something she wanted to voice to Peter quite yet, however. Even though she trusted him, it was always safest to keep quiet about that sort of suspicion whenever possible. Unsubstantiated rumors did no one any good and often did a great deal of harm. Besides, she might not be right about possible enemy activity and she would hate for Peter to think her an alarmist. That was the sort of accusation that men so often leveled at women and one that she did not intend to contend with along with everything else being said about her. She decided to seek out Avis after they had more information available.

'And miss out on the chance to see what someone has to say about our mystery man? Certainly not,' Billie said reaching for her uniform cap and sticking it on her head. 'I'm ready if you are.'

FIFTEEN

The armaments factory was too far out from the center of the city to be easily reached on foot, so they headed for the first tram car stop and waited for one to come into view. Once again Peter asked Billie to be the one to flash her badge in order to mount the tram car without the need for a ticket. There was something about his insistence on her taking the lead in such matters that didn't sit quite right.

Although she had accepted his previous explanation when they visited Mr James, the ARP Warden, it hardly seemed to be the same situation with the tram conductor. But perhaps he had simply wanted to give her one more opportunity to be perceived as the one in a leadership role. The tram driver had raised an eyebrow in surprise when he spotted Peter over her shoulder standing there passively, but he had simply waved them both aboard without an actual comment beyond his quizzical glance.

As the tram wended its way through the city, she felt a sudden pang. She wished she could share the experience with her brother Frederick. He had been missing since Dunkirk and every day hope for his return grew fainter. To her knowledge, Frederick had never ridden in a tram, and she suspected he would have found the experience to his liking. Her brother had always been interested in all things mechanical. She felt herself smile as she imagined Frederick sitting directly behind the driver making a nuisance of himself by asking a great many questions about how the whole thing worked.

It was funny the sorts of things that people in the city took for granted that she had never encountered before arriving in Hull. The height of the buildings, the ceaseless rumble of traffic along the streets, the profusion of cinemas, restaurants and dance halls. She wondered if Peter ever gave any thought to how miraculous the tram system truly was.

They rode on in silence and she was surprised at how comfortable it was to be in his presence without the need to speak. He wasn't the most talkative of men in general and the clamor of the open vehicle and the constant hum of conversation around them would have made the effort to speak all the greater. Besides, the thing that was most on her mind that she would wish to share with him were questions about the case. It would not do to speak of such things in front of members of the public. Not only would it be a breach of police procedure to discuss an ongoing case where they might be overheard, it occurred to Billie that knowing how easily someone could convince strangers of their identity would serve to damage public morale. If people on the home front lost heart she was quite certain they would stand very little chance of coming out on top.

Peter shifted in his seat and stood, grasping the leather strap hanging from the ceiling to steady himself. Billie rose and as the tram jolted to a stop, she lost her footing and careened against him. He reached out with his free hand to steady her and for just a split second her heart clutched with fear. Despite the fact that the tram in no way resembled that small room in the police station at the end of the hall, feeling a colleague's arm wrapping around her waist brought the whole scene flooding back to her.

She pulled away and hoped she had not given offense. As she glanced up at Peter's face, she could not quite decipher the emotion she saw playing across it. It might have been concern or it might have been regret. But if it was regret, she did not know what caused it. Did he regret having distressed her or did he regret not being able to hold her pressed against himself for a longer stretch of time? He stepped back to allow her to slide out from her spot near the open window and into the exit corridor.

As she descended the steps after thanking the driver, she forced herself to push the episode entirely out of her mind and to return to the investigation at hand.

'How far is it to the armaments factory?' she asked as Peter stepped down on to the pavement behind her.

He raised his hand and pointed to a building at the far end of the block. 'That's it right there,' he said. Without the weight of Dennis Partridge's boxes slowing him down, Peter resumed his usual swift gait. Billie hurried to keep up with him and in no time they stood in front of a security guard who asked for identification before permitting them to enter the building. Once more Billie was the one to reach into her jacket pocket to pull out her badge. The guard waved them through and after explaining the reason for their visit to a blonde receptionist with an impressively constructed hairdo they were asked to take a seat while she telephoned to someone from the hiring department. After a few moments another woman in a dark navy gabardine suit appeared and introduced herself.

'Constables, I understand you wish to speak with someone about one of our employees. I'm Mrs Monroe, the head of the personnel department, and if you'll come right this way, I'd be happy to answer any of your questions,' she said.

She gestured for them to follow her down a long corridor past a large room filled with a couple dozen fresh-faced young women seated at typewriters. They turned down another hallway and she pushed open the door to a private office where she indicated they should each take a seat.

'So, tell me, what exactly is this about?' she asked.

'We wish to verify that the man named here was in fact in your employ,' Peter said pulling the stack of pay envelopes from his inner pocket and sliding them across Mrs Monroe's desk.

She lifted a pair of reading glasses from the chain holding them around her neck and settled them across the bridge of her nose before reaching for the envelopes. She thumbed through them quickly and then spun around in her chair and yanked open the metal drawer of a filing cabinet placed along the wall. She deftly flicked through the files before removing one and sliding the drawer shut with a bang. She spread the folder open on the desk between them and nodded.

'Our records indicate that we hired a man named Dennis Partridge about two months ago. Unfortunately, there is a note here stating that Mr Partridge has not turned up for work for the last two days and has not rung to give us any warning that he would be absent. I'm afraid his ongoing employment with us is not guaranteed in light of his unexplained absence. We expect our employees to be unwaveringly dedicated to the war effort and such absenteeism is not tolerated,' Mrs Monroe said.

'I'm afraid he won't be in any position to work for you

any longer regardless of your position on absenteeism. I regret to inform you that Mr Partridge was found dead earlier this week,' Peter said.

'I suppose that is a compelling excuse,' Mrs Monroe said. 'I'm sure that he will be missed although I cannot speak about him personally never having met the man. Is there anything else you think that I can do for you?'

'You could point us toward someone who would be in a position to speak about him. We understand that he was a lorry driver for the factory. Is there perhaps a supervisor he reported to on the premises?' Peter asked.

'Certainly, there is,' Mrs Monroe said running her finger along the top piece of paper in Dennis Partridge's folder. 'Bryant Smalley is the supervisor's name. He has an office at the loading dock area and should be there now if you wish to speak with him.'

'That would be most helpful,' Peter said shifting as though he meant to rise.

'Would it be possible for us to copy down any names and contact information for references with previous employers or acquaintances that Dennis Partridge might have used in his application?' Billie asked.

'Generally, that's not the sort of information that we give out,' Mrs Monroe said peering over the top of her glasses at Billie.

'I expect you don't generally receive such requests from the constabulary. I assure you we would not be making the request if it were not necessary,' Billie said.

'I suppose it won't do any harm,' Mrs Monroe said flipping through the sheets of paper before handing one of them over.

Billie removed her police notebook from her jacket pocket along with a pencil and quickly began copying the information on to the day's entry. There were three references listed all from far-flung locations. Each of them was with companies that had need of lorry drivers. One was a commercial bakery, another was a building supplier and the third a coal merchant. Billie snapped her notebook shut and passed the paper back to Mrs Monroe. After making enquiries about how to reach the loading docks they left her behind and set out for the far side of the building complex.

'Did you notice anything strange about that conversation with Mrs Monroe?' Peter asked.

'Do you mean the fact that she exhibited no curiosity about how Dennis Partridge died?' Billie asked.

'Exactly,' Peter said. 'Even for someone as efficient as she seemed to be I find that odd.'

'I suppose it could be that we've all become so accustomed to hearing about unexpected death that it is losing its ability to shock. But still, it did strike me as strange,' Billie said.

Was it that people simply did not wish to know the truth about how others had died? Or was it more likely that there were so many tragedies playing out in each and every individual's life that an unexpected death no longer provoked much curiosity? Billie supposed it was also possible that Mrs Monroe was one of those people with so little imagination that she simply was not curious about why two constables would appear out of the blue in her office making enquiries about an employee.

Perhaps the sort of person who was best suited to be responsible for private information on hundreds of employees was as incurious as possible. It might be in everyone's best interest for such a person to simply fill in forms and file them away without giving what they contained any further thought. But then again, it could just be that she either knew something about what had befallen Dennis Partridge already or she thought it in her best interest not to appear particularly interested.

Billie mulled the matter over all the way out to the loading docks. The sound of men calling to each other in loud voices and letting out intermittent bursts of laughter reminded her of Constable Drummond and her other colleagues gathering around his desk and jeering. She told herself once more to stop dwelling on things that had already passed. She followed Peter as he strode out towards a knot of men standing around smoking and talking.

'Good afternoon. I wondered if any of you might know Dennis Partridge at all? I understand he got his assignments from Bryant Smalley,' Peter said.

'I know Dennis, but he hasn't been in for a few days. What do you want with him?' a burly man with bright blue eyes asked.

'I'm sorry to tell you this but Dennis Partridge is dead,' Peter said.

Billie watched the faces of each man in turn as the news registered. Several of them seemed far more surprised than had Mrs Monroe. Perhaps they were simply not as good at hiding their emotions. Or perhaps they had been actual friends of his.

'Was he in some sort of an accident?' one of the men asked.

'Now why would you say that?' Peter asked. 'Was he a bad driver?'

'I didn't say that. I didn't say I meant a lorry accident. Accidents come in all kinds, and he was a young guy. I wouldn't have thought he would've had a heart attack or something,' the man said.

'It wasn't an accident. He was murdered,' Peter said.

Billie kept her attention focused on a slight man standing off to her right. His hands trembled as he attempted to light a cigarette. It took several tries before he managed to flick the lighter into flame. His nerves seemed to settle as he took a deep drag and let out a billowing puff of smoke as he exhaled.

'Who would want to go and murder Dennis?' another man asked. 'He seemed harmless enough to me.'

Billie noticed several of the men in the group sneaking glances at the one who had difficulty lighting his cigarette. There was definitely something they were not giving voice to that she felt sure would provide them with a line of enquiry.

'We'd like to take a statement from each of you,' Billie said. She felt rather than saw Peter glance over at her in surprise. But he didn't question her in front of the men.

'That's right. In an investigation like this one statements from friends, family and acquaintances are vital for solving the crime. Who wants to be first?' he asked.

Some of the men shrugged and others took a step back as if they were not willing to cooperate. Billie noticed that the man with the fit of nerves was attempting to slink away.

'I think that we'll start with you,' she said pointing to him. 'If you just step this way, sir, it'll only take a moment or two.'

'I'm due to make a delivery just about now,' he said.

'If you have time to smoke a cigarette, I expect you have

time to speak with the police about something so important. That is unless you have something to hide?' she said.

The man shrugged. 'I've got nothing to hide. I didn't like Dennis and it won't do any good to lie about it. So, ask me your questions.'

Billie noticed Peter singling out another man to be questioned. Satisfied he had the rest of the employees well in hand she turned her attention back to the man standing beside her.

'Let's start with your name,' she said as she opened her notebook and held her pencil above a blank page.

'Stan Reynolds.'

'And why is it that you didn't like Dennis Partridge?' Billie asked.

'I didn't think it was right that he was carrying on with another man's wife, especially not a man who was serving his country overseas while Dennis stayed here getting up to all sorts of no good,' he said before taking another drag on his cigarette.

'You sounded as though you know that for a fact. Are you quite sure?' Billie asked.

'Doreen Cook is the wife of my best mate, Harry. I made the mistake of introducing her to Dennis one night when a bunch of us met up at the pub. He made his intentions towards her clear from the moment she arrived. It didn't take long before the two of them were carrying on,' he said.

'Showing an interest and having that feeling returned are two different things. Are you certain that Mrs Cook reciprocated his feelings?' Billie asked.

'I caught them at it one night when I went round to see how Doreen was doing. I promised Harry that I would keep tabs on her while he was gone and so I did. Not long after that night at the pub I dropped by thinking I'd just stay a while and play cards or listen to the wireless with her, you know, to keep her spirits up. When she answered the door, her hair was all mussed up and her lipstick was smeared across her chin. And it's the first time she's ever answered the door in her dressing gown.'

'Did you see Dennis Partridge there too?' Billie asked.

'I did indeed. He was sprawled across the sofa looking like

he owned the place. The man wasn't wearing a shirt,' Stan said dropping his cigarette to the concrete floor and grinding it out under his boot. 'I told Doreen what I thought about her behavior and how disgusted I was by the way she had betrayed her husband while he was off facing God knows what trying to keep those of us back on the home front safe. She didn't even try to deny it.'

'Did you tell her husband what you saw?' Billie asked.

'I hated to, but yeah, I did. It's not the sort of thing you want to put in a letter, so I waited until he was home on leave. I took him out for a drink and told him just what I'd seen with my own two eyes,' Stan said.

'How did he take the news?' Billie asked. She tried to keep the excitement out of her voice, but Harry Cook seemed like a very good suspect, especially if he came home from time to time.

'He seemed sore about it, of course. But he told me not to say anything to anyone else. He didn't want Doreen's name dragged through the mud,' Stan said.

'When did this happen?' Billie asked.

'Maybe I've said enough,' Stan said looking down at his shoes.

'If you are keeping back anything that might be vital to this investigation, you're going to find yourself in a great deal of trouble,' Billie said. 'When did you tell Harry Cook about the affair?'

'I guess it was about four days ago. But I'm sure that Harry wouldn't have done anything stupid. After all, he's one of the good guys,' Stan said.

'I'm going to need Doreen Cook's address,' Billie said.

'She lives in an apartment over on Noyce Street. Number 73, apartment B.'

'Is there anything else you think you should tell me?' Billie asked.

'I don't have anything else to say.'

Billie watched as he strode off towards a line of lorries and took a clipboard from a spot on the wall nearby. He clambered up into the cab and the engine roared to life. She joined Peter and the other men as she watched the lorry pull away from the building. For the next half hour, she and Peter questioned the remaining men. Once they had concluded the interviews Billie filled Peter in on what she had learned from Stan Reynolds.

'It sounds like we ought to speak with this Doreen Cook and find out if her husband is still on leave. Good work,' Peter said. 'How did you know to single him out for questioning?'

'He was the only one who looked nervous when you mentioned that Dennis Partridge had been murdered. His hands were so unsteady he had trouble lighting his cigarette,' Billie said.

'Well, he gave us a much better lead than anybody else that was here,' Peter said. 'The rest of them only seem to know him very slightly or had a favorable impression of him.'

'Or at least that's what they said they thought about him. I don't know that we ought to assume anything at this point in the investigation,' Billie said.

'Why don't we head over to the Cook's apartment now? I'd like to see her face when we give her the news,' Billie said. 'That is, if it is news to her. If her husband is involved because she was having an affair with the victim, I would guess that she might already know.'

'Before we leave, we should take the opportunity to look through his employee locker. One of the men I spoke to while you were busy with Mr Reynolds mentioned that all of the people who work here have one.'

Billie nodded and fell in behind Peter as he strode off to the far side of the loading dock area. Nestled against the wall ran a bank of lockers. Most of them didn't have a lock keeping them shut, but the one with Dennis Partridge's name on it did. In just a couple of minutes, though, Peter had located an employee who knew where to find a bolt cutter. Billie was not entirely sure if breaking into the locker in order to search it was entirely legal, but it was too late to voice an objection. Besides, it wasn't as though they were about to get permission from Dennis himself.

Peter stepped back after applying the bolt cutter and nodded that Billie should be the one to do the honors. A freshly laundered shirt hung on a hook inside the locker and a paper sack giving off a pungent smell of rotting food sat on a shelf at the top. She crouched down and peered at the floor of the locker where a pair of highly polished boots sat. She removed them and placed them carefully on the floor beside her. They were just the sort of thing that would give the impression of being part of a uniform.

Next, she removed a large square biscuit tin. It was the sort of thing her mother had kept to hold an assortment of items in from packets of seeds for her beloved garden to buttons she had collected from cast-off garments. Billie removed the lid. Carefully she reached in and pulled a handful of small bundles of paper out of it. She held them up for her partner to see. Peter stepped towards her and reached out for one of the items. He examined it carefully and then let out a low whistle.

'Now where do you suppose he got these?' he said tapping a new and unmarked national identity card with a finger. Billie carefully examined the one she held in her hand. It was the same as the two that had been found with Dennis Partridge's body, if that was in fact his name. It was also the same as the one she carried. She supposed it was identical to all those distributed throughout the country. There was nothing about it to suggest that it was not a genuine card from the government. But she could think of no good reason why a member of the public would have a stash of blank national identity cards secreted away among his possessions.

'I have no idea whatsoever. I should think that something like this would not be the easiest thing to get one's hands on,' Billie said. 'At least I would hope that they were well secured by authorized government personnel.'

'We'd better take everything in this locker back to the station with us for further investigation. After that, we will head out to interview his girlfriend, but I don't want to take the chance of leaving something as valuable as these in this locker,' Peter said.

Billie felt the knot return to her stomach, the one that had formed there when she had considered that there might be more to Dennis Partridge's multiple identities than just simple greed.

SIXTEEN

In what felt like no time Billie and Peter had reached the police station, placed the items in an evidence box and alerted Sergeant Skelton as to the status of the case. Although the sergeant rarely had complimentary things to say about his direct reports, if Billie had to guess she would've said he seemed favorably impressed by their progress. He had even turned and included her in his nod of approval when Peter mentioned that she had been the one to spot Stan Reynolds's bout of nerves when murder was mentioned.

He agreed with their assessment that Doreen Cook should be questioned and, if possible, her husband should be located. It was the first solid lead they had in the case and one he was eager for them to pursue. Billie could not believe her luck at the sergeant's insistence that she be included in the questioning and was once again allowed to head out of the station. It was almost as if he was as eager for her to be far from her colleagues as she was.

The address Stan Reynolds had given for Doreen Cook was close enough for them to head there on foot. As much as Billie enjoyed riding the tram or one of the many coaches that zigzagged across the city, she always felt as though she learned more about her surroundings when she traveled on foot. Besides, after the excitement of the day and the slight case of nerves that had built up as she anticipated interviewing a witness, she appreciated the opportunity to stretch her legs and burn off any pent-up energy.

As they approach the apartment building, Peter slowed. 'I think you ought to be the one to take the lead with this witness. After all, she might be more inclined to open up to another woman,' he said.

Billie's stomach gave a flip-flop. She didn't think of herself as prudish exactly, but her experience with extra marital affairs, or any affairs of the heart for that matter, was extremely limited.

One of the things she had not become accustomed to about the job was how much of it felt like it comprised of a breach of etiquette. There was really something rather nasty about asking such sordid questions, especially of strangers. Although when she came to think on it, it would not be any less distasteful to pry so unwelcomely into the private lives of her nearest and dearest.

Still, if she wanted to gain the respect of her fellow officers, she would need to be willing to do whatever the job required of her. Before she had donned her uniform, she never would have expected to help locate missing persons, take down purse snatchers, or to get to the bottom of a murder enquiry. It was just one more thing she was going to need to adjust her thinking on and to become adept at handling. She was certain that soldiers on the front, men like her father and her brother, did not turn away squeamishly because something was distasteful.

She nodded and grasped the handrail leading up the steps to the apartment door. She knocked forcefully on the glossy black paint and stepped back as she withdrew her badge from her jacket pocket in readiness. After a moment with no answer, she knocked again, this time louder still. When there was still no response, she tried the handle and finding it turn smoothly pushed open the door and stepped into a short, dimly lit corridor. Four different doors led out from the hallway and even in the gloom she was able to make out the one with Doreen Cook's name printed on the slip of paper and tacked to the side.

This time her knock yielded a response. Billie held out her badge to a woman dressed in evening attire. The woman's hair was elaborately arranged on her head and her makeup was expertly applied. False eyelashes and deep red lips gave her a dramatic appearance and one that seemed at odds with the hour of the day as well as the modest little apartment Billie could see over the woman's shoulder. Billie thought the look she saw on the woman's face was one more of resignation than surprise. With the most cursory of glances at Billie's badge she stepped back and waved them inside.

'Has one of my neighbors been complaining again? It was Mrs Gordon, wasn't it? She's had it in for me ever since I moved into this place,' the woman said.

'We aren't here on any sort of a complaint call. We have some questions to ask of Doreen Cook. Would that be you?' Billie asked.

The woman arched a perfectly plucked eyebrow. 'Well, that makes a change. Yes, I'm Doreen. What can I do for you?' She took a seat at a small wooden table in the kitchenette area and tapped a cigarette out of a pack. She gestured towards the other seats in an invitation to join her. Billie took the closest chair and waited for Peter to remove his notebook from his pocket and place it in plain view.

'We were given your name by a man named Stan Reynolds. He says that he is good friends with your husband, Harry,' Billie said.

'That's right. Stan and Harry are the best of mates. What's all this about?' Doreen asked. 'Nothing's happened to my husband, has it? Or to Stan?'

'Not to my knowledge. Do you also know a man named Dennis Partridge?' Billie asked.

Doreen immediately seemed interested in a speck of dirt clinging to the surface of the table. She scratched at it with a long, lacquered fingernail and Billie thought it was in an effort to buy time before answering.

'I've met Dennis on a few occasions,' she said.

'How would you describe your relationship?' Billie asked. She felt the word relationship stick in her throat as if she had swallowed a bug. Part of her felt as though she was hovering above herself and looking down at the stranger asking such impertinent questions.

'I don't know that I would describe it as a relationship. Why do you ask?'

'We were told that you and Mr Partridge were quite close. Do you deny that?' Billie asked.

'Sometimes we have a laugh or two. I don't know that I would describe that as any sort of closeness. Is that what Stan told you?' she asked.

'Stan Reynolds is the one who told us that you and Mr Partridge knew each other well. He suggested that the relation-ship was a romantic one,' Billie said.

She hoped that her cheeks were not as flushed as she feared

that they were. It would hardly help for her to be perceived as a professional if the mere mention of a romantic relationship brought a furious blush to her face. All the while Peter continued to make brief notes in his notebook and from her quick glance at his face, there was nothing to indicate he found the topic of conversation the least bit unnerving.

'So, what if it is? What's he got to do with Stan or the constabulary for that matter?' Doreen said lifting her chin defiantly and taking a deep drag from her cigarette.

'We also understood from Mr Reynolds that your husband had been home recently. Is that correct?' Billie asked.

Once again, a guarded look crossed Doreen's face. 'He was back on shore a few days ago but he's gone again. He just signed up with the new ship.'

'He's in the merchant navy, isn't he?' Billie asked.

Doreen nodded and tapped her cigarette against an overflowing ashtray in front of her. Billie glanced at it and noticed it contained stubs from a variety of different brands of cigarette. It appeared that Doreen was someone who frequently entertained guests. But only one brand of cigarette in the ashtray had lipstick traces. The shade looked very like the one Doreen was wearing.

'That's right. He just got back in on one ship and took a few days at home with me before signing on with his next vessel. He's back-and-forth a lot is my Harry. Some of his trips are long and some of them are short. That's the life of the merchant navy men,' she said.

'It's a dangerous job. You must be very proud of him,' Billie said.

'That it is. And you're right, I am proud of him. You'd think the country would be more appreciative of all that the merchant navy does. When I think of the risks that they take and how little they're paid for their efforts, I just about see red,' Doreen said.

'I don't really know anything about the average pay for a merchant navy man. Aren't they part of the Royal Navy?' Billie asked.

'I wish they were. But no, they're not. They're all free agents which I suppose is one of the appeals to the job. They're free to sign up for any voyages of interest to them and to spend as much or as little time at sea as they'd like. So, unlike the Royal Navy they aren't at the beck and call of their government. But they are only paid when they're at sea and if a ship goes down and they're stranded, they are not paid for the time that they spend bobbing about in a lifeboat waiting for rescue, nor are they paid for their previous labor because the ship didn't come safely into port. And lately, there are a lot of ships that don't make it into port,' Doreen said.

'But the merchant navy is responsible for all the supplies that manage to reach our shores. How is it possible that they are so poorly compensated when the risks are so great?' Billie asked.

'I wish I had a good answer, but I don't. I've tried encouraging Harry to sign up for the Navy or even some other line of work, but he won't hear of it. He loves being a free agent and if he were being honest, I think he would also admit that he loves the risk.'

'So, you'd say your husband's a bit of a daredevil?' Billie asked.

'Absolutely. My Harry is the most fearless man I've ever met.'

'Would you say he has a temper to match his fearlessness?' Billie asked.

'What's this all about? Two police constables would not come to see me in the middle of a workday to discuss the finer points of my husband's character. I'm not saying anything else until you tell me why you're really here,' Doreen said stubbing out her cigarette and leaning back in her chair with her arms across her ample bosom.

'Dennis Partridge was found murdered. Stan Reynolds suggested that you were carrying on an extramarital affair with him and that he had disclosed that fact to your husband. We are here wondering if it's possible that your husband is the one who killed him,' Billie said.

Doreen's eyes widened in surprise. 'I suppose that explains why I haven't heard from Dennis lately. But to answer your question, no, I am absolutely certain my husband did not kill him in a fit of jealousy.'

'Most husbands would be inclined to take action if they

found out their wives were seeing another man. Do you expect us to believe that Harry is so different?' Billie asked. She glanced over at Peter as if to get his agreement with her statement. He nodded and fixed his attention on Doreen.

Doreen shrugged her bare shoulders and Billie was once again confronted with the inappropriateness of her dress for an afternoon at home. 'Harry knew exactly what he was getting into when he married me and never complained about it.'

'And what was he getting into when he married you?' Billie asked.

Doreen pointedly looked Billie up and down, then turned her gaze on Peter and winked. She looked back at Billie. 'You seem awfully young and fresh faced. Are you sure you want to hear all this?' she asked.

Billie was quite sure she did not want to hear any of it, but as it fell within her duty she was determined to do so.

'You needn't be concerned on my behalf. Please answer the question,' Billie said.

'My husband met me in what I will refer to as a professional capacity.' She looked over at Peter again. 'We would get together whenever he was on shore, and it turned out we suited each other in most ways. He makes me laugh and I make him feel at home. What I do with my time when he's away is not something he worries about. And considering how little he's paid, he's not unhappy about what I'm able to contribute to the household budget.'

Of all the things Billie had considered Doreen might say about the reasons why her husband would not have been involved with the murder, an arrangement such as the one she described would not have ever occurred to her. That said, if one took the morality out of it, the arrangement seemed to be eminently practical.

'Do you think I've shocked her?' Doreen said leaning towards Peter and tapping the hand holding his notebook. Billie found her question even more discomforting than the revelation about how she earned her money.

'I doubt it. And I am absolutely certain WPC Harkness can speak for herself,' Peter said.

'Why do you think that Stan Reynolds would have felt the

need to be so defensive on your husband's behalf? He came out and admitted that he detested Dennis Partridge because of the way you were behaving towards him in your husband's absence,' Billie said.

'Stan wasn't being defensive on Harry's behalf. He hated Dennis because I took him on as a client and I would not do the same for Stan. I expect that he wondered what would happen to me if the police came knocking on my door. And it's possible that he might be jealous enough to want to get Harry in trouble.'

Billie felt the enthusiasm following a potential lead draining away. Perhaps Harry had nothing to do with it after all. She made a mental note to follow up with Stan Reynolds. It sounded as though he had at least as much of a motive as Harry. In her limited experience, most men did not like to be made to feel less desired than their peers. But while they were there the least they could do was to ask for more information.

'If you are so certain your husband was not involved with his murder, do you know if Dennis had anyone else who might have a reason to harm him?' Billie asked.

'I suppose that I would start with the trouble he had at work,' Doreen said.

'No one at his employer mentioned any trouble,' Peter said.

'It was not exactly the sort of thing they would want to advertise, now was it?' Doreen said.

'Enlighten us,' Peter said.

'It doesn't reflect particularly well on the company if one of their lorry drivers runs someone down while on the job, now does it?' Doreen said.

Billie and Peter exchanged a glance.

'Dennis knocked someone down with his lorry?' Billie asked.

'Not just knocked him down. He killed him.'

'Do you know the details of what happened?' Billie asked.

'Details, no. It happened a few weeks ago, that much I remember. Dennis came to see me not long after he left the police station. He didn't really want to talk about what had happened more than to say that he felt terrible about it. My job is more about taking a man's mind off his troubles than giving him a place to rehash them,' Doreen said.

'Did the accident take place here in Hull?' Billie asked.

'I believe so. If not right in the city center than in one of the towns nearby. He wasn't a long-distance lorry driver so it would have been on a route that was within a distance he could have driven during the course of his shift,' Doreen said. 'I do know that a kid was involved. He was so broken up about the whole thing I made an exception and let him stay the night.'

'This is all very helpful, but we will still need to speak with your husband,' Billie said.

'I wish you good luck with that, Constable,' Doreen said. 'Communication with ships at sea is not the easiest thing in peacetime. I can assure you it hasn't gotten any better, especially not for the past few weeks.'

'If you can provide me the name of the ship he's on it would be very helpful,' Peter said.

'The *Belinda Marie*. She's registered with the Christchurch Company,' Doreen said. 'Do I have any reason to be worried about what I've told you?'

'About your employment?' Billie asked.

'Yes.'

Billie looked over at Peter. She had no idea how the constabulary should handle such information. While what Doreen was up to was criminal behavior, pursuing it would be a distraction from a far more serious criminal investigation. Unless it turned out that her activities had some bearing on the death of Dennis Partridge, she had no desire to look into the matter further. In fact, she would really rather simply let it drop.

'We are pursuing a murder enquiry not some sort of a vice operation. Unless our investigation calls your story into question or turns up a new lead that brings us back to you, I wouldn't give it a great deal more thought. I'd say we all have more important things on our minds with the world being what it is than how people find a little bit of happiness in the privacy of their own homes,' Peter said. He pushed back his chair and stood.

Billie followed suit and thanked Doreen for her time before following her partner out into the small hallway. She waited for the door to close firmly behind them before turning to Peter with a question. 'Is that really the way that the constabulary responds to admissions of prostitution?' Billie asked.

'Honestly, I've never been in exactly that sort of situation before. None of my police training has told me what to do under those circumstances. It just seemed to me that dragging her down to the station would have served no good purpose,' he said. 'Do you disagree with the way I handled it?'

'No. Perhaps I should have done but it seems to me that the best use of our time and energy is to focus on the murder enquiry. I think you handled it really well,' Billie said.

Peter made his way back outside then stopped under the shade of an elm tree and leaned up against it as he took off his hat and smoothed back his sandy colored hair. Billie stepped under the leafy canopy, glad for a moment of respite.

'I'm impressed with the way you led that interview. You didn't let her rattle you and she really was trying,' Peter said.

'I think what you mean is, I didn't let it show. But she did manage to shock me. I wasn't expecting her to admit what she did for a living or to confide that her husband knew all about it,' Billie said.

'That's assuming he does know what she's up to. We only have her word for it. Not to mention that the consequences of selling your favors are a lot lighter than serving a sentence for murder. Maybe it's just a question of her thinking quickly on her feet,' Peter said.

'Do you think she's telling us the truth about how difficult it is to make contact with a merchant navy ship?' Billie asked. 'Or do you think she just told us that in order to buy some time for them to get their stories straight?'

'Communication with ships isn't easy right now, I'll give her that much. But I don't think it's impossible or quite as difficult as she made it out to be. I expect that she would want to get in touch with him before we did even if she is telling the truth,' Peter said. 'It's also possible that we won't be allowed to pose our questions if the captain of the ship has given orders that his crew are not to be distracted. With all that's going on right now, I can't say that I would blame him if he did.'

The Battle of Britain had made the war seem all the more real somehow. It was as if all of the months of preparation and sacrifice were coming to a head. While Hull had not been the target of ceaseless air raids like some other locations, there had been a change in the atmosphere in the city that was palpable. Even though the majority of the battle was being waged in the air, there certainly had been fallout for those trying their best to navigate the seas.

'You think she was telling the truth about the danger to the merchant seamen and the unequal amount of pay they receive?' Billie asked.

'That much is true. It's practically criminal what those men go through in order to get supplies to us. No one who's worked at the docks for any length of time is unaware of how much we owe to all of them.' Peter placed his hat back on his head and pushed away from the tree trunk.

'Surely, we at least have to try to call him,' Billie said.

'I agree that the constabulary needs to try to make contact, but I think it might be better coming from someone with a higher rank than you or me. This is the sort of thing that the sergeant is great at managing,' Peter said.

'So, what do we do now? Do we return to Stan Reynolds to ask him more questions or do we try to find out about the accident Dennis Partridge supposedly was in?' Billie asked.

'Now we clock out. We've made great progress, but I've got to be on time for my night shift at the docks. And you've been on all day, haven't you?'

The time passed so quickly when out in the field that she hardly even noticed how many hours had gone by. She was about to protest that she could keep on without him when she remembered that it was that evening that she had promised to attend the Women of Work meeting.

'I do have plans this evening, come to think of it. What do you propose for tomorrow?'

'I think we ought to start by trying to track down the accident. After all, Stan Reynolds should be easy enough to locate. We don't even know if this accident actually occurred so we could ask some of the other constables on the shift if they remember any accidents involving a lorry driver and child recently. That's the sort of thing that would be hard to forget if you had heard about it,' Peter said. 'What about you? Do you have any ideas?'

'It seems to me that not only would that be the sort of thing constables would remember, but it would've also been news-worthy. What about checking back issues of the *Hull Daily Mail*?'

'Where would you be able to get your hands on back issues? The newspaper is buying back editions because of the paper rationing.'

Peter made a good point. She had been surprised to notice advertisements placed by the *Hull Daily Mail* in each edition of their own newspaper stating that they would buy it back for a small sum. Still, she knew that not everyone took advantage of the offer.

'The library should have them. Even the reading room in Barton St Giles kept back issues of the local newspapers. I'm sure my cousin Lydia would not allow a big city library to do any less,' she said.

'Why don't you head on over there tomorrow and I'll go to the station to make enquiries. Agreed?' he said.

She nodded. 'I'll see you in the morning,' Billie said. Peter lifted his hand then crossed the street. As she watched his retreating back, she wondered if there was a reason he was finding ways for her to stay away from the station. But no matter the reason she thought it a good plan. Besides, she never needed any coaxing to visit the library.

SEVENTEEN

B illie double checked her handbag to reassure herself that the tube of coral lipstick and change from the one-pound note sat safely inside it. She set off for the Guildhall with plenty of time to spare. The evening was a warm one and she did not want to have to hurry. She was surprised how quickly she had become accustomed to the cooler temperatures of the north. When she had first arrived, she had felt the need to keep on a thick, woolly jumper she borrowed from Lydia whenever she was not in uniform. She had been grateful for the warmth of her constable's jacket when she had first donned it. But as the weeks had passed and June turned to July the temperatures had risen along with her tolerance for the salty breeze and cool, damp air.

As she strode along the pavement now, she admitted to herself that she felt slightly nervous about the meeting. While she looked forward to seeing Trudy again, she was not entirely sure what to think about defining herself as a working woman.

With her thoughts to keep her company, she arrived at the Guildhall in what felt like no time. Room 203 was easy to locate, and she paused only momentarily outside the door noticing a flutter of nerves as she considered introducing herself to a group of strangers. But, if she could face down criminals in the street, surely she could say hello to a few like-minded women. She stepped through the door and looked for Trudy's familiar face. It seemed that her new acquaintance had been looking for her as well because she hurried forward to greet her.

'I was sure that you would come,' Trudy said beaming at her. 'I'm so glad you made it. I saved you a seat with me.' She gestured towards a pair of chairs near the front of the room. Billie followed her and after they had settled themselves in their seats, she remembered the lipstick and change. She slipped them from her handbag and passed them over to Trudy.

'Tangee,' she said. 'I've heard that it matches the territorials' uniforms beautifully.'

'That's what a recruiting officer told me when she was trying to convince me to sign up,' Billie said. 'Are you in the territorials? I never thought to ask you what you did for work.'

That was one of the other things about meeting so many new people in the city. Unlike in her small village, she did not already know everyone's history and occupation along with all of their family connections. It was funny how she had taken information for granted when it felt as though she had known it all her life. But in a city full of strangers, she had no such background about any of them. She chided herself slightly for a breach of etiquette in not being more curious at Hammonds department store.

'I work for the local bureau of the national service,' she said.

'What do you do there?' Billie asked.

'I'm a clerk. I mostly do sorting and filing. I'm actually rather a good typist, but I try not to let anyone know as it's not a job I want to get stuck with,' she said.

'I'm afraid I didn't think of that when I signed up for the constabulary. I've ended up typing a lot of reports for fellow officers since I've been there,' Billie said.

She thought back to one particular report she had typed for Peter after their first shift together. She still remembered the look on his face when he read the way she had written up their individual roles on an arrest. He had chided her for giving him credit where it was due to her. And as difficult as it had been to withstand the stares of her fellow officers as he had criticized her in front of the entire squad room, it had proven a turning point in their partnership. Perhaps she did not regret having admitted to her typing skills, after all.

An older woman stepped to the front of the room and called the meeting to order. The seats filled up with women of all ages and manner of dress. Some of the women wore the sorts of clothing she would expect to see for an evening out at the cinema or to visit a restaurant. Others wore uniforms from various branches of the women's auxiliary services. One young woman seated nearby wore a greasy coverall, her hair covered in a kerchief. She looked as though she had come straight from a long day of physical labor.

It appeared as though there were members who were loath to miss a meeting even if it meant coming straight from work regardless of how they were turned out. She settled back in her chair and turned her attention to the welcoming remarks. The agenda that evening included a presentation by a member who had recently visited the United States. Billie found the entire talk entertaining and enjoyed herself beyond her expectations. By the time the meeting concluded Billie decided that she would be happy to attend another. When the applause died down, Trudy turned to her.

'So, what did you think?'

'I enjoyed the meeting very much,' Billie said. 'Are all the presentations given by members?'

'Usually. After all, who would know better than we do what a working woman would value? For example, members have given talks about continuing education, caring for children as a working woman and dealing with trouble from male colleagues.'

'What kind of trouble?' Billie asked.

'The sort that comes up when a supervisor or even someone on your own level gets it into his head that he fancies you and won't take no for an answer,' Trudy said.

Billie leaned forward in her chair. Maybe someone had some idea what she should do about her predicament.

'What did the speaker suggest should be done?'

'She said that you could try speaking to your supervisor, especially if you are lucky enough to work for a woman. That said, many supervisors are not the least inclined to be helpful. Some of them even blame the woman reporting it for encouraging the behavior.'

Billie's stomach clenched. That was exactly her worry about bringing the troubles with Drummond to either the sergeant or Avis.

'So can anything be done?'

'She suggested something I've used several times myself. It can work quite well, especially if you nip things in the bud.'

'What was that?'

'She said that if they don't listen when you rebuff their

advances, tell them you already have a sweetheart, preferably a large angry one. Why do you ask?' Trudy said.

The urge to unburden herself to Trudy was almost overwhelming. Then she thought of how it might sound as though she were criticizing the constabulary and she thought better of it. She could consider the advice without discussing it with an acquaintance.

'I was just curious about the content of the presentations. It sounds very useful,' Billie said.

'Does that mean we can count on you to become a member?' Trudy asked. 'You'd make a wonderful addition to the group.'

'I will if you'll have me,' Billie said.

'We would love for you to join. While you're at it, you could put in a good word about us with the other female constable. She would be more than welcome too.'

Billie wasn't sure that Avis was the joining sort, or even if she would have time for such things considering the fact that her position with the constabulary was far from her only job. Still, it wouldn't hurt to pass on the invitation.

EIGHTEEN

All the way to work the next morning Billie debated mentioning to Avis the trouble with Constable Drummond. She had no idea if the older woman would take her side, or what would likely come of it even if she did. While the idea of using an imaginary sweetheart to dissuade Drummond's attentions was not appealing, it might be the most effective way so long as she found an opportunity to mention one. Still, if Avis joined the club too it might make an opening to discuss less comfortable aspects of the job.

When she arrived at the station, she found her supervisor in the women's cloakroom tidying her neat bun. Avis turned at the sound of the door creaking open and looked her up and down.

'Why do you look as though you are about to face a firing squad?' Avis asked. 'You haven't had another run-in with Sergeant Skelton, have you?'

'No, nothing like that. I was just thinking about the meeting I attended last night,' Billie said.

Avis slid a hairpin into place and then gave Billie her full attention. 'Which meeting was that?'

'It was for the Women of Work Club.'

'I've heard good things about them. Didn't you enjoy yourself?' she asked.

'I did. There was a very interesting presentation on America,' Billie said.

Avis snorted. 'I'm sure that there were much more interesting things that could be discussed than allies who fail to show up when called upon.' She crossed her arms over her chest and pressed her lips into a stiff line.

Billie scolded herself silently for mentioning the topic of the talk. Elaborating on something as unpopular with Avis as the Americans would not make her interested in joining herself.

'Someone filled in since the scheduled speaker had to cancel at the last minute. It sounds as though they are generally very serious in the topics they discuss,' Billie said. 'The leadership asked me to invite you to join too if you are interested.'

'I'll give it some thought. It's one of my fondest wishes that now that young women are able to join the force, they might make a career of it. A club like that could prove useful in promoting the cause,' Avis said.

'Do you really think that a career with the constabulary is a possibility for women?' Billie asked.

Avis's arms crept back over her chest. 'I would like to think so, but speaking frankly, I really don't know. Women turned out in droves to serve as constables during the Great War and look where that got us,' she said.

Billie had heard that there had been a large number of WPCs in the past, but that their numbers had dwindled in the intervening years until there were so few as to be practically nonexistent. That was until war had been declared and women had been needed once more.

'Why aren't there more women on the force?' Billie asked.

'The main reason given for eliminating women from the force at the end of the last war was the notion that a woman's place was in the home. There was also a lot said about the fact that men were the ones who should get priority for any jobs available. With the economic downturn those post-war years brought, good jobs were hard to find. Nobody thought women ought to be allowed to have any job that a man wanted.' Two bright spots of color had appeared on Avis's usually pale cheeks.

'Were there a great many women who served?' Billie asked.

'There certainly were. Did you know there was actually a women's police training college established at that time?' Avis asked.

'I had no idea. It must not still be in existence,' Billie said.

'No, it isn't. The situation was disheartening, but it can't all be laid at the feet of men. Much of what happened had to do with the suffrage campaign. Some of the most passionate suffragettes ended up creating two different women's police forces. When leadership in those two groups disagreed about how women should go about trying to win the vote, it caused a rift that weakened the cause of suffrage and of women in the constabulary.'

'That sounds like a missed opportunity,' Billie said.

'It was. I was absolutely heartbroken when it all broke down,' Avis said.

'Were you one of the constables who served the first time around?' Billie asked.

Avis nodded. 'I was just about your age when I signed up. Those years were the proudest of my life. It was especially gratifying to help protect Belgian refugees. You would not believe the way that members of our own country tried to take advantage of them as they were huddled in camps waiting for the war to end.'

'I had no idea that women constables were involved with something like that,' Billie said.

'We were indeed. We also made it our business to handle crimes against women and children and also to hold female criminals accountable for their actions. The male constables typically came down on one side of the issue or the other. They either assumed that women were incapable of behaving criminally or they treated them roughly even when they had been the victims of violence,' Avis said.

'And still no one seemed to see the value of having women remain on the force after the war ended?' Billie asked.

'The women constables did, but it made no difference whatsoever. We were tossed out lock, stock and barrel. One day I was wearing the uniform and the next I was out on my ear,' Avis said.

'It's almost surprising that you were willing to take up the responsibilities once more when they were offered considering what happened last time,' Billie said.

'I don't find it surprising at all. It's a job I've always wanted and when the opportunity became available, I grabbed it with both hands. And this time, I don't intend to give it up no matter what,' Avis said.

Billie looked at the determined set of Avis's jaw. She didn't want to say or do anything that would jeopardize either of their chances of a long-term career. No, she would keep her problem with Constable Drummond to herself.

NINETEEN

J ust as she had suspected, the library contained a vast collection of back issues of not only the *Hull Daily Mail*, but several other newspapers as well including those of smaller outlying towns and national outlets like the London *Times*. Within a few moments she had gathered up several weeks' worth of issues of the local paper and had spread the oldest one open on a long oak table in a quiet section of the reference area of the library. While there were many fascinating things to be found in each of the June issues, none of the papers she checked contained what she was looking for.

But the first week of July yielded fruit for her efforts. There in black and white Dennis Partridge's name jumped out at her. According to the paper he claimed to have been making a routine delivery for the East Riding Armaments Factory when a young lad dashed out into the street in front of him. There were no witnesses to the accident and the child was rushed by ambulance to the nearest hospital.

She heard the newspaper begin to rustle and realized that her hand had started to shake. A lump swelled in her throat and the vision of the village constable in Barton St Giles appearing at her door twisting his cap round and round in his hands swam unbidden in her mind's eye. She knew it was her duty to read on to discover what had become of the child, but she dreaded doing so.

It seemed that the job of being a constable brought a good many difficult emotions to the fore. If she had been asked to guess what might be the most challenging parts of the job before she had signed on, she would have said learning the various rules and regulations and being involved in the physical apprehension of violators. She had not realized the most difficult thing would be the emotional load one had to learn to carry.

Billie set the paper aside and reached for the next most

recent edition. She felt a wave of relief as neither it nor the
next one mentioned the accident again. But the morning paper
of the third day revealed more details. The child, identified as
Trevor Ward, was in a critical condition at the Hull General
Hospital. His parents John and Mabel Ward and his older
brother Colin were said to be keeping vigil at his side night
and day. Doctors were not available for comment. The police
stated that the investigation was ongoing.

Billie reached for another newspaper and searched for any
of the pertinent names. A few days later she found a small
notice that Trevor Ward had died as a result of his injuries.
The following day he was listed among the obituaries, a heartbreaking addition to a list of names involving people far older
than his own eight years. The family address was listed for
cards of condolence.

Billie drew out her police constable's notebook and added
the family members' names, the accident date, the name of the
hospital, the day of Trevor's death and the Wards' home
address. She thought it possible that she might be able to
uncover minutes of the police court also covered by the newspaper. But she thought it would be far more efficient to simply
look into the police files directly. Surely Sergeant Skelton
would be able to point her in the right direction once he had
names and dates to rely upon. She returned the newspapers
to their stack and glanced up at the large clock on the library
wall. Rather than telephone Peter she would simply wait and
tell him in person. It was no more than a fifteen-minute walk
from the library to the station, less if she hurried.

Special Constable Upton's Police Notebook

Peter entered the station and headed straight for his desk.
The boxes from Dennis Partridge's boardinghouse sat just
where they had left them the day before. He glanced over at
the cluster of desks beyond his own and noticed that several
of them were occupied. Constable Drummond and Constable
Thompson each sat looking as though they had very little to
do. In fact, Constable Drummond had his feet propped up on

his desk and his fingers interlaced behind his head. Sergeant Skelton was nowhere in sight.

Peter turned his back on them and slid the box beneath his desk. He fetched the box from WPC Harkness's desk and stowed it away with the other before he heard Constable Thompson call his name.

'So, Upton, how's the investigation you stole from us been going? Are you making any progress?' Constable Thompson said.

Peter walked over to the other two men. There was no need to carry on a conversation that everyone entering the station might overhear. It wouldn't do the public perception of the constabulary any good for there to be obvious tension between officers.

'I wasn't aware that I had stolen an investigation from you,' Peter said.

'I guess it would be fairer to say that you let your partner do the dirty work and then you just tagged along for the ride,' Constable Drummond said. 'It looks like WPC Harkness has worked Sergeant Skelton round her little finger. Now, how do you think she managed that?'

Peter felt his pulse begin to pound. Constable Drummond reminded him of his stepfather, a man he had tossed off a gangway and into the murky water below at the first opportunity once he realized how the man had been mistreating his mother. Constable Drummond gave off a similar sort of menacing aura. Was there any possibility that WPC Harkness would involve herself romantically with such a man? It seemed at odds with everything else he knew of her.

But it did sound as though Constable Drummond was trying to put him in his place. Did he feel possessively towards WPC Harkness? Did he think he was complimenting her by implying that she was behaving inappropriately in order to gain favor with the sergeant? It didn't seem like the sort of thing most men would say about a sweetheart.

'All I know is that the sergeant sent us out to make some enquiries. If you don't like how he's handing out the assignments, I suggest you take that up with him. Neither WPC Harkness nor I have that sort of clout.'

Constable Drummond swung his feet down off his desk and pushed back his chair. 'I meant no offense. We were just wondering how it's going.'

'We're making some progress, but something came up this afternoon that I wanted to ask other officers about. Have either of you heard anything about an accident between a lorry driver and child during the last few weeks?' Peter asked.

From the stubborn set of Constable Thompson's jaw Peter was sure that even if he had witnessed the incident firsthand, he would deny knowing anything about it. Sure enough, Thompson shook his head silently.

'That rings a bell, but I don't remember any of the details. I don't think it involved anyone in this station though,' Constable Drummond said. 'Do you think it has any bearing on the case?'

'It might. In fact, it's one of the better leads we've got. A witness we interviewed yesterday said that the victim was involved in some sort of accident, and she suggested that the child's family might've had a reason to wish him harm,' Peter said.

'I'm assuming that the we you mean is you and our pretty little WPC,' Constable Drummond said leaning forward.

'Constable Harkness and I have continued to investigate the case together at the sergeant's request,' Peter said. 'Do you have a problem with that?'

'Oh, I don't know that I have a problem with it, but I would say I think it's a little unfair that the sergeant hasn't been spreading around the wealth. Why should you get to monopo- lize all of her time and attention? Shouldn't we all get a crack at her?' Constable Drummond said.

'Skelton assigned her to be my partner. If you have a problem with that you should take it up with him. And for the record, I have no intention of trying my luck with WPC Harkness, at least not in the way that you are implying,' Peter said.

Constables Thompson and Drummond exchanged a smirk. 'It sounds like you're too much of a gentleman to have made any headway with her. If you ask me, she could use someone who is inclined to take a firmer hand with her,' Constable Drummond said.

'And I suppose you think that you are the one to do it?' Peter said.

'I am already working on it. There's the lucky girl now.' Constable Drummond lifted his chin to indicate a spot behind Peter's back.

Peter turned to see WPC Harkness smile at him as she hurried in his direction. He willed her to keep her eyes firmly fixed on him and for that look of enthusiasm in place on her face, but to no avail. She must have felt Constable Drummond's leer as she made her way across the room because her steps slowed and her jubilant grin slipped away in an instant. It was as if a light switch had flipped and all the glow had blinked out of her. Peter didn't know exactly what had transpired between them, but he was concerned it had not been something that she had deliberately encouraged. A spurt of anger shot through his chest like a bout of heartburn.

But unlike the trouble with his stepfather, this was a matter that seemed less clear cut. Not only was he unsure as to what exactly had occurred, it was not necessarily his place to do anything about it. WPC Harkness was his colleague, not a family member or even a close friend, and to take a high-handed approach to her troubles might create more problems than it would solve. She might even resent him for meddling. Unsolicited interference might be construed as a belief that she was not capable of taking care of herself, and from what he had already learned of her over the past few weeks, that was not the case.

Instead, he turned his back on Constable Drummond and hoped his body formed a visual barrier between WPC Harkness and their fellow officers. He took a step towards her and spoke in a voice pitched low enough not to be overheard.

'You look like you have a lead,' he said.

Her eyes lit up once more as she turned her gaze on his own rather than focusing on the men seated beyond him. 'I do indeed. It seems that Doreen Cook was telling the truth about the accident.'

TWENTY

The Ward family lived on the north side of the city. Billie had hoped that their residence would be a walkable distance from the station, but Peter assured her that the distance would best be covered by using one of the city's coaches and so she found herself once more seated beside him as they rumbled through the busy streets. Her thoughts turned to the interview ahead and she tried to imagine what she might say to someone who had lost a loved one in a similar way as she had done. She was deep in thought when Peter spoke.

'You're awfully quiet. Usually, you're peppering me with questions about everything under the sun when we are out on patrol. Is there something on your mind?' he asked.

Billie was not sure how to respond. Peter had not been one to share much about his own personal life and she felt uncertain as to how welcome details of her own past would be. Besides, should her own experiences really influence the way in which she interacted with the public? Was it not the duty of a police officer to approach each and every case with as much neutrality as possible? Her experience with Constable Drummond and the reaction of the sergeant to what he had witnessed between them made her all the more wary of showing the private side of herself to a colleague. She turned slightly in her seat hearing the vinyl beneath her make a squelching noise.

'I know that the Ward family might well have good reason to have murdered Dennis Partridge, but I wish we did not need to intrude upon their grief,' Billie said. Did she imagine it or did some tension ease from Peter's expression?

'You get used to prying after a while. Besides, if it has to be done it is better that we are doing it than a pair of heavy-handed thugs like Thompson and Drummond,' Peter said.

Billie turned to look him full in the face. She had not considered that Peter might not approve of one of their colleagues. He was remarkably disinclined towards gossip and although that was one of the things she admired about him, it had given her very little indication that they might share the same opinion about Constable Drummond. Was it possible that there might be someone in the department that she could trust to back her up if she decided to complain about him?

'I'll bear that in mind,' she said.

They disembarked the coach at the end of a tree-lined avenue filled with modest but tidy houses. It was not as well-to-do as Linden Crescent, where she lived with her cousin, but it was very pleasant, nonetheless. As they made their way along the pavement, she admired the householders' efforts at planting victory gardens in their small front gardens along with the pots of colorful flowers and neatly clipped privet hedges.

The Ward family home blended easily with its neighbors. There was nothing to indicate that anything traumatic had befallen them. That was until they started up the short walkway to the front door and Billie noticed that blackout curtains were still drawn across each of the windows as if no one inside the house could find the effort to manage the simple task of opening and closing them.

A dog barked inside the house in response to the knock Peter landed upon the door. The barking grew to a crescendo until finally Billie heard the sound of a bolt being drawn back and the door hinges creaking. In front of them stood a man in a baggy camel-colored cardigan that looked two sizes too large for him. His feet were bare and there was something so pathetic about the sight of them that Billie cringed with the forced intimacy. Once again Peter waited as she drew out her own badge and held it towards the man in front of her. He let out a sharp gasp and took a step backwards.

'Please don't be alarmed. We aren't here with any bad news,' she said quickly pocketing her badge once more. 'Are you John Ward?'

It took a moment for the man to find his voice. It crackled dryly as though it had been months since he had last used it. 'I am. Why are you here?'

'We have a few questions for you involving your son Trevor,' she said.

'You'd best come in then,' he said backing away from the door and drifting down the hallway, his bare feet slapping against the linoleum floor. She followed him and heard Peter behind her press the door firmly into place. As she moved along, she noticed signs of dishevelment. Unopened post lay strewn on the floor where it had been pushed away from the letter slot by the opening and closing of the front door. A hall table held a half dozen vases filled with flowers that had long since faded and scattered their wizened petals on its surface.

The dog that had barked so ferociously to alert Mr Ward of their presence was the only sign of animation in the house. He capered along after his master as though by the sheer force of his will he could raise his spirits. He kept looking back over his shoulder at Billie as if to plead for some assistance in returning his household to normal.

Mr Ward turned and passed through an open threshold into a small sitting room where more vases of dead and dying flowers covered every possible surface. A woman who seemed even less present somehow than Mr Ward sat in an upholstered chair and did not even glance up as they entered the room.

'Mabel, we have some visitors,' Mr Ward said, his voice as discordant as it had been at the door.

The woman looked up and her mind seemed to register the fact that the visitors were both clad in police uniforms. She clutched something to her chest tightly and Billie could barely make out in the low light that what she held appeared to be a boy's pajama top.

'Have you come to tell us you've arrested the man who killed our son?' she said.

Billie took a few steps towards her, and the dog raced forward and placed himself in her path.

'We are here to speak with you about Dennis Partridge, but I cannot tell you that we have made an arrest,' Billie said.

'You think it was an accident too, don't you?' Mrs Ward said. 'Why won't anyone believe us? Trevor knew better than to run out in the street.'

Mr Ward came around and stood at his wife's side. He placed his hand on her shoulder and looked at Billie.

'I do not have an opinion on the cause of the accident. We have come to speak with you on a different matter,' she said.

'Has he gone and killed someone else?' Mrs Ward asked. She reached up and clutched her husband's hand with her own. The tone of her voice alarmed the dog who let out a low growl.

'Dennis Partridge has not been involved in any further accidents to our knowledge. But he is the reason that were here. Would you please tell me about your whereabouts between noon and eight p.m. three days ago?' Billie asked.

'What right have you to ask us questions like that? Why are you here?' Mr Ward asked.

The dog growled again. Peter stepped towards Billie's side, then crouched down and extended his hand to the dog who sniffed it delicately. Peter reached forward with his other hand and began to scratch the dog's ears.

Reassured that she was not about to be attacked Billie continued. 'Dennis Partridge was found dead three days ago and we are asking anyone who might have had reason to hold a grudge against him to provide us with that information,' she said.

Mrs Ward squeezed her husband's hand even more tightly. 'Serves him right,' she said.

'My wife and I have been home ever since our son's funeral,' Mr Ward said.

'Is there anyone else who can verify that?' Billie asked.

'Our older son Colin has been in and out ever since,' Mr Ward said. 'You could ask him.'

'You didn't happen to have any guests who were here to condole with you during the hours in question, did you?' Billie asked. 'A visit would help to verify your whereabouts.'

'Are you calling my husband a liar?' Mrs Ward asked. 'It's bad enough that no one believed us when we insisted that Trevor would never have dashed out in front of traffic. To be accused of lying is another matter entirely.'

Billie couldn't help but feel she had bungled the interview. Despite the fact that she ought to be adept at questioning a grieving family, it seemed she had done a remarkably good job of offending them instead. Perhaps it was time to be more forthcoming.

'That was not my intention. I know how hard it is to lose a family member so suddenly and to an accident that seems to have no resolution. I have no desire to make your lives any more difficult than they already are,' she said.

'What would you know about it?' Mrs Ward asked.

Billie stepped towards the only open spot on the nearby sofa and took a seat. She leaned forward on her elbows and gave her full attention to the woman seated across from her.

'Back in May my mother was struck and killed by a motorist while walking along a country lane. Because of the blackout whoever knocked her down was able to drive off unobserved. No one was ever held to account for what happened to her. I cannot claim to know the grief of losing a child as I have none of my own. But I do know how terrible it is to lose a loved one so suddenly and without having the answers to why it happened,' Billie said.

'And yet you still come asking us a thing like that knowing how painful the subject would be?' Mr Ward asked.

'As part of my job I have to ask these questions. I cannot say for sure what I might have done had I known the identity of the person who killed my mother. I would like to believe that I would have controlled my emotions and allowed the legal system to take its course, but I cannot tell you with any real certainty that that is exactly what would have happened. I can only imagine how much more difficult it would be to leave justice to the courts if I had lost a child,' she said.

'You did not say how Dennis Partridge came to die,' Mr Ward said.

'He was murdered,' Peter said giving the dog's ears a final stroke and getting to his feet once more. 'Which is why we need to verify your whereabouts at the time of his death.'

'As I said, my wife and I were here then just as we are now. None of our neighbors were so presumptuous as to intrude upon our grief. The only person we've seen besides you is our son Colin,' Mr Ward said.

'Where is Colin now?' Billie asked.

'I'm not sure. Do you know?' Mr Ward asked turning to his wife.

'I'm never sure where he gets off to lately. With the schools being subject to closure during the air raids I'm never certain where to find him. He's a good lad and is always home to sleep in his own bed,' Mrs Ward said.

'So, Colin is a school-aged boy?' Peter asked.

'Yes, he's sixteen. He's considering leaving school and getting a job, but after what happened to his brother, I've been trying to convince him to leave the city to stay with my sister in Sussex,' Mrs Ward said.

'Now Mabel, you know he's not about to leave us. Besides he's too invested in his work with the air-raid patrol,' Mr Ward said. Billie thought she heard a faint stirring of pride in Mr Ward's voice as he spoke of his elder son.

'What exactly does he do for the air-raid patrol?' Billie asked.

'Right now, he's acting as a messenger, but he hopes to be promoted to a warden before he's old enough to enlist in the services. He seems to have been making quite a good impression on the man in charge of our district, at least from what Colin has had to say,' Mr Ward said. 'I would hope you would be able to take the word of a lad like that.'

'We will be sure to ask if he can confirm that you were home on the date in question. Do you have any idea where we might be able to track him down?' Peter asked.

'He spends a lot of his time at the air-raid patrol headquarters for our district.' Mr Ward said.

'And where might that be?' Peter asked.

'They were given the use of a couple of spare rooms in the Methodist Church over on Gerrit Street,' Mr Ward said. 'If you ask the air-raid patrol warden, Mr James, I'm sure he'll know where to find him.'

TWENTY-ONE

Special Constable Upton's Police Notebook

'Are you all right?' Peter asked.

WPC Harkness stood at the base of the Wards' front steps staring off at something in the distance. She drew in a deep, shuddering breath, as if she hadn't inhaled since leaving the Wards in their sitting room. In all the weeks since she had arrived in Hull, he had never asked what had brought her to the city. He knew that she had received an invitation from her cousin to visit and had decided to stay, but he had not imagined that her move was based on something besides a desire for a change of scenery. He felt heartily ashamed of himself. Would he have done half so well on the job had his own mother been struck down so unexpectedly?

She turned to him. 'Why do you ask?'

'It's just that I didn't realize that questioning the Wards might drag up difficult memories for you. If I had known about the loss of your mother, I would have volunteered to handle the interview on my own,' he said.

'That's kind of you, but it's not as though I can do this job and avoid people who have also lost loved ones.'

'Still, you could have told me. I'd like to think that you don't need to keep secrets from me,' he said.

Her eyebrows lifted slightly as she met his gaze. 'I'll bear that in mind. Although, I wouldn't say that I was keeping my mother's death a secret. Until today there was no reason for it to have come up in conversation.'

Peter had to admit that she had a point. Their discussions had centered around police procedures and actual cases. They had spent little time discussing anything that did not involve the job. He had to wonder if he would have expected one of the male officers to mention such a tragedy. Still, he had to consider what else she was keeping to herself. A girl who could hide her grief as well as Billie, might be just as good at keeping her own counsel about harassment from Constable Drummond.

'I suppose you're right,' Peter said thinking it best to let the matter drop. If she wanted to bring it up in future that was her choice. 'What did you think of them?'

'They struck me as people who were turning in on themselves more than ones who were inclined to seek vengeance. Still, they mentioned something interesting at the end of the interview, don't you think?' she said.

'I do indeed. What are the chances that there are two men named Mr James serving as the air-raid patrol warden for this very district?' Peter asked.

Mr James did not respond to the knock on his door. After a moment or two the sounds of excited barking could be heard rolling down the narrow alleyway along the side of the building and Peter followed the noise until he reached a small back garden behind the house. Mr James stood dressed in his ARP uniform clipping a vest to a clothesline stretched between the building and a post supporting a neglected wooden birdhouse. From the scowl stamped on his face as he recognized them, it did not appear he was pleased by the interruption.

'I don't suppose that you are here to return my keyring, are you? Or are you here in response to my complaint that someone seems to be messing about in the shelters when they aren't being used during an air raid,' he said as they approached.

'Actually, we are here on another matter entirely,' Peter said.

Mr James jammed a clothes peg down on the shoulder of the vest and reached for a sock from a wicker basket on the ground nearby.

'You'd best get on with it then. As you can see, I've got my work cut out for me. My wife is off visiting her sister and it's left me responsible for her work as well as my own,' he said. 'The dog thinks it's a bit of fun which is holding me up all the more.' Mr James gestured towards the dog, no larger than a well-fed tomcat, who had a sock held firmly between his paws. If Peter had to guess, Mr James was not any more pleased with being in charge of it than he was to be tasked with the laundry.

'Do you know a lad by the name of Colin Ward and his family?' Peter asked.

He was glad that they had already met Mr James and there would be no need to present him with identification. While Peter thought that WPC Harkness had believed him when he made the excuse for asking her to show her own badge, he was not entirely sure how many times he could ask her to do it before she became suspicious. Besides, he had missed taking charge of questioning someone in the course of an investigation. While WPC Harkness did an admirable job, he had not joined the constabulary to simply sit on the sidelines all of the time.

'Yes, I know Colin and his parents. He's a messenger boy for the air-raid patrol. A nice lad,' Mr James said. 'Why do you ask?'

'If you know him, I'm sure you are aware of the tragedy involving his younger brother, Trevor,' Peter said.

'Such a terrible thing to have had happened,' Mr James said turning away from the clothesline and giving them his full attention. 'I can't imagine anything worse than losing one's child.'

'Do you know anything about the manner in which Trevor Ward met with his accident?' Peter asked.

Mr James tipped his head to one side and squinted slightly. 'I only know what the family told me. Trevor was run down by a careless lorry driver,' he said.

'Do you know the name of the lorry driver?' Peter asked.

Mr James crossed his arms over his chest. 'Something Partridge, I believe. Colin mentioned it once or twice.'

'Did Colin mention anything else?' Peter asked.

'Like what?' Mr James said widening his stance slightly.

'Did he say anything about wishing him harm?' Peter asked.

'I'm sure I can't recall. If he did, it's more than understand-able, wouldn't you say? The man ran down his younger brother after all,' Mr James said turning back towards the basket of laundry.

As he bent over to retrieve a shirt WPC Harkness spoke. 'Did you happen to know Mr Partridge yourself?' she asked. 'Had you ever met him?'

Mr James straightened and kept his back to them as he raised the shirt to the clothesline. 'Not that I can recall. It's a big city after all and one could hardly expect to know all the people who call it home.'

Peter watched as Mr James took his time attaching the shirt to the clothesline with an abundance of care.

'So, I suppose you would be surprised to learn that Dennis Partridge is the name of the man who came knocking at your door claiming to be an air-raid shelter inspector,' Peter said.

Mr James let go of the shirt and the unpinned side of it flopped limply away from the clothesline. He turned towards the pair of constables with what seemed to be a genuine look of surprise.

'That would surprise me very much. Why on earth would he pretend to be an inspector? My understanding from accounts in the paper was that he worked as a lorry driver for one of the armaments factories here in the city,' Mr James said.

'So, you did know a bit about him then,' WPC Harkness said. 'More than just what Colin reported to you.'

Mr James looked from WPC Harkness back to Peter. 'The entire situation was devastating for poor young Colin. I did follow the accounts of it in the newspaper very closely. I did not want to ask him for any details that would dredge up painful feelings, but I felt it my duty to the community to have some idea whether or not he would be available and reliable as a messenger for the air-raid patrol. I did not want to burden him or his family in such a distressing time, but the role he fulfills is a vital one.'

'Can you think of any reason why the man who killed his younger brother would have been interested in secretly gaining access to air-raid patrol shelters in the district where Colin serves?' Peter asked.

'Honestly, Constable, I can think of no reason whatsoever. Surely you're not connecting Colin with what happened to that man in the shelter, are you?'

'We are looking for connections with people who might

have had a grievance with the victim, and I can think of no greater grievance than the one the Wards would have had with Mr Partridge. Can you?' Peter said.

'I cannot think of anything worse. But I can't imagine that Colin would have had anything to do with someone's death. I've known him for months and have found him to be a trust-worthy and responsible young man.'

'You said that he's been terribly distressed by the death of his brother. Do you think that it's possible he's also distressed by guilt about what happened to Dennis Partridge?' Billie asked.

'I'm sure I couldn't possibly recognize the difference between those sorts of distress having not experienced either one for myself,' Mr James said. 'But I hope you haven't gone and said anything to upset anyone in that family. They have suffered enough.'

'You sound like you think quite well of them all,' Peter said.

'Certainly, I do. The Wards have lived in this district for years and years and I have counted myself lucky for them to be of my acquaintance,' he said. 'They didn't deserve to have something like this happen to them. Trevor was shaping up to be just as likable a boy as his older brother. It's a blow to the entire community.'

'From the reports in the newspaper there were many people who attended the enquiry at the police court. I expect that considering how much you esteem the family you would have been there to show support,' WPC Harkness said.

Peter thought his partner was rather good at catching people up in falsehoods. He wondered how much of it had to do with her natural ability as an investigator and how much of it could be attributed to her upbringing as a rector's daughter. Surely the sniffing out of wrongdoing was part and parcel of her father's role, wasn't it? Not that he knew a great deal about the responsibilities of rectors having been raised by his Irish mother as a good Catholic. Still, he imagined them to be concerned with righteous behavior and lying could not be reconciled with that.

'Well, of course I was. The entire neighborhood wished to

turn out to support them but considering how limited the number of spots in the courtroom were I thought myself lucky to have been able to procure a spot.'

'That makes it seem all the more surprising then that you did not recognize Dennis Partridge as the man involved in the accident when he came face-to-face with you on the day that he died,' WPC Harkness said.

Mr James crossed his arms over his chest once more. 'All I can say is that I did not recognize him. You can believe me or not as you see fit. He presented himself as a city inspector and I had no reason to doubt him. The man who I saw at the police court was dressed in a suit and named Dennis Partridge. The man that appeared on my doorstep was wearing coveralls and carrying a toolbox. He showed me an identity card with the name David Phillips. I cannot fault myself for not recognizing that they were one and the same. I don't expect either of you would have either.'

Peter watched as WPC Harkness took a few steps towards the clothesline and gave it her full attention.

'Do you happen to know where we could find Colin at this time of day?' Peter asked. He was not quite sure what WPC Harkness was up to, but he wanted to give her time for it.

'That's the sort of thing you should ask his parents, isn't it?' Mr James said. 'I'm only supposed to keep tabs on him during the hours he volunteers for the air-raid patrol.'

'His parents don't seem to know what he gets up to much of the time. I think that they are barely holding themselves together and have perhaps let Colin look after himself more than they would have done in the past,' Peter said.

'I'm sure that I can't shed more light on that than his parents can. The unpredictable closure of the schools has left most of our remaining children at loose ends. Although I appreciate having Colin here, I can't help but think he would have been better off evacuating. Certainly, Trevor would have been,' Mr James said.

As soon as war had been declared parents had been encouraged to join the government scheme of evacuating children from vulnerable areas. Thousands of them had set out from Kingston upon Hull on the third of September 1939. It had been heartrending to see the downhearted looks on the faces of so many of the city's women. And although it was not in the best interest of the nation's children, Peter could understand why so many parents had decided to ask that their children be returned to them as the early months of the war dragged on. There had been so little real enemy action prior to the events at Dunkirk and he could well understand how easy it would have been for parents to justify their return.

His mother had said much the same thing. She had revealed one evening during his weekly visit how relieved she was that a choice like that had never been one she had to face. She confessed that she was not entirely sure she would have had the strength to send him off even if it would have been for his own good. Something in the way she referenced vulnerable children at the mercy of strangers had stuck in his mind. His mother was not someone who talked about her past very often, but he had gained the impression that there had been something she would rather have forgotten involving children and strangers.

In the case of a family like the Wards the consequences of either never evacuating their children in the first place or recalling them back were dire. He wondered how the Wards could possibly justify keeping Colin in Hull after what had happened to his brother. Was it that they could not bear to be parted from both of their sons? Had Colin simply refused to leave? Or did they view him as practically a grown man and someone who would be a valuable asset to his city?

Did the fact that they kept him in Hull support the idea that he was not responsible for what had happened to Dennis Partridge? Would they have had the foresight to consider that if he were guilty, it would be in his best interest to send him far from the scene of the crime? Or would they have considered that his sudden departure might make him appear even more suspicious? No matter what the answer, Peter was more convinced than before that they urgently needed to question the boy. Surely someone would know where he could be found.

He looked over at WPC Harkness who had stepped away from the clothesline. 'Would you happen to know the names of some of Colin's friends?' she asked.

'I know he's often seen with Paul Harper. He's another one of the volunteers.'

'Do you know where we might find Paul Harper?' Peter asked.

'When he's not volunteering for us, he helps out at his parents' corner shop on Sumner Street,' he said. 'Now, if you don't mind, I'd like to finish up hanging out the wash and get on with fixing my tea.'

'Thank you for your time. And if you see Colin, please let him know that were looking for him,' Peter said.

TWENTY-TWO

WPC Harkness followed him out of the small yard and into the alley before she turned to him excitedly.

'What was so interesting about that clothesline?' Peter asked. 'You seemed quite taken with it.'

'Did it strike you that it was strung very tautly and that the line was a brilliant white?' she asked in a low voice.

Peter thought back to the scene that had unfolded in Mr James's small garden. Nothing about the clothesline had struck him as particularly unusual.

'Aren't clotheslines supposed to be pulled taut?' he said.

WPC Harkness nodded. 'Theoretically they are supposed to be, but the weight of the laundry ends up pulling them down over time. Generally, they've got a bit of slack to them. And one of the things that has struck me about life here is how things that are white in the country are much greyer in the city. I suppose it's all of the exhaust from vehicles and chimney stacks that does it,' she said.

'What does this have to do with Mr James and his clothesline?' Peter asked.

'It looks to me that Mr James has recently put up a new clothesline,' she said. 'And I have to ask myself, what happened to the old one.'

'Dennis Partridge was strangled by a length of clothesline.'

'That he was,' she said.

'Did you believe him when he said that he didn't recognize Dennis Partridge?' he asked.

'I really can't say for sure. It's so easy to take people at face value, especially when they present you with proof of who they say they are. And from what we found among Dennis Partridge's possessions, it seemed that he was practiced at presenting himself as someone he was not.'

'Perhaps it is too much to imagine that he might murder

someone just because he felt sorry for a victim's family,' Peter said. 'Still, I would feel better if we could speak with Colin and find out whether or not he had something to do with this.'

'I know we shouldn't go into such things with any sort of closed mind or personal agenda, but I hope that no one in the Ward family has had anything to do with this. It's heartbreaking enough already,' she said.

'What did you think about Mr James's complaint that there have been more disturbances in the air-raid shelters?' Peter asked.

'It brings to mind the question of what happened to Mr James's keys. And what kind of things do you think have been going on in an empty air-raid shelter?' she asked.

'Probably it's just kids using them as a place to mess about away from the eyes of critical adults,' Peter said.

He thought back to the many hours he had spent as a kid looking for just such an opportunity. Disused warehouses down at the docks were popular with his peers and on occasion he had joined them. When he was quite young there had been the thrill of independence that came with seeking out hiding spots in darkened alleys or even in some of the more densely overgrown parts of city parks.

As he grew older places that provided privacy were more prized if they included creature comforts that might appeal to female classmates. Not that he wanted to share such memories with WPC Harkness. He did not want to step over the line of propriety with a female colleague by even mentioning such a thing.

'I attended an event with my cousin Lydia the other day and the chief constable was there,' WPC Harkness said.

Peter hadn't thought that she was the sort of person who might boast about her connections to the higher-ups in the city. She had not ever made mention of the fact that the chief constable was a family friend despite the fact it was common knowledge in the department. She also had not bragged about the chief asking for her to participate in a high-profile case just after she was hired on to the constabulary. It seemed strange that she might do so now.

'I assume the event connects to our case,' Peter said.

'The chief constable mentioned that as much as he would not like to broadcast it to the general public, crime has been steadily rising since the outbreak of war. The cover of darkness that the blackout provides has made it easier than ever for otherwise law-abiding citizens to turn their hands to crime. Perhaps the air-raid shelters might factor into that somehow,' she said.

'In which way? Like a place to stash ill-gotten gains?' Peter asked.

WPC Harkness shrugged. 'Maybe. Do you think it's possible that Dennis Partridge wasn't killed by someone who actually knew him? Do you think maybe he surprised a stranger who was up to no good in the shelter and that person killed him to keep him from telling anyone what he saw?'

Peter stopped in his tracks. WPC Harkness had opened up an entirely new line of enquiry and one that he felt embarrassed not to have thought of before. 'You might be on to something there. What do you suggest as our next move?'

'I think that we should still try and speak with Colin Ward, but we might want to consider the problems at the air-raid shelters Mr James complained about. I don't imagine that whoever killed Dennis Partridge would be foolish enough to use that shelter again, but the other ones might be worth checking out,' she said.

'Let's try that corner shop where Colin's friend works first and then we'll decide what to do next,' he said.

Peter couldn't say for sure, but he thought he detected a spring in WPC Harkness's step that he had not seen since Sergeant Skelton had asked him to get her out of the station house. He hadn't realized how much he had missed seeing the eager look on her face whenever they went out on patrol. He even missed the way she peppered him with questions nonstop. He told himself he would go out of his way to do what he could to see that upswing in her mood continue. He didn't, however, give himself permission to consider why such a thing mattered to him as much as it did.

WPC Harkness's Police Notebook

Something had been nagging Billie in the back of her mind for days. It was as if a bit of music floated through her thoughts, but she couldn't quite remember the words. She knew it had to do with the case, but what exactly she was trying to put her finger on eluded her. And something about their conversation with Mr James only made it all the more irksome.

She hurried her pace as Peter moved along the pavement at his usual breakneck speed. As they turned one corner and then another, she caught sight of a street sign and something clicked. Sumner Street. She came to a complete stop as she looked at it trying to remember where she had seen that before. It wasn't the address of any of the suspects in the case, nor was it a street she remembered traversing at any point in her time in Hull. She closed her eyes and allowed her thoughts to drift as she sorted the word Sumner through recent memories.

Her eyes flew open and she noticed that Peter had continued on ahead of her. She raced to catch up and called out to him. He turned at the sound of her voice and waited for her to catch up.

'You look like you just had a breakthrough,' he said.

'I think I might have. It's the street name, you see,' she said pointing up to another sign bearing the name Sumner on the corner ahead of them. 'That was the name on one of the national registry identification cards we found in Dennis Partridge's toolbox, I think.'

'It might've been. But why has that gotten you so worked up?' he asked.

'Earlier on the day that we found Dennis Partridge's body Sergeant Skelton had put me on the reception desk. A woman came in and lodged a complaint about a man whose last name was Sumner. I think they may be one and the same,' she said.

'What was the complaint about?' He asked.

'She said that he had promised to help her son get a job with the Ministry of Supply and that he had needed money for a train ticket to London to speak with a contact he had there on behalf of her son,' Billie said.

'Do you think that the woman killed him over a train ticket?'

'I don't know how she might connect with the case, but if it's the same man, at the very least it would give us a better sense of his movements before he died,' she said. 'Perhaps he may have said something in passing that she would remember and could help us.'

'Do you think that it's a better lead than speaking with Colin's friend?' Peter asked.

'I don't know that it's better but maybe it would be worth our time to split up,' she said.

'I don't know about that. It seems like we make a pretty good team,' Peter said. 'Besides, you've been the lead investigator so far. It doesn't seem like it would be right for me to push on without you.'

Billie looked him in the face. As much as she had found Peter to be surprisingly open-minded about how much she could contribute to the constabulary, his eagerness for her to be in charge of the investigation beggared belief.

'Is there something you're hiding from me?' she asked.

'Like what?' he asked. His gaze shifted to a spot on the pavement somewhere near her shoes. There was no doubting it now. Peter was trying to keep something from her.

'Like why it is that you are being so generous about me taking a leading role in all this? After all, you've been with the constabulary longer than I have. If one of us should be in charge, it's you. I can't imagine that I would be any good at getting to the bottom of a murder if I couldn't notice that something was not adding up with you,' she said.

Peter let out a deep sigh. He raised his gaze to her face and seemed to have come to a decision. 'I didn't want to say anything because I kept hoping it would turn up, but I suppose it's gone on too long to still believe it might,' he said.

'What did you hope would turn up?' she asked.

'My badge. I haven't been able to find it for days,' he said.

Billie thought she could detect a slight flush to her partner's cheeks. While her father and brother had been famous for mislaying their possessions from pocket knives to woolly socks to sermon notes, she could not imagine either of them misplacing something as important as their identification. Peter struck her as more responsible than her brother and less absent-minded than her father. In fact, she could not imagine him losing his badge at all.

'That doesn't seem like you. What do you think could have happened to it?' she asked.

'I'm damned if I know. I suppose it's possible that it fell out of my uniform jacket pocket one day when I was walking home after a shift. Sometimes when it's warm I see no reason to keep my jacket on when I'm off duty and I slip it off and just sling it over my arm. I suppose it could have fallen out anywhere along the route between the station and my boardinghouse,' he said.

'You also could have been pickpocketed. It's not as though that never happens in the city,' she said.

It never happened in her village in Wiltshire she was happy to be able to say, but Lydia had warned her about the perils of cutpurses. And her first shift with Peter had involved arresting a purse snatcher. Although what someone might want with a police constable's badge left her feeling decidedly uneasy.

'I suppose I could have been. It's not as though the city doesn't have its fair share of light-fingered citizens,' he said.

'Don't you think you ought to report it to Sergeant Skelton?' Billie said.

'There was a constable who lost his badge not long before you arrived,' Peter said. 'He told Sergeant Skelton about it and was told that that was fine since he wouldn't be needing it anymore.'

Billie felt her stomach clench with cold. Peter was the only person on the constabulary besides Avis that she felt was on her side. The chief constable seemed pleasant enough, but he was too far removed from daily operations to make much of a difference to her on the job. If Peter were to be dismissed from the constabulary, she wasn't sure how much longer she would be able to stick it out if left on her own with men like Constables Drummond and Thompson.

'Then I guess we had better not tell him about it after all,' she said. 'Maybe it will turn up before you have to mention it.'

'You'd really keep quiet about it?' he asked.

'Of course. Why wouldn't I?' she asked.

'Some of the other constables might be tempted to take me down a peg with the sergeant,' he said.

'Why would anyone want to do a thing like that?' she asked.

She kept her gaze firmly on Peter's face and was surprised at the look of discomfort she saw there. Was there some sort of tension between her partner and some of the other members of the force? She thought she was quite skilled at reading a room, but she could not honestly say she had seen any trouble brewing between him and any of the others. Although, if she were to have to guess she would have said that perhaps Peter was more favored by the sergeant than were the other officers. Perhaps there was some sort of envy that he was more aware of than was she.

'Let's just say Constable Drummond and I have had words lately,' he said.

Billie's stomach gave another cold squeeze. What sort of words had they had? Had Constable Drummond told him something ugly about her? Had he shown distaste for what Constable Drummond might have said? She felt even more conflicted about what had happened in the canteen. Had something she had done led to her partner falling out with his fellow constables?

She couldn't bring herself to ask him exactly what had happened. She wanted to clear things up, but the words stuck in her throat. She swallowed as if to shove them down somewhere where they wouldn't trouble her for the present.

'So, what should we do then if we shouldn't split up?' she asked. She wasn't certain but she thought she saw a flicker of relief pass over Peter's face as she changed the subject back to the work at hand. Maybe he was no more eager to discuss what had happened with Constable Drummond than she was herself.

'Since we're already here let's try to see if we can find Paul Harper and Colin. If we can't, we can always head back to the station to check the statement you took from the woman that lodged a complaint,' he said.

'That sounds like a good use of our time. After all, I don't expect the reports are going anywhere and I don't think that the woman who lodged the complaint seemed like much of a flight risk. I might not even be right about what I'm remembering,' Billie said.

'And even if you are there's no guarantee that it'll lead anywhere. It doesn't seem like anything in this case is helping to get to the bottom of why anyone would have wanted to kill him. Maybe it really was just that he interrupted something criminal and got killed for it,' Peter said.

TWENTY-THREE

Paul Harper was right where Mr James suggested he might be found. Billie was grateful for Peter's solid presence at her side as she held out her badge to the young man. She had a sneaking suspicion that he would have refused to speak with her had she visited on her own. He had given her badge a suspicious look as though he didn't quite believe it was authentic.

His parents stole glances over at them from across the busy store where customers prevented them from causing any direct interference. From the look on Mrs Harper's face, Billie was quite sure that the woman was worried about what sort of mischief her son might have gotten up to that would require a visit from a pair of constables, even if one of them was only a woman.

'We are looking for Colin Ward and we were told that you are a good friend of his. You don't know where we might find him right about now, do you?' Billie asked.

Paul looked from Billie to Peter and back again. He glanced over her shoulder at the long counter supporting a brass till and shook his head.

'Colin and I are pals, but I don't know where he keeps himself every minute of the day. Maybe he's helping out with something for the air-raid patrol. You should check with Mr James,' Paul said.

'Mr James is the one who sent us looking for you,' Peter said.

'Well, he's not here so I don't know where he might be,' Paul said shifting his gaze to a door at the side of the store. Billie suspected that it led to a storage room and wondered about the possibility of entering it without a search warrant.

'Does he have a girl he fancies, or some kind of activity he participates in like football or cricket?' Peter asked.

'He doesn't have time for anything like that, not with his

work at the air-raid patrol and keeping an eye on his mother after what happened to his younger brother,' Paul said.

'Does his mother need keeping an eye on?' Billie asked.

Paul pressed his lips together as if he had said too much. He glanced past Billie's shoulder once more and seemed to change his mind. 'She's been in a really bad way since Trevor died and Colin's father doesn't want her left alone. I don't want to get her in to any trouble by telling you this, but they are worried she's not quite in her right mind,' he said.

'How about Colin? Does he seem weighed down by grief about his brother too?' she asked.

'He hasn't been himself lately, if that's what you're asking. But who would be? What happened to Trevor was a real blow. I know so many people are losing loved ones between soldiers lost on the front and people being killed in the air raids, but this was a different thing altogether.'

'In which way?' Billie asked.

'It was the kind of terrible accident you'd read about in the paper and think it was just about the most horrible thing you'd ever heard of. At least, that's what I used to think before war broke out. Now it seems that something terrible happens every day,' Paul said with a shrug.

Billie had to agree with him about the way that what constituted a tragedy had shifted in only a few short months. She didn't think of herself as a callous or hardhearted person, but over the weeks and months her capacity to feel shocked by the number of soldiers listed as missing or dead in the newspapers on a daily basis had faded. Bombing deaths and houses reduced to rubble were common enough occurrences that they did not produce the same sense of disbelief they once did. It seemed all the more terrible, though, that someone as young as Paul could be so jaded.

Perhaps that was one of the most discouraging things about war. Loss of life and property were searingly difficult, to be sure. Billie wondered about the long-term effects on young men like Paul and Colin. Surely, they should have kept more innocence for longer, shouldn't they?

'Do you think that's the only thing that's on your friend Colin's mind?' Peter asked.

'Probably not. But just on its own his family situation would be enough to make anyone seem changed, don't you think?' Paul asked. 'Is there anything else you want to ask me? We've got a queue forming and we close in less than an hour. My mother is waving for me to help her out.'

'That should be it for now. But if you see Colin, let him know that we would like to speak with him. If you ring or drop by the Central Police Station someone will get in touch with us,' Peter said.

Paul nodded then pushed past Billie, squeezing between small throngs of middle-aged women clutching string bags in one hand and small children in the other. He ducked behind the counter and spoke directly into his mother's ear. Billie wished she could have overheard the conversation given the look that passed across the woman's face. It flitted from relief back to concern and Billie did not think it had much to do with the impatient clamor of her customers. Peter angled his head towards the exit, and she followed him out the door.

'Did you believe that he didn't know where we might find Colin?' Billie asked.

'I thought he was holding something back,' Peter said. 'I'm not sure that it was Colin's whereabouts, but it was something that he didn't want to discuss with us for sure.'

'What he had to say about Mrs Ward makes the family all the more suspect in Dennis Partridge's death too,' Billie said.

Peter stopped in a patch of shade cast by one of the nearby buildings.

'I thought so too. It sounds as though any one of the Wards might have been capable of killing him. Both Mr Ward and Colin are easy enough to imagine being strong enough to do it, but if Mrs Ward is as unbalanced as Paul made her sound, perhaps she would have found a surge of strength herself,' Peter said.

Billie had never been one to give credit to the notion that people with an unbalanced mind were possessed of unnatural strength. It seemed the sort of thing one read in the more lurid sort of Gothic novel. And she had read more than her fair share at the reading room back in Barton St Giles. And although it was a genre she particularly enjoyed as entertainment, she did

not think that it had much to do with the business of life. That
said, she did not disagree with Peter that Mrs Ward could well
have been capable of strangling Dennis Partridge.

'I should think that even without the balance of her mind
being disturbed, Mrs Ward could have easily done away with
him. Given the darkness in the shelter she likely could have
surprised him. And since the life was choked out of him with
the help of a length of clothesline, she probably would have
had the strength. If he had been manually strangled, I think
it would have ruled her out, but the clothesline keeps her easily
on the list of suspects,' Billie said.

Peter looked at her with an eyebrow raised. 'You sound as
though you know a great deal about murder methods.'

'You forget that my cousin is the head librarian. It's amazing
what you can learn given access to enough books,' Billie said.
'Do you have a library card?'

'As a matter fact I do, but I would have to admit it's been
a while since I've used it,' Peter said. 'But clearly if I want
to keep up with you, I should dig it out soon.'

Billie felt a faint glow of pride as she did every time
someone complimented her on her job performance. She had
not ever expected to be told by a colleague, especially not
one that she admired, that he was trying to keep pace with
her. What would her mother say, she wondered as she stood
there basking in the compliment? Although her mother had not
wanted to see her daughter join any of the services and likely
would have protested that the constabulary could be considered
to be one of them, she also insisted that anything Billie turned
her hand to she do with competence. She had to think that her
mother would have been at least a little proud of the way she
contributed to solving the cases to which she was assigned.
Even though this one was proving a challenge to make any
headway on whatsoever, Billie felt as though she really was
giving it her all.

'Well, as much as it would please me for you to head off
to the library for a new armload of reading material, I doubt
very much Sergeant Skelton would approve. So, what do you
think our next move should be? Do we keep looking for Colin?'

'Paul said that the shop closes in less than an hour. What

if we head into the café across the street and wait for him to leave? I don't know about you, but I could use a cup of tea and a bite to eat. We could follow him and see if maybe he does actually know where Colin could be found,' Peter said.

Billie looked across at the restaurant on the other side of the broad avenue. There was a plate-glass window partially obscured by window boxes overflowing with bright blooms. Despite the fact that they were in the heart of the city in the midst of a war someone had thought it worthwhile to at least attempt to brighten things up with a profusion of cheerful flowers. It seemed the ideal spot to refresh oneself and as she considered the possibility of sitting down for a light meal, she realized that she was famished.

'Do you think he'll spot us watching for him?' she asked.

'I doubt it. They're too busy in the shop to pay any attention to what's happening out on the street. Look for yourself,' Peter said inclining his head towards the shop window behind him.

Billie glanced through the glass and confirmed that Peter was right. If anything, the activity in the shop had become even more frenzied in the short time since they had stepped out the door. It looked as though every housewife in the neighborhood had descended upon the Harpers' corner shop clamoring for items for their evening meal. She nodded in agreement with his suggestion and upon spotting a break in the traffic dashed across the street. He followed her at a slightly more genteel pace and reached the curb just as she was yanking open the café door.

The inside of the restaurant, or maybe just being inside it with Peter, brought back the memory of the day she had met him in a café not unlike the one in which they now stood. Fortunately for all of them this one was not about to go up in smoke. They found a table with an easy view of the shop and waited for the waitress to arrive. Billie suddenly felt overcome by shyness.

Although she and Peter had been partnered out on the beat regularly since she had joined the constabulary, they had never had occasion to sit so formally together at a table. There had been occasions, of course, when they had stopped for something to eat from a street-side vendor or one or the other of them had brought enough of a bagged lunch to share while sitting on a park bench.

But the atmosphere in the restaurant was somehow different. Even though they were merely colleagues, a fact for which she was grateful after what had happened with Constable Drummond, she could not deny that it was the type of situation that to an uncomfortable degree resembled a date. The impression was reinforced all the more when the waitress did appear at the side of the table and Peter waited for her to place her order before he instructed the waitress on his own.

There was no denying that being colleagues made social situations awkward. Where did the lines of courtesy and professionalism cross? It was the sort of thing that might be a point worth raising at the Women of Work Club. She must have been lost in thought longer than she realized because when she lifted her gaze from the spot on the snowy white tablecloth in front of her, she found Peter searching her face.

'You seem to have a lot on your mind. Is there something wrong with the restaurant?' he asked. He glanced around as if to make sure that there was nothing untoward happening in the bright and welcoming space.

'I was just thinking about an organization I've recently joined and what they might have to say about certain social norms,' Billie said.

'Which organization is that?' Peter asked.

Billie suddenly wished she had not brought up the topic. What would Peter say about organizations of women supporting each other in the workplace? Would he and the other constables think her disloyal if she sought encouragement from outside the constabulary? Even so, the meetings were reported in the *Hull Daily Mail*, and should her name appear in the paper, it seemed likely that at least one constable would spot it there and mention it to the others. It would be easier if she told her partner about it ahead of time.

'It's the Women of Work Club. I just joined it,' she said.

'I didn't know there was such a thing,' Peter said leaning back in his chair and fiddling with his roll of cutlery. 'I can see how something like that might be of use to someone like you.'

'What do you mean "someone like me"?' she asked.

'I mean that it can't be easy to be one of the only women on the job. Navigating the situation must be trying at times and I would think it would be useful to have people to discuss that with who might understand what it's like to be you,' he said.

Billie felt a lump rising in her throat. Was it possible that even if he had heard gossip and crude talk from Constable Drummond that he had not believed her to be the one who had encouraged such behavior? But before she could respond Peter shoved back his chair and got to his feet. He waved for the waitress and asked her to cancel their order. Billie looked out through the window once again and spotted Paul Harper hurrying along the pavement with a large rucksack strapped to his back. She grabbed her handbag and moved to the window.

TWENTY-FOUR

Paul Harper's figure grew smaller and smaller as he quickened his pace. Peter practically broke into a trot as they left the café behind and attempted to follow him. Billie could barely keep up, but she was not about to ask him to slow down. Paul kept casting glances over his shoulder, but fortunately his attention was on the same side of the street as the family store had been. He paid no mind whatsoever to the opposite side of the broad avenue. Billie was glad of the heavy traffic that flowed between them and provided cover.

Paul turned right at the corner several blocks past the store and Billie thought for a heart-stopping moment that they had lost him. But the traffic lights were in their favor, and they managed to cross the street and catch sight of him just as he turned another corner. They slowed their steps so as not to alert him to their presence and Billie was pleased to see that he had slowed down as if he were no longer concerned he was being followed.

As they made their way along, she had a sense that she might have been in this section of the city before. She could not remember a time when she had taken the same exact route but some of the landmarks seemed familiar. After about five more minutes of following Paul, she realized that they were in the same neighborhood as one of the air-raid shelters that Mr James had mentioned in his original complaint.

Sure enough, Paul glanced one last time around him furtively then stepped up to a low-slung shelter. He knocked on the door and although Billie could not see who opened it, the portal swung open, and Paul stepped inside.

'Do you think Colin is in there?' Billie asked.

'There's one way to find out,' Peter said. She raced alongside him as they crossed the street and made straight for the shelter themselves. Peter stepped up to the door, raised his hand and knocked on it with several blows. The door opened and a boy of about sixteen with sandy-brown hair and over-sized ears stood framed in the opening.

'Colin Ward?' Peter asked. Wordlessly the boy nodded. 'We have some questions to ask you.'

Peter placed a broad hand on the door and swung it fully open. There, in the center of the shelter, sat a folding table with a large display of goods spread upon it. To Billie's eyes it appeared to be a miniature version of the Harper's corner shop. Paul's rucksack sat open on the floor beside the table and through the opening in the top she could see a brown-paper-wrapped parcel peeking out. In addition, there were several oil lamps, some hooks and coils of wire as well as folding chairs and a pair of camp beds. Unless she missed her guess, not only were the boys looking to sell black-market goods, but they were also offering up the same items that had been reported stolen by Mr James.

'Colin was just helping me out,' Paul said.

'Helping you out with what?' Peter asked.

'We're just earning a bit of extra spending money, that's all,' Paul said.

'Are these items stolen from your parents' shop and air-raid shelters?' Billie asked.

'Stolen?' Colin said, his voice wavering. 'You never said anything about anything being stolen. I thought your parents were in on this, too.' He looked over at Paul with what Billie believed was genuine surprise.

'I'm not saying anything,' Paul said. 'You keep your mouth shut, too.'

'I guess we're going to have to take this to the station,' Peter said reaching for his handcuffs. 'Turn around, Colin.'

As Peter snapped the handcuffs around Colin's wrists the boy began to tremble. His knees wobbled and before he could collapse Peter pushed him gently towards a bench placed against a nearby wall. Billie stepped forward and ordered Paul to put his own hands behind his back. But unlike his friend, Paul thrashed around, doing his best to make her job all the more difficult. Once again, she was glad for Peter's presence as she dealt with him.

'See, I told you we'd be heading back to the station soon.

I just didn't know that it would be with such a result in hand,' he said as he began gathering up the items spread across the table and placing them into Paul's rucksack and a sailor's ditty bag lying discarded upon the floor.

He shouldered the larger of the two bags and handed the rucksack to Billie. The furniture and other items from the shelters would have to stay. There was no way to carry it all. Despite her burden's smaller size, she felt weighed down by its contents and was glad once more for Peter's presence. It was going to be a long walk back to the station with both the evidence and suspects in hand.

All along their walk from the air-raid shelter, every time it seemed that Colin was about to say something, Paul admonished him to keep his mouth shut. They separated the boys as soon as they reached the station. They left Paul on a bench in front of the reception desk under Sergeant Skelton's watchful eye and led Colin to an available interview room for questioning.

Peter removed his cuffs and indicated Colin should take a seat. The pair of constables seated themselves in chairs across a wooden table from him. Billie couldn't help but think how young he looked sitting there under the harsh light of the overhead bulb, his face blanched with fear. It was just as the chief constable had said. Opportunities for indulging in criminal behavior abounded under the war regulations and citizens of all stripes decided to take their chances.

'You know it's a serious offense to sell rationed goods on the black market,' Peter said.

'I was just trying to help out a friend,' he said. 'It didn't seem like we were really doing anything wrong.'

'I think you know it was very wrong. There's a reason for the ration and trying to get rich off the backs of your neighbors is a form of treachery,' Billie said letting the words sink in.

The Treachery Act that had passed back in May was the most stringent law concerning wartime activities to date. It had been enacted in order to allow for prosecution of those foreign nationals found on their shores or indeed their own citizens who were working against the common good. It was not possible to legally accuse a foreign national of being a traitor when operating for the good of their own people, but it was possible to rename it treachery. The burden of proof had been considerably lowered in order to allow for more sweeping use of the regulation and the punishment extended all the way to execution. Billie felt queasy as she watched the meaning of what she said register on Colin's pale face.

'Paul said that his parents were having to pay higher prices for the things they sold in the store, and it was just a way to recoup their losses,' he said. 'I had no idea it could be considered treachery. Please, my parents couldn't stand to go through anything else.'

'Because of the accident with your brother?' Billie asked.

Colin nodded his head slowly and Billie had the impression that he wanted to lay it down on the table and sob.

'We interviewed your parents and they seemed like they are having a very hard time dealing with your brother's death. I've heard that's the case for you, too. But perhaps what was really bothering you was knowing that you've been involved with something as illegal as this business with the black market goods,' Peter said.

'I feel just terrible about both,' Colin said. 'Do we have to tell my parents?'

'I'm not sure that we will be able to keep from telling your parents. This is a very serious matter. And to think we wanted to talk to you about something else entirely,' Billie said.

'Something else?' Colin said, his eyes widening even more.

'Did your parents tell you that Peter and I had stopped by to ask them about the man who struck your brother with his lorry?' she asked.

'They didn't tell me that the police had come by, but they did say they had heard that Dennis Partridge had died,' Colin said. 'Why do you ask?'

'Did they tell you that Dennis had been murdered?' Billie asked.

'They didn't say that. Who killed him?' Colin asked.

'We were hoping you might be able to help answer that yourself,' Billie said.

That wasn't quite the truth. She hoped very much that Colin had no idea what had happened to Dennis Partridge. But despite the fact that she wished for him to be in the clear, he started to shake just as violently as he had when Peter had snapped the handcuffs on his bare wrists.

'I didn't kill him, I swear,' he said. 'I just found him.'

'You found Dennis Partridge murdered?' Peter asked.

'Paul thought that maybe we might be able to get into one of the air-raid shelters to use as a temporary spot to set up shop. We tried a couple and then found one where the door was unlocked. But when we stepped inside Dennis Partridge was there on the floor, stone cold surrounded by saleable goods,' Colin said holding out a ring of keys to Peter.

'Why didn't you ring for help at the nearest police phone box?' she asked.

'Would you have done that if you were me? After all, we were looking for a place to sell black market goods and I stumbled across the body of the man accused of killing my brother,' Colin said.

His voice cracked and he began to sob in earnest. Billie pulled out a freshly laundered pocket handkerchief from her uniform jacket and slid it across the table towards him. While she waited for the storm of sobbing to subside, she thought about what he had said. When he had managed to pull himself together, she renewed her questioning.

'You said that Dennis Partridge was accused of killing your brother. You sound as though he wasn't the one responsible for Trevor's death,' Billie said.

Colin slumped even lower in his chair and exhaled deeply. It was as though all of the fight had gone completely out of him.

'Dennis Partridge might have hit Trevor with his lorry, but it wasn't his fault that my brother died. It was mine,' he said.

He looked up at Billie and she thought she had never seen so much sadness in any one face. She wanted to reach across the table to give his hand a squeeze, but it was not for her to do, not in her position as a police constable. If she had accepted her father's curate Ronald's offer of marriage, it would have been her place as his wife when confronted with someone in such distress, but that was not the role she had decided upon.

So instead, she sat up a bit straighter and swallowed down her emotions.

'How is it that you think you are complicit in your brother's death?' she asked.

'Trevor had become curious about where it was that I was going in the afternoons without him. I caught him snooping around my room and trying to follow me. He was just a kid and I know he would have told our parents everything if he found out what I was up to,' Colin said, drawing in a ragged breath. 'The day he died I was trying to give him the slip. I knew that he was following me and at the last minute I dashed across the street. I was on my way to meet Paul in an alleyway not far from his parents' shop where we had agreed to meet a few neighbors in order to sell them some sugar and bacon. I didn't ever think he would chase after me like he did.'

Billie felt her heart catch in her chest. She knew exactly how Colin felt. Even though he had not been the one behind the wheel, she completely understood how he felt as though he had been the reason his loved one had died. She still felt an overwhelming sense of responsibility for her own mother's death despite the fact she'd been nowhere nearby when the accident had occurred.

If she had gone home before dark her mother would not have been out looking for her and would not have been struck down by a motorist who had not been able to see her in the blackout darkness. She was absolutely certain the look on Colin's face was the same as the one she wore when Constable Bridges had delivered the news to her on the day of her mother's tragic accident. It took all the self-control she possessed to keep her hands in her lap instead of reaching across the table to comfort him.

'Do your parents know what really caused your brother to dash across the street into traffic?' she asked.

'I couldn't bring myself to tell them. They both were so angry at Dennis Partridge that they didn't look for answers anywhere else. My mother kept asking why Trevor would have done such a thing when he knew better, but everyone assured her that sometimes boys just don't think. I know that I didn't when I tried to lose him that day.' Colin dissolved into tears once more.

As Billie sat there wondering what on earth she ought to do, it occurred to her that the one good thing that had come of the interview was that she doubted very much that Colin would have been the one to kill Dennis Partridge. If anything, she thought it far more likely that the boy would be more inclined to take his own life. What she didn't know was how his parents would be able to endure the loss of both sons should he do so.

TWENTY-FIVE

Although Billie was exhausted from her shift, she could not bring herself to head home before double checking her memory about the name given to her by the woman who had complained on behalf of her job-seeking son. She let Peter believe that she was headed home as she had gathered her personal belongings from the women's cloakroom, as she did not want him to feel that he needed to work as late as she did.

While he never complained about it, Billie was acutely aware of the fact that as well as serving as a special constable, he worked at his reserved occupation inspecting the docks. Peter was burning the candle at both ends without regard for his own need for rest or recreation. She certainly wasn't going to be the one to encourage him to delay getting home to supper any longer than had already been required of him by dint of the interviews with Colin Ward and Paul Harper.

She waited in the women's cloakroom until she was quite certain he was gone for the day, then slipped back out into the hallway and made straight for the bank of filing cabinets where archived reports were kept. She pulled out the report brought in by Mrs Geraldine Hayes and ran her finger along the words printed there searching for the surname Sumner. Right there in her own handwriting her memory was confirmed. Donald Sumner was listed as the name of the man who had accepted money from Melvin Hayes for travel to London in order to help seek a better position for the young man.

Next, she went to a large room at the back of the station where evidence was stored on rows of shelves. It took a while to locate the boxes she and Peter had carried from Dennis Partridge's boardinghouse, but after a few moments she did so. She carried the boxes to a table in the center of the storage room and lifted their lids. Riffling down through the items she pushed aside articles of clothing and personal possessions until she laid her hands on the two registration cards found with Dennis Partridge's body. Opening each in turn she found what she was looking for. There, neatly penned was the name Donald Sumner with the false address listed.

She returned the evidence boxes to the shelves and made her way back to the bank of filing cabinets. She pulled out a folder containing the information gathered thus far on the Dennis Partridge investigation and searched through it for the police artist sketch. She lifted it from the file and folded it in half carefully before placing it in her uniform jacket pocket. Before leaving she decided it would be wisest to apprise Avis of her intentions. She found her superior officer in her small office at the far end of the station.

Avis answered on the first knock and Billie took a seat in the guest chair opposite Avis.

'You look as though you have something on your mind, WPC Harkness,' Avis said. 'I have been keeping tabs on your investigation from a distance and it seems as though you've been very busy.'

'We've been busy, but I don't feel as though we're making much headway. Something has come up, though, that I wanted to ask you about,' Billie said. 'It may have more to do with your extracurricular efforts than those you do for the constabulary.'

Avis looked past Billie's shoulder as if to ascertain that the door was firmly closed. She lowered her voice and leaned forward slightly. 'What's on your mind.'

'I know I mentioned to you earlier that the victim in the case I've been working on was found with more than one national identity card in his possession at the time of his death,' Billie said.

'Yes, I remember. Did you get to the bottom of that?'

'I'm not sure I would say that. The addresses on the cards turned out to be fakes and when we finally did manage to identify him and track down his actual residence, we discovered he had even more of them. It turns out that he was using a false identity to gain access to air-raid shelters, but I've come across something else as well,' Billie said.

'Which is?'

'A woman came in earlier in the week lodging a complaint that a man claiming to have ties to the Ministry of Supply had offered to help procure a job for her son with that agency. The name he gave was one of the ones on a falsified registry card,' Billie said.

'And what of it?' Avis asked.

'We've just arrested two young men for selling black-market goods in one of the air-raid shelters. One of the boys confessed to having found the victim dead in the shelter, but that he did not want to report it for fear of being blamed for his death,' Billie said.

'Are you suggesting that the claims this man made of being connected to the Ministry of Supply might also be connected to the sale of black-market goods?' Avis asked.

Billie nodded. 'It had crossed my mind that in order for them to sell more than one of the boy's family's allotted share of goods that they had to obtain them somewhere. At an event with Lydia a few nights ago I happened to encounter the chief constable. He mentioned in conversation that there are growing concerns about abuses in the system by people in positions of trust.'

'Are you suggesting that it's possible that someone in the Ministry of Supply killed him in order to silence him about black-market supplies?' Avis asked.

'I'm suggesting that it's a possibility. Every lead we turn up seems to lead basically nowhere with this man. He had enemies, to be sure, but I think it possible that someone who could be held accountable for treachery might be inclined to silence him before he could betray them,' Billie said.

'You might be right, but until you have more information, I don't think I should send this to my superiors. It might be a large problem, but until we have more facts I would rather that they remained able to concentrate on the charges that we know for sure are very real,' Avis said.

'I suppose you're thinking of the airfields and factories,' Billie said.

'The sale of black-market goods, especially foodstuffs, is a real problem and I'm not dismissing it in any way. But day after day the Luftwaffe is destroying aircraft and the means to build replacements. I don't think it's in anyone's best interest to distract the powers that be from putting a stop to that. A large part of my job is to help filter and prioritize what reaches them. Right now, the most important thing is to plug leaks about where our most important military assets can be found,' Avis said.

'With your permission I'd like to follow up on some questions for the woman whose son was interested in the job with the Ministry of Supply. That may be where the most good could be done if this is a matter of treachery on the part of a government official,' Billie said.

'That sounds like a good way to proceed. What do you plan to tell Peter?' Avis asked.

'I thought I would simply suggest that Geraldine and Melvin Hayes be questioned because of the false registry card. I would let him draw his own conclusions about any connection to the Ministry of Supply. I think it would draw more attention to my thoughts on that line of questioning if I were to try and hide it from him in some way,' Billie said.

'He is a bright and inquisitive constable, so I expect you're right. I would feel better if you took him along with you for the questioning. Anyone who would be willing to kill someone over their knowledge of black-market bacon might be just as willing to cause harm to a small female constable. And we already don't have enough WPCs to suit me,' Avis said bestowing her one of her rare smiles.

Billie scraped back her chair and left Avis's office feeling a renewed sense of purpose. The questioning of Mrs Hayes and her son could wait until the next day. She would just have to think carefully about how she questioned them in front of Peter. Fortunately, she had all evening ahead of her to think.

She stepped out of the station, her mind on the next day. The crowds steadily thinned as she crossed Alfred Gelder Street and away from the people heading towards Paragon Station. The evening was fine and she decided to cut through the Queen's Gardens on her way home rather than sticking to the streets. She was pleased that she had enough familiarity with the city that she could recognize shortcuts.

The gardens were not filled with flowers as they would have

been before every available bit of land had been converted to growing food. Still, it was pleasant to walk among so much greenery in the middle of the city. As she stopped to admire a well-tended patch of potatoes a hand reached out and gripped her sleeve.

She wheeled around, her heart beating wildly.

'I thought that was you,' Constable Drummond said, keeping his large hand clamped around her arm.

She tried to take a step back, but he held her firmly in place. She glanced around, alarmed at how few people had chosen to enter the garden that evening. She commanded herself not to panic. After all, what harm could he do in broad daylight in public? Still, she had no intention of allowing him to make free with his hands as he had at the station.

'Let go of me,' she said with as little quaver in her voice as she could muster.

He smiled at her and increased his grip. 'Is that any way to speak to a friend?'

'We aren't friends.'

'You know, you ought to learn to be nice to me. I'm not a bad chap once you get to know me.'

'I know you as well as I intend to,' she said attempting to yank her arm away once more.

'Now, what kind of nonsense is that? I've half a mind to drag you off into that cozy bit of shrubbery and teach you the only thing a WPC is really good for.'

He tugged her arm in the direction of a clump of rhododendrons taller than either of them. She reached up with her free hand and before he could react brought her police whistle to her lips. Constable Drummond recoiled from the piercing blast, throwing his hands up to cover his ears. She sprinted off as fast as her legs would carry her and reached the edge of the gardens where she joined a small queue wending its way on to a tram. As she collapsed on to a seat, she caught sight of Constable Drummond emerging from the park with a look of fury clear to see even from a distance.

TWENTY-SIX

Special Constable Upton's Police Notebook

It had been a long day, but one Peter felt had finally led to some sort of result. While he could not claim to have been pleased to land a young lad like Paul Harper in as much trouble as he and WPC Harkness had managed to do, he did not hold with black-market activities. The ration, at least to his mind, was a very sensible precaution and one that was designed to fight that most evil of enemies, low morale.

He thought it unlikely that either Paul or Colin would face the most serious consequences for their actions as they were both just boys. Paul's parents, however, would be brought before the police court and if they were lucky would simply face stiff fines. The fact of the matter was that either or both of them could be sentenced to hard labor. When he had mentioned the nature of Paul's and Colin's arrests to the sergeant he had felt relieved when his superior said that the real target should be the suppliers of the excess sugar and bacon that merchants like the Harpers used to access the materials.

Sergeant Skelton reminded him that for the most part people in positions of trust either directly or indirectly stole from government stores in order to provide shopkeepers like the Harpers with goods to sell. He even indicated that there were more times than anyone wished to acknowledge that people who were employed by the government to safeguard the nation's food supply were profiting by such underhanded dealings. It seemed that the chief constable's confession to WPC Harkness about the increase in criminal activity because of an excess of regulations had more than a little truth to it.

After a day on his feet walking the beat and witnessing the result of people's poor decisions, Peter always felt a deep desire for a bit of peace. It was on days such as this that he felt the lack of a home and wife of his own acutely. Generally speaking, he was well satisfied with his lot, his small room in the boardinghouse and the lack of responsibility that his bachelor state allowed. But now and again he found his thoughts turning towards what he imagined it would be like to be headed to his own private space, however humble, to be greeted by someone who counted it a privilege to read his mood and to accommodate him.

But his landlady Mrs Cummins had no such duty to fulfill. She was far more interested in chattering at him no matter how he might insist he wished to head straight to his room and refresh himself in solitude. Before the blackout he might have spent pleasant hours wandering the city bathed in streetlights and illuminated signs, people-watching as folks dressed up in finery passed him by, headed for nightclubs and cinemas. There was something so soothing about finding oneself in the midst of a crowd with which one need not interact.

But since the blackout had removed as much light as was possible from the public thoroughfares, there was not much people-watching to be had. And truth be told, he felt far less comfortable being out in the open knowing that on any given night he might have to seek temporary shelter somewhere. He thought of WPC Harkness and the look that had been on her face as she stood with him in the corridor outside the interview rooms. She had taken the troubles the boys found themselves in at least as much to heart as had he.

When she mentioned Colin's confession and how responsible he felt for his younger brother's accident, her face gave away how pained she had felt by the encounter. Her recent sharing of confidence that had told him of her own mother's death gave him some insight into why she had taken the news particularly badly. Even though he was not looking forward to his room at the boardinghouse, he was comforted by the notion that WPC Harkness would have no such difficulty herself that evening.

He had accompanied her back to her cousin's home weeks earlier after the two of them had sheltered from an air raid underneath heavy wooden pews at his mother's Catholic church. Lydia's house had awed him although he had tried not to show it. It was one of the more modern sorts of homes that he was entirely unaccustomed to. He had made an excuse and had left WPC Harkness on the doorstep rather than accepting her invitation to come inside for a drink. He had made his excuses, citing the lateness of the hour and the distance from his own bed. But the fact of the matter was he felt intimidated by the outside of the house. He couldn't imagine how much more awkward he would feel inside it.

But he expected such a location would fit WPC Harkness just fine. She always appeared so neat and tidy even when the heat of the day left him feeling a sodden, perspiring mess. When they had the rare opportunity to sit on a bench side-by-side and break for a bit of lunch, she always managed to consume a sandwich or piece of fruit without marring her lipstick or dusting the front of her police uniform with crumbs. He could not imagine her depositing great clods of earth on fancy carpets or marring the upholstery with grimy fingers.

He took a steadying breath as he rounded the corner on to his own street and braced himself as he approached the door to the boardinghouse. He mounted the steps and placed his hand on the knob hoping that there would be no one in the hallway beyond. If luck was with him, he might be able to sneak up to his room, carefully navigating the second and seventh stairs that creaked so loudly underfoot, without attracting the notice of Mrs Cummins. As he pushed open the door and slipped inside the house, he cocked his head listening for the sound of any other residents. Hearing nothing, he pressed the door into place behind him and turned towards the stairway. But before his hand touched the newel post, Mrs Cummins's voice called out to him from the sitting room.

'Is that you, Peter?' she asked.

He thought about holding his tongue and hurtling up the stairs, but rejected the notion. He had too much self-respect to slink about like a recalcitrant child or a common criminal. Perhaps if he were to drop broad hints, or even simply state that he had no intention of socializing that evening he might beat a hasty retreat with his dignity intact.

He threw his shoulders back and strode to the sitting-room door. 'It is. Is there something you wish to speak with me about, Mrs Cummins?'

Although he deliberately hovered on the threshold, Mrs Cummins waved him in. 'I want to speak with you about a list I've compiled from your fellow lodgers,' she said, fluttering a piece of paper in his direction.

He left the safety of the threshold and crossed the room to take it from her. As he did so he noticed Mary Parker seated in a chair placed near a window overlooking the street. He suspected Mary of having alerted Mrs Cummins to his arrival. He felt irrationally irritated at her for delaying him from reaching the peace of his own room. But he gave no vent to his irritation, but rather nodded to her before turning his attention to the list.

In Mrs Cummins's neat, but slightly childish hand, he read:

One pair of enameled cufflinks
One small magnifying glass with a silver handle
One coin purse with a snapping clasp
One cigarette lighter
One ornate brass lady's compact

'What is this a list of?' he asked.

'Items that have been reported missing by your fellow lodgers,' Mrs Cummins said. 'I had hoped that Mary's missing coin purse was a question of her misplacing it, but there are far too many items that have gone missing for such an innocent explanation.'

Peter turned towards Mary Parker. 'You still haven't found your coin purse?'

'No, and I have looked for it everywhere. I've torn apart my room here at the boardinghouse and searched my workstation and locker at the factory as well. It's not in any of the pockets of my clothing and there's simply nowhere else I can think that it could be,' she said.

'Do you know the last time you had it for sure?' he asked.

'Well, that's the thing, Mr Upton,' Mrs Cummins said. 'I asked that question of each and every one of your fellow lodgers who have lost one of the items on this list. They all seem to have gone missing the very same day.'

'And which day was that?' Peter said.

'The last time anyone remembers having had the items on this list was the day before that man came here posing as an RAF billeting officer,' Mrs Cummins said.

'Do you think that he is the one responsible for the thefts?' Peter asked.

'I cannot say for sure. But I would say that he moved about the building methodically and without oversight. I had things on the hob and in the oven and I certainly couldn't let my lodgers' supper burn, now could I?' she asked.

Peter did not make a response, but rather sent a look at Mary Parker who smiled at him. The only thing Mrs Cummins served as frequently as burnt food to her lodgers was food that was undercooked. Her heart was in the right place, but her skills did not lay in that direction no matter how vigilantly she attended to those duties. Still, it would do no good to mention it to her.

'So, what you're saying is, this man who presented himself as a billeting officer was allowed to wander through the building all on his own?' Peter asked.

'I gave it no thought at the time. Billeting officers have to be allowed to inspect the premises in order to know exactly how much space you have to squeeze in more boarders. I had no reason to doubt his word and left him to get on with what he claimed was his work,' Mrs Cummins said. 'I feel just terrible about it now.'

Peter recalled how easily Dennis Partridge had convinced Mr James that he was an air-raid shelter inspector. It was easy to see how he might have come off as entirely credible to someone like Mrs Cummins as well. Too many people trusted those in uniform without giving it a second thought. It was clever, but far too easily pulled off, in his opinion.

'Don't go blaming yourself. He managed to fool at least one other person and took advantage of his trusting nature as well.' He looked over the list once more. 'All of the items on this list seem like things that could easily be secreted away in pockets without alerting anyone to the fact that they were hidden there. A small coin purse or pair of cufflinks would not make an obvious lump in his clothing, and he could easily have run off with them with no one the wiser,' Peter said.

He thought about the date Mrs Cummins mentioned and realized that it was the last time he remembered seeing his badge. The day before the billeting officer had appeared he had worked an extra-long shift at the docks and had not spent any time serving as a special constable. It wasn't until the next day that he realized his badge was missing. He had left it in the bureau in his room thinking it should be secured as it had been every other time he had left it there.

Perhaps he had not been careless after all. A policeman's badge was just as easy to slip into a pocket as a pair of cufflinks or coin purse. And it would have been even more valuable for someone like Dennis Partridge than any of the other things he had acquired in the boardinghouse that day. With his proclivity for assuming identities not his own, how much mischief could he have made with a constable's badge? With a sinking feeling he realized that he was going to have to confess its loss to Sergeant Skelton whether he wanted to or not.

But it did occur to him that perhaps he might be able to track down the other missing items. Certainly, Dennis Partridge could have offloaded them somewhere between the time he stole them and his unexpected death, but perhaps one or two of them could be found among his possessions boxed up so neatly by his landlady. His fellow lodgers' possessions might be in safekeeping right at the police station.

'I can't make any promises, but I may have an idea where some of these things have gone. I should know by the end of my shift tomorrow,' he said. With that he made his excuses and headed for his own room, trying to figure out just exactly what he was going to say to the sergeant.

TWENTY-SEVEN

WPC Harkness's Police Notebook

Billie stayed on the tram, caring little in which direction it was headed until her legs stopped trembling and she was out of sight of the Queen's Gardens. By the time she had disembarked and boarded a bus headed towards Linden Crescent the hour was long past her usual time to return home.

Her heart pounded in her chest and her palms grew slick with sweat as she left the safety of the crowded bus and headed for Lydia's house as quickly as she could without breaking into a run. She raced up the steps, burst through the door and sagged against it. She still could not quite believe what had happened. She removed her cap and placed it on the hall table next to her cousin's sky-blue handbag and matching pair of gloves. Her reflection in the mirror hung above the table looked as distressed as she felt.

'Is that you, Billie?' Lydia called out from the sitting room. 'They've kept you rather late tonight, haven't they?'

For a fleeting moment there was nothing she wanted more than to head straight up the broad stairs for a bath and an early night, tucked up in bed with a favorite novel. But Lydia did not deserve to be ignored and with a longing glance at the stairs she headed instead towards the sound of her cousin's voice.

Lydia too seemed settled in for a quiet night spent reading. She sat in her usual spot on an elegantly upholstered settee, a book opened on her lap. She glanced up as Billie entered the room.

'What on earth is the matter?' Lydia asked, swinging her feet to the floor and rushing towards Billie with her slim hands outstretched.

Billie simply shook her head and willed herself not to sob.

Lydia led her to the couch, and urged her to sit before crossing the room to the glass-and-chrome side table she had set up as a bar. With practiced ease she plucked cubes of ice from an awaiting bucket and dropped them into a tall glass. She added a healthy splash of gin and topped it with soda water from a crystal and mesh siphon.

She held the glass out to Billie who took it with the tiniest smidgen of guilt. Her mother had not approved of strong spirits and while Billie had found that a cocktail every now and then had not turned her into some sort of degenerate, she never accepted one without the sound of her mother's voice ringing in her ears. Still, her mother was no longer able to chide Billie about anything at all.

'Has something happened at work?' Lydia said settling once more on the settee opposite.

She turned her attention completely on Billie. Lydia had a remarkable gift for making one feel as though they were the center of the universe when she focused upon them. Unlike so many other people of Billie's acquaintance, Lydia never seemed to be waiting to speak rather than actually listening. Billie took a sip of her drink before she felt equal to the task of speaking.

'I'm not exactly sure what happened. I can't seem to make sense of it in my own mind, let alone to try and express it to someone else,' she said. That queasy feeling she had had in the canteen swept over her once more and she found it difficult to meet Lydia's gaze. The spot on the plush carpet between them was so much easier to look at.

'That doesn't sound like you. You're such an articulate person,' Lydia said. 'Come, tell me what happened. Surely it can be sorted out.'

Billie looked Lydia in the face and let out a long exhalation. 'It seems that I have somehow given the wrong impression to one of my colleagues,' she said.

'What sort of wrong impression?' Lydia asked.

'I am not sure how I did it, but it appears I have encouraged Constable Drummond to believe I harbored some sort of romantic interest in him,' Billie said. She forced herself to keep her eyes from seeking out the pattern on the carpet once more.

'Did he say something to give you that feeling?' Lydia asked.

'Not exactly. It was more what he did with his hands,' Billie said feeling the heat rising to her cheeks once more. Lydia gave a sharp intake of breath and leaned forward.

'Do you mean to say that one of your colleagues placed his hands on you?' she asked.

'He came up behind me unexpectedly while I was doing the washing up in the canteen and wrapped me in an embrace,' Billie said.

'Had anything passed between you that prepared you for such an overture?' Lydia asked.

'I've barely spoken to the man. Mostly I work with Peter, the sergeant and Avis. We've never walked the beat together, nor have we worked together on anything in the station house either. I really don't know what I could have done to encourage him,' Billie said.

'You must have been completely taken by surprise.'

'I was shocked. I should have pushed him away immediately, but somehow, I simply froze in place. It was as if my mind and body were no longer working together,' Billie said.

'What a scoundrel,' Lydia said. 'How did you put a stop to it?'

'I didn't. Sergeant Skelton came in just then and Constable Drummond stepped away from me.'

'I hope the sergeant sent him off with a flea in his ear at least.'

'That was the worst part of the whole wretched mess. I believe the sergeant thought that it was a consensual embrace. He said something to the effect of being sorry to disturb our canoodling, but that we ought to get back to the job at hand,' Billie said.

'How ghastly. And how like that Sergeant Skelton. From what I've heard from Avis Crane he's never been supportive of the idea of women serving in the constabulary. I suppose it's no surprise that he would have assumed that a woman in the work-place would be inclined towards loose morals,' Lydia said.

Billie's cheeks blazed with heat. 'I'm afraid that my reputation has been damaged by what happened.'

'Did you speak with Avis about the incident?' Lydia asked.

'No, I didn't. I was so embarrassed I couldn't face speaking about it again. Besides, I didn't want to make any trouble with my colleagues. Tattle-taling to my superior didn't seem like the best way to salvage my reputation,' Billie said.

'You cannot be sure it was spoken of, can you?' Lydia asked.

'I feel quite certain the matter was discussed. Later, while I was working at the reception desk, I heard Constable Drummond say my name and then something else I couldn't hear. A whole group of other constables started laughing and jeering.'

'Did this happen today?'

Billie took another, larger sip of her cocktail. She shook her head. 'The incident in the canteen happened earlier in the week.'

'Then there has been something else that has distressed you today.' Lydia leaned forward squeezing her hands together in her lap. 'Is that why you are late getting home?'

'This evening, Constable Drummond must have followed me out of the station. He caught up with me as I was passing through the Queen's Gardens.'

Billie heard Lydia's sharp intake of breath. 'Did he harm you? Were you interfered with in any way?'

'He grabbed me by the arm and wouldn't let me go. I don't want to repeat exactly what he said, but I am afraid that if I hadn't thought to blast my police whistle in his ear he might very well have done so.'

Lydia rose from her spot on the settee and crossed the short distance between them. She sat on the sofa next to Billie and reached out to clasp her hand.

'This isn't your fault. I know from sad experience how frequently one can find oneself in such an uncomfortable position through no fault of one's own,' Lydia said.

'But surely no decent man, certainly no police officer, would behave in such a way without believing his attentions to be welcomed, would he?' Billie asked.

The idea that someone in a position of authority would behave in such a way shocked her. She knew that she had been raised in an indisputably sheltered way. After all, even young men in the village of her close acquaintance had displayed very little interest in her, at least romantically. Being the rector's daughter had provided some sort of invisible cloak of protection from that sort of behavior. Her only real experience with such matters had involved a proposal of marriage from her father's curate, offered purely out of a desire to protect both of their reputations rather than from any particular romantic feelings on his part.

'I'm sorry to say that such things occur far more often than they should. And they don't seem to be constrained to any particular sort of job or social standing. From dockworkers to politicians, the country is simply heaving with chancers who think nothing of putting their hands where they ought not.' Lydia reached up and tucked a lock of stray hair behind Billie's ear.

It was such a maternal gesture that Billie felt a lump rise in her throat. All of the confused emotions she had kept bottled up throughout the day threatened to release themselves in a spate of tears. She forced herself to breathe in slowly and to not give in to a burst of uncontrollable sobbing.

'Do such things like that take place at the library?' Billie asked. She always thought of libraries as a haven of sorts. She found it utterly disheartening to know that something so ugly might occur within its confines.

Lydia arched an eyebrow and nodded. 'No place is sacred, it seems. I've been cornered in the storage room, in the stacks, and even once behind the desk right in front of a patron. And that doesn't begin to list the times I have put up with unsolicited comments and unwanted caresses before or after city council meetings, while volunteering at charitable organizations or even while riding a city tram.'

Billie's eyes widened. She had difficulty imagining that anyone would be so bold as to clasp Lydia in an embrace she had not requested. She always seemed so completely self-assured and poised. The notion of her enduring something like that boggled the mind.

Of all the things her mother had warned her about, such widespread malfeasance had not been among them. She had worried about Billie's posture, her tone of voice when speaking to her elders and the breadth of her home-keeping knowledge. She warned her not to speak with strangers, of which there were few in Barton St Giles, not to wander too far into the woods on the outskirts of the village, and not to wear cosmetics which would brand her a harlot.

She had never voiced concern that Billie would be subjected to the sort of manhandling Lydia described. Nor had she ever shared her own experience of such things. Perhaps as the wife of the village rector she remained as untainted by such abuses as Billie did herself.

'The worst thing is, I feel even more reluctant now to appear before the city council to encourage them to allow additional women to join the constabulary. At first I was hesitant to agree because I felt unqualified to speak on the subject as any sort of an expert. Now I'm not sure I should encourage any other women to place themselves in such a position,' Billie said.

'I can understand your concern, but I think that the more we normalize the notion of women participating in the work-force, the more I have to hope that this sort of behavior will eventually fade out of existence.'

'Do you really think so?' Billie asked.

'I don't think it is in anyone's best interest to look at the future with pessimism. After all, no one enters any sort of conflict if they don't have the smallest bit of hope of triumphing in the end, do they?' Lydia asked.

'So, I suppose that means you wouldn't be willing to help me to make an excuse to the chief constable in order to get out of the council meeting?'

'Certainly not. What I would be happy to do is to accompany you to speak to him about what has happened, if you like.'

'Thanks all the same, but I think that might be the very worst thing I could do. Employing a personal connection to the chief isn't likely to endear me to my colleagues under the best of circumstances. I cannot imagine it would help in this one.'

'You could report him to the sergeant. Isn't he in charge of the male constables at the station?'

'I'd be too embarrassed to speak with Sergeant Skelton about it. Besides, I feel like I am finally making some headway with him, and I wouldn't want to do anything to jeopardize that,' Billie said. She took a sip of her cocktail and pressed the cool glass against her flaming cheek.

'Then why not speak to Avis? Surely, she could help you,' Lydia said,

'I'd hate to put her in the middle of this. She has enough trouble with our male colleagues herself, especially the sergeant,' Billie said. 'Although I don't see why that should be the way. Without women volunteering to pitch in the whole country is going to collapse.'

'That's the spirit. Anger is a much more useful emotion than shame, especially when it comes to things that are not one's own fault. I've encountered similar situations throughout my life and while it doesn't get any easier, it is possible to learn to speak up for oneself and to refuse to be embarrassed by the actions of others.'

'I'll bear that in mind. If you don't object, I think I'll make an early night of it.'

Lydia reached out for her empty glass and gave her a kiss on the cheek. 'I'll make you a cup of cocoa.'

But despite the cocktail, the Horlicks and the comfort of her bed, sleep eluded her. She dreaded the thought of seeing Constable Drummond in or out of the station. But what bothered her even more was what he might say about the incident to their colleagues. What if Peter heard something about her that lowered her in his eyes. For some reason she did not wish to dwell upon, that seemed the most difficult thing of all.

TWENTY-EIGHT

Peter made a beeline for her when he entered the police station the next morning.

'Do you remember the contents of the boxes we took from Dennis Partridge's boardinghouse?' he asked without even pausing to greet her.

'I remember many of them, but it might just be easier to take a look. Why do you ask?' Billie said.

'Follow me,' Peter said, inclining his head towards the hallway. 'Do you know if the boxes are still in the evidence room?'

Billie nodded. 'I was just checking on them yesterday, so I know that they are there,' she said. Peter hurried ahead of her, and she raced along trying to match his long, loping stride.

Before she could pass through the door of the evidence room, he was running his finger along the cartons searching for the one containing Dennis Partridge's belongings. She headed for the shelf containing his possessions and pointed them out. They each carried a box to the table in the center of the room and Peter began removing items and spreading them out across the table.

'What are you looking for?' Billie asked.

'A pair of cufflinks, a cigarette lighter, a woman's compact, a change purse, a magnifying class and my badge,' Peter said.

'I remember spotting a lighter and a pair of cufflinks, but I think I would've noticed if your badge was among the items. What makes you think it would have been? Do you think you dropped it into the box when we first brought them back to the station?' Billie asked.

'I think that Dennis Partridge was a thief. Not only was he posing as an RAF billeting officer, but several of my fellow lodgers also reported the items I listed missing from their rooms after he had been there. Mrs Cummins said that she had not accompanied him to the individual rooms because she had housekeeping duties to attend to. He could've helped himself to any of those items and I was hoping against hope that my badge might be among them,' he said.

'I can see why you would like to get it back and also how a constable's badge would suit somebody who was already so interested in impersonating people in positions of trust,' Billie said.

She began methodically removing each of the items from the box in front of her. The cigarette lighter and pair of cufflinks were indeed among the items held there. The other carton also contained a magnifying glass and a brass compact. Although Billie had not really expected to find it, she was somewhat disheartened to see it did not contain Peter's badge. They went through the items once more, carefully checking the pockets and even the linings of the clothing so carefully folded up by Dennis Partridge's solicitous landlady.

'I guess it was too much to hope for. I didn't find Mary Parker's coin purse either,' Peter said, scooping the items carefully one by one back into the box and replacing the lid.

'Are you sure that your badge went missing at the same time as the items your fellow lodgers lost?' Billie asked.

'Absolutely. Mrs Cummins said that he arrived during the day while I was working at the docks. I always leave my badge in a bureau drawer in my room when I'm not on duty for the constabulary. It wasn't until the next day when I went to get dressed to come in for a shift here that I noticed it was missing. I had used it several times out on the beat two days earlier when presenting residents with blackout-violation summonses,' he said.

'But you do think that the cigarette lighter and other items belong to your fellow lodgers?' she asked.

'I'm certain of it. I've actually seen the lighter and the compact being used in the public spaces of the house.'

'So that confirms one thing for us, then, doesn't it,' Billie said.

'What's that?' Peter asked.

'We know that not only was Dennis Partridge someone who impersonated people in positions of authority, he was actually a thief.'

'But that doesn't get us any closer to finding out what happened to him, does it?' Peter asked.

'I'm not sure if it does or if it doesn't. But it does make me more inclined to believe that he was the one, as Mr James originally suggested, who was stealing items from inside the air-raid shelters. I also wonder how he came to have suggested to Mrs Hayes that he could get a job for her son. Did he actually steal that money from them too? I'm not sure that one sort of theft is all that different from another,' Billie said.

'I'm not really sure either. But since you mentioned his connection to Mrs Hayes and her son, does this mean that you verified that Donald Sumner was one of the names listed on a registry card and that it was the one she claimed he used with her?' Peter asked.

'I did check it, that's how I knew about the cigarette lighter and cufflinks being in the boxes. I've cleared it with Avis to go and question the Hayes about his visit to them as Donald Sumner.'

'Do you have their address?' he asked.

'They are over on Polk Street,' Billie said. 'Does this mean you want to go with me?'

'It's better than standing around here stewing about my badge. And if I'm out of the building I have a good excuse for not telling Sergeant Skelton that it's missing just yet,' Peter said.

'What are we waiting for then?' Billie said. She slid the box back on to the shelf and headed for the door with Peter right on her heels.

Polk Street was in one of the parts of the city with which Billie had the least familiarity. The homes were modest but well-kept and as she followed Mrs Hayes into her sitting room, she thought the space exuded middle-class respectability. The types of needlework projects her mother would have admired were on display throughout the room: on pillows, chair covers and even in frames hung upon the walls, there was the evidence that someone devoted a great deal of time and skill to the hobby. Mrs Hayes motioned for the constables to make themselves comfortable on a small sofa placed near a well-swept hearth.

'It's nice to see that the constabulary is taking my complaint so seriously. After how little satisfaction you seemed capable of providing when I reported the incident at the station earlier in the week, I did not expect such a courtesy,' Mrs Hayes said.

'We do our best to get to the bottom of the concerns of our residents,' Peter said. He opened his police constable's notebook and propped it on his knee. Mrs Hayes nodded with approval as though it was a sign he was prepared to undertake a thorough investigation.

'We are here to ask you a few questions about the man who came by and spoke with your son about a job with the Ministry of Supply,' Billie said. 'That is the correct governmental branch, isn't it?'

'Well, that's what he said. Now I'm not quite so certain. After all, we've heard nothing more from him. The more I think on it, how would a man connected with the gasworks have a contact at the Ministry of Supply?'

'I'm sure you mustn't blame yourself. It seems that the man in question was highly skilled at fooling a great number of people by telling them he worked for one service or another in order to gain access to their homes. The gasworks was just as good an excuse as any of the others that he gave,' Billie said.

'What a menace. I do hope you've managed to catch up with him,' Mrs Hayes said. 'Will you need me to identify him?' She leaned forward eagerly.

'It would be a great deal of help to us if you could tell us if you recognize the person in this sketch,' Billie said, holding out the artist's rendering of Dennis Partridge.

'That's him,' Mrs Hayes said, pointing at the proffered sheet of paper. 'It's a jolly good likeness.'

'I seem to recall from your report that the man who your son gave the money to called himself Donald Sumner. Is that correct?' Billie asked.

'That's right. I remembered because I have a cousin named Donald and we always used to visit that side of the family in the summer. At the time I thought it was sort of a sign of good fortune for that to be his name.'

'I'm afraid his real name was Dennis Partridge,' Billie said.

'His name *was* Dennis Partridge? Has something happened him?' Mrs Hayes said.

'I'm sorry to report that he's been murdered,' Billie said.

'Suits him right running around telling people a passel of lies,' Mrs Hayes said, nodding vigorously and crossing her arms over her ample bosom.

'You haven't happened to have noticed any items missing from your home since he visited here, have you?' Peter asked.

Mrs Hayes's eyes widened in surprise. 'No, nothing like that. The money my son gave him was entirely out in the open. I cannot say that I've noticed that he also helped himself to things behind our backs.'

'Is your son here right now?' Billie asked.

'No, he's at work.'

'Where is he employed?' Peter asked.

'Melvin works for the council as a clerk. Most days he spends at City Hall,' Mrs Hayes said.

'Do you think he might have held a grudge about being swindled?' Billie asked.

'What are you implying?' Mrs Hayes asked.

'We are just looking into every possibility.'

'Are you suggesting that my Melvin had something to do with that man's murder?' Mrs Hayes asked.

'I'm not suggesting anything. I'm just asking if he's expressed any anger towards him,' Billie said.

'I suppose you'll be wanting an alibi or some such nonsense,' Mrs Hayes said.

'That would certainly be a good way to clear your son of any possible connection to what happened to the victim,' Peter said.

'When did he die?' Mrs Hayes said. 'I shall have to know that in order to tell you where my son might have been at the time.'

'He died sometime during the hours between one in the afternoon and midnight four days ago,' Billie said.

'Four days ago,' Mrs Hayes said casting her eyes up towards the ceiling as if searching it for an answer. She snapped her fingers and got to her feet. She hurried to a small drop-front desk on the far side of the room and reached into a cubbyhole crammed with papers. She came back and stood in front of the sofa, thrusting the sheet of paper at Peter.

'It can't have been the same man, so Melvin has no reason to have been involved in what happened,' Mrs Hayes said.

Peter looked over the piece of paper and handed it to Billie.

'What does this telegram have to do with your son's alibi?' Billie asked.

'Look at the date,' Mrs Hayes said, pointing towards the telegram. 'It arrived here three days ago. A dead man couldn't have sent a telegram asking for more money, now, could he?' she said.

Billie read through the message in her hands. The sender was listed as Donald Sumner, and it had in fact been received at the local post office three days earlier. The message requested additional funds for overnight lodging as the contact at the Ministry of Supply would not be available until the following day. Billie felt her heart sink as yet another lead dissolved into nothing. Although it was possible that there was still a connection between whoever Donald Sumner was and the victim. There still might be a thread between them and a possible wrongdoer well positioned at the Ministry of Supply.

'Do you mind if we take this telegram into evidence?' Peter said.

'Not one bit. Since it clearly exonerates my son from any complicity in whatever happened to your victim, I would feel better for it to be in police custody. With all of the air raids, you never know what might go up in smoke. If you've put it in evidence that will hopefully make some documentation as to Melvin's claims of innocence,' Mrs Hayes said. 'Now, if you don't have any further questions, I'd like to get on with my day.'

They took their leave of her, and Billie turned to Peter feeling defeated.

'That didn't turn out exactly how I had hoped,' she said as they left the house on Polk Street behind them.

'I'm still not quite ready to face the music with Sergeant Skelton quite yet. Why don't we try the post office and ask about this telegram? There are too many unanswered questions to take anything at face value,' he said.

'Do you know where the post office that received it is located?' Billie asked.

Peter looked the telegram over carefully. 'It says it was handed in at the office closest to this address. It's right on our way back to the station,' he said.

'We'd be remiss not to stop and ask questions,' Billie said.

TWENTY-NINE

As they walked along, she couldn't help but wonder what her own mother would have done if a pair of constables had arrived on her doorstep asking questions about Billie's brother Frederick. Not that he was the sort of person to get in trouble with the law, or anyone else for that matter, but she could well imagine her mother would have been at least as fierce in her defense of him as was Mrs Hayes of Melvin. Which begged the question, could a mother's word really be trusted when it came to danger towards her children?

She had seemed so certain that the sketch was of the man she had seen her son giving money to. How could she have been so mistaken? Were witnesses often so easily swayed? Did they change their memory of events based on new suggestions presented to them or things they perceived as irrefutable facts? And what about Melvin himself? Surely, he should be on the list of people to question directly?

And why would someone with a job working for the city council be so tempted to switch positions? Did he think that he could earn more money or that such a position would offer more opportunities for advancement? It wasn't as if his job as a clerk would be so vastly different than working at the Ministry of Supply. Or was it that he wanted to have access to things to sell on the black market? Could he and the victim have been in cahoots somehow?

They arrived at the post office before she had time to come to any conclusions. In fact, Peter had to call her name to break her train of thought in order for her to follow him inside.

There was a queue in the post office almost as long as the ones Billie saw every day at the butchers, the greengrocers and at the corner shops. Before she had come to Hull, she had always thought of cities as being anonymous sorts of places where no one would have a sense of neighborliness, but over the weeks that she had been there she had come to realize that cities were simply clusters of much smaller towns, much like villages themselves, and that people knew their neighbors just as well as people had back in Wiltshire.

So it was with no surprise that she watched and overheard the people pass the time in the long queue by chatting about the neighbors they all lived among. A pair of women perhaps ten years her senior compared the cost of jumper wool at one shop versus another. Behind her a man well into his senior years was regaling a much younger one with a tale of fine fish he had caught the week before. An elderly woman slid a passbook across the counter along with a pound note and asked that it be added to her savings account.

As the line moved steadily towards the front Billie felt more at home in the city then she usually did. It reminded her so strongly of her neighbors back in Barton St Giles that her heart gave a squeeze. Being in the post office also reminded her that she owed her friend Candace another letter. Despite the fact that her companion had been sent to the center of the country working on something too secret to share, she faithfully sent newsy letters of daily life to Billie at least once a week.

Finally, Billie and Peter reached the front of the queue and were beckoned to the window by a woman not much older than Billie. Without waiting to be prompted this time, Billie removed her badge from her uniform jacket pocket and held it up for the woman to see.

'What can I help you with, Constable?' the woman asked, her voice tinged with curiosity.

'We have a question about a telegram received at this office three days ago and we wondered with whom we could speak about it,' Billie said.

'I was on shift at the window during business hours three days ago so I expect that any questions you have would best be directed to me,' she said.

Peter stepped forward and slid the telegram they had taken from Mrs Hayes across the counter.

'Do you remember this telegram coming in?' Peter asked.

The woman lifted it and inspected it carefully. 'Those are

my initials at the top, so I am the one who processed this request.' The woman's eyes shifted back and forth as if she were reading through the lines of text. 'As a matter of fact, I do remember this telegram coming in because it was a bit peculiar.'

'Peculiar in which way?' Billie asked feeling her heart rate begin to speed up ever so slightly. Peter had leaned just a bit closer towards the window and as a result towards her as well.

'Well, generally when someone goes to the expense and trouble of sending a telegram, they don't send it to their own home,' the woman said.

Billie shifted slightly and looked up at Peter. He raised an eyebrow at her and she basked in the feeling of being part of a team, and one that was making progress on an important goal.

'Are you saying that a member of the household at the address to which this was sent was responsible for sending it?' Peter said.

'Exactly. Although I suppose it's possible that the sender was doing it on behalf of someone else,' she said.

'Who was the sender?' Billie asked.

'Melvin Hayes, although that wasn't the name he signed at the bottom of the telegram,' she said.

'How do you know that it was Melvin Hayes who sent this telegram?' Billie asked.

'Well, I suppose it's a bit embarrassing to admit, but he was in my eldest brother's class at school and as a girl I always rather fancied him. He never paid any attention to me, of course, being so much older, but it always reminded me of my childhood when he would come in for a roll of stamps or to put money in his savings account,' she said. 'I was too embarrassed to remind him who I was because I'm afraid I had been rather obvious in my feelings towards him as small girls are wont to do.'

'You said that he seemed to be sending the telegram on behalf of someone else?' Billie asked.

The woman tapped her finger against the telegram. 'The message is signed off Donald Sumner. That's not Melvin's name, now is it?' she asked.

'Did he say anything about the telegram that struck you as

unusual besides the fact that he was having it sent to his own household?' Peter asked.

'I wouldn't say that he mentioned anything about it, but I can tell you that I remember he paid to have it sent priority, which is not something most people do. Who would waste an extra sixpence especially if they could have just told the person they lived with instead of relying on a telegram to do it for them?'

Billie had not been much in the habit of sending telegrams herself, but she knew that the Postal Service had added a priority service to their offerings not only as a way to increase the speed with which the telegram might reach the recipient, but also to disassociate such missives from their reputation as exclusively a conduit for bad news. For several years the Postal Service had heavily publicized telegrams as a way to share birthday greetings or wedding announcements and offered special gold envelopes with red and blue borders and a dove logo displayed upon it. Since the use of telegrams to deliver such tragic news throughout the course of the war had grown, she could well imagine how often senders might be willing to part with a few extra pence in order to avoid upsetting the recipients of their urgent news.

But no matter how much Melvin Hayes might not wish to distress his mother by sending a telegram that might be viewed as something to fear when it arrived, it still did not explain why he had sent it in the first place. The only thing she could think of as a reason was that Melvin Hayes had been conspiring with the man who called himself Donald Sumner to squeeze money from his own mother.

Noticing the queue swelling behind them and having no other questions it seemed likely the postal clerk could answer, Billie reached for the telegram and thanked the woman for her time. Peter asked for her name and carefully wrote it down in his police notebook before following Billie to the exit.

'That was an unexpected piece of information, don't you think?' Billie said.

'It certainly brought up more questions,' Peter said.

'Do you think that Melvin Hayes and Donald Sumner were

working together to extract money from Mrs Hayes?' Billie said.

'That's one possibility, but I can think of another,' Peter said.

'What's that?' Billie asked.

'Mrs Hayes was convinced that her son could not be involved in Dennis Partridge's murder because Donald Sumner sent her a telegram a day after Dennis had died,' Peter said.

'So, if Melvin Hayes is the one that actually sent the telegram, Dennis and Donald could be one and the same person after all,' Billie said.

'I think that's likely considering the reaction Mrs Hayes had to the artist sketch of our victim,' Peter said. 'I guess the only thing to do is to interview Melvin Hayes and ask him why he sent the telegram to his mother.'

Billie wasn't so sure. Melvin might deny that he was the one who had sent it. After all, it was only his word against that of the postal clerk and it might be easy enough to claim that she had simply confused him with someone else. Although it would be more difficult to explain away the fact that the telegram had been handed in right there in the city of Hull and not from London as its contents implied. She still thought it would be more useful to speak with Mrs Hayes once more and to see her reaction when confronted with the fact that her son was actually the real sender.

It seemed like it would be better to speak to her before Melvin was able to come up with some sort of plausible excuse. Mrs Hayes seemed like the sort of woman who would not refrain from telling her son over the evening meal about a visit from the constabulary. After all, who would not wish to discuss such an unusual event with their nearest and dearest?

'I think we'd be better off confronting Mrs Hayes with what we've just discovered first. We can always locate Melvin afterwards and I think it would be worth seeing her reaction when Melvin will not have had time to explain away our findings,' Billie said.

'All right then. Mrs Hayes first and Melvin after,' Peter said looking both ways before sprinting across the avenue towards the Hayes residence.

THIRTY

I t could not be said that Mrs Hayes looked happy to see them. In fact, she held her handbag draped over her arm and had opened her front door just as Peter landed the first knock upon it. If Billie had to guess, she had the air about her of a woman who was on her way out and did not wish to be delayed.

'I'm afraid we're going to need another few moments of your time,' Peter said.

He planted himself on the threshold in such a way as to imply that Mrs Hayes would not be exiting the building. She stepped back and slapped her handbag down on the hall table with such force that a letter slid off a stack of post and tumbled to the floor. Billie bent to pick it up and replace it. Mrs Hayes appeared not to notice as she stood staring at Peter with her hands placed on her broad hips.

'Well, what is it then? First, I don't feel as though you took me seriously and now it seems I cannot be rid of you,' Mrs Hayes said.

Billie stepped to Peter's side and took the lead. 'We've just been to the post office where your telegram from Donald Sumner was handed in. Would it surprise you to know that the clerk who processed the telegram claims that your son is the one who brought it in?' Billie asked.

Mrs Hayes shook her head slightly as if to attempt to dislodge Billie's words from her ears. 'Nonsense. The telegram was from Donald Sumner. It said so right on the bottom of it.'

'Your son Melvin sent it himself from the local post office. He paid extra for it to be sent as a priority and enclosed in a gold envelope. Clearly, he wanted to get it to you straightaway,' Billie said.

'But how can the postal worker be sure it was Melvin?' Mrs Hayes said, one hand moving towards the base of her throat.

'Apparently her brother went to school with your son and as a young girl she was rather taken with him. Her initials were the ones on the telegram and the office that it was handed in at is in fact the local one, not London, as the body of the message suggests.' Peter said.

'There's really no reason why she would lie about a thing like that,' Billie said.

'Are you implying that there is a reason that my son might have to lie?' Mrs Hayes said.

'There are two reasons that suggest themselves readily and neither of them place your son in a very good light,' Peter said.

'It is possible that Melvin wanted to gain money from you without admitting to being the one asking,' Billie said. 'Or it may be that Dennis Partridge and Donald Sumner are in fact the same person and he wanted to make it look as though the man you met was still alive when the body was discovered.'

'I don't believe my son would be involved in anything like you're suggesting. He would not steal from me, nor would he harm anyone else.' Mrs Hayes appeared outraged by their suggestion. Her confusion and tentativeness had turned to defensive fury. Bright splotches appeared on her cheeks and instead of grasping at her throat she jabbed her index finger straight at Billie.

'Is your son at work at the city hall today?' Peter asked.

'Of course he is. Where else would he be?' Mrs Hayes said, her voice ratcheting up in volume and filling the small hallway. 'You aren't thinking of going and troubling him there, are you?'

'We are going to need to speak with him as soon as possible. It cannot be helped if our conversation takes place at his place of employment,' Peter said.

'But a visit from the police at his workplace will irreparably damage his reputation,' Mrs Hayes said. 'It might cost him his post and that would result in him being eligible for military service.' Mrs Hayes dropped her hand once more and Billie could see that the older woman was beginning to shake. While she did not like to take advantage of people in times of distress, sometimes it was the most expeditious way to get to the bottom of something.

'If you allowed us to take a look at Melvin's room, we might find something to exonerate him there. Perhaps this is all just some sort of big misunderstanding,' Billie said.

'Follow me,' Mrs Hayes said, her voice regaining a bit of its strength and purpose. She grasped the railing of the stairway to her right and practically raced up the steps.

Billie followed her and Peter brought up the rear. A ripple of trepidation washed over Billie as she followed Mrs Hayes into the depths of the house. What would such a woman be willing to do to protect her son? She could be leading them into some sort of danger rather than into her son's room. Once again Billie was grateful for Peter's solid presence. There was something quite comforting about having another person to face difficulties with head-on.

Mrs Hayes stopped in front of a door near the end of the second-floor corridor and pressed down on the latch. The door swung open with a creak, and she stepped aside to allow the constables to enter.

'Take all the time that you want, but I will be standing here watching you to make sure you aren't leaving any sort of evidence that would implicate my son in wrongdoing,' Mrs Hayes said as she filled the doorway with her imposing figure.

The room was spacious and flooded with light from two tall windows. Blackout curtains hung to either side of them and a gas meter clung to the wall nearby. Billie headed for a small writing desk placed beneath one of the windows and began looking through the things tucked away in its cubby-holes. Pencils and a sharpener as well as a penknife and pencil shavings filled one compartment and stationery supplies filled another. A third held a few curl-edged photographs. The woman featured in each of them appeared to be a younger version of Mrs Hayes. Some of them also depicted a small boy. In the earliest photographs a man was also present. Billie wondered if he was Mr Hayes and what had become of him.

She never liked looking through other people's private possessions and it felt all the more uncomfortable to do so with Mrs Hayes looking on. She clucked her tongue indignantly every time Billie reached out to touch items in the desk. Fortunately, the desk was small and she quickly completed the task. Peter had made straight for Melvin's bed and turned back the covers, carefully searching between the layers of fabric and under the mattress. Billie crossed the room and pulled open the doors to a walnut wardrobe.

A man's jacket and pair of trousers hung neatly from a rail at the top of the wardrobe. Three white shirts and an overcoat took up room there as well. The wardrobe reminded her of one in her brother Frederick's room back at the rectory with its stack of small drawers for holding things like socks as well as folded stacks of pajamas and, in Frederick's case, small treasures he wished to keep away from the prying eyes of his family members. Billie had found a stack of love letters from local girls in one such drawer after Billie's mother had received a telegram that informed her that Frederick was missing in action.

Sifting through Melvin Hayes's drawers brought that painful memory flooding back and Billie felt her throat constrict as she moved aside a hand-knit, thick, woolen jumper. It was very like the one her mother had made for Frederick for Christmas the year before. She had sent it along with a gift from Billie of books in order to cheer him up as he spent his first holiday away from home.

As she slid her hand beneath this jumper her fingers touched what felt like metal. She pulled the jumper from the drawer and peered inside more closely. There, lying in the bottom of the drawer, was a box similar to the sort one might see in a safety deposit room at a bank. She lifted it out and carried it over to the bed where Peter had smoothed the coverlet back into place.

She lifted the hinged lid and looked inside. The box was approximately the size and shape of a file drawer from a card catalog at the library. And inside it, arranged neatly one behind the other, were folded wedges of card stock. She reached in and pulled out the very first one in the row. Her heart began to pound wildly in her chest as she recognized it for what it was.

She held it out to Peter whose eyes widened in surprise.

She ran her fingertips along the contents of the box and realized that there in front of her were dozens and dozens of blank
national registry cards. And there at the back of the drawer
was something at least as surprising. She dipped her hand in
once more and held the item out to Peter whose expression
turned from surprise to shock tinged with relief.

'If I'm not mistaken, that's your badge,' Billie said.

'What's that you found?' Mrs Hayes said stepping into the
room and attempting to peer over Billie's shoulder.

'We found sufficient evidence that we're going to need to
ask you to accompany us to the police station,' Peter said
slipping his badge into his pocket.

'Whatever you found in here has nothing to do with me,'
Mrs Hayes said.

Billie marveled at how quickly Mrs Hayes had gone from
being the sort of woman who was willing to do whatever it
took to protect her son, to claiming she had no part in whatever
he might be up to. For all the ways in which she and her
mother had not seen eye to eye, she could not imagine her own
parent would ever abandon her child with such speed. Although,
she hadn't been as quick to defend Billie in the face of criticism either. Perhaps that was how such things often went. But
it hardly mattered what Mrs Hayes had to say at that moment
in Melvin's room. What mattered more was what she was not
going to be able to say to her son before the police had a
chance to speak with him.

'We're going to have more questions for you before we get
to the bottom of this and the only place to conduct such an
interview officially is at the police station. You will have to
accompany us, but we can manage it with as little or as much
attention to that fact as you wish to create,' Peter said.

'What my partner means to say is that your neighbors need
not think that anything untoward is happening if you accompany us quietly. If you don't, I expect that your name will be
the most frequently spoken around everyone's tables this
evening,' Billie said.

Mrs Hayes clamped her lips into a firm line, then bobbed
her head. 'Let's get on with it then,' she said.

Peter stepped up behind her and Billie closed the lid on the metal box and tucked it under her arm. There could be absolutely no good reason for a City Hall civil servant to have a cache of blank national registry cards in his possession. But there were innumerable bad reasons for him to do so. What she didn't know for sure was if one of them was murder.

THIRTY-ONE

Special Constable Upton's Police Notebook

'What's all this then?' Sergeant Skelton said as Peter guided Mrs Hayes to the front desk at the station and asked if an interview room was free.

'Mrs Hayes is helping us with our enquiries, and we wanted to make sure she remained here while her son is questioned in connection with the Dennis Partridge murder,' Peter said.

'Sounds like you're making progress on that then,' the sergeant said.

'I think we're finally making some headway,' he said. 'WPC Harkness has gone down to place some items in the evidence room, but we would like to head out again as soon as possible.'

'Room three is available. I suppose that means you want to leave her in someone else's keeping while you're gone?' the sergeant asked.

'I'd like to see this case through, and I know that WPC Harkness feels the same,' Peter said.

'You're not suggesting that I should babysit her, are you?' Sergeant Skelton said.

'I was thinking more of someone like Constables Drummond or Thompson for the job,' Peter said.

The sergeant looked Mrs Hayes up and down. The woman would not stop mumbling under her breath about the way the police were no better than the Germans with their high-handed invasion of people's homes and false accusations.

'I think that Constable Drummond is just the person for that task,' he said as he turned towards the back end of the station and raised his voice. 'Drummond, I've got an assignment for you.'

Constable Drummond hurried to his feet with an expectant look on his face. He pushed past Peter with a swagger, completely ignoring Mrs Hayes.

'What is it, Sergeant?' he asked.

'I'd like you to take this lady down to interview room three and make sure she doesn't leave it until I tell you that she may,' the sergeant said.

'What do you want me to interview her about?' Constable Drummond asked, turning his attention to Mrs Hayes for the first time.

'You misunderstand me. I don't want you to interview her about anything. There's no need to speak with her at all. All I want for you to do is to make sure she doesn't leave,' the sergeant said. 'Do you think you can handle that?'

'We have cells for that, don't we?' Constable Drummond said.

'This lady has not been arrested. We merely wish to keep her under our watchful eye for a while. But if you don't think you're up for the task, I suppose I could ask someone else to help you with it. You and Constable Thompson are thick as thieves lately. Although, it seems to me that this is a sort of job that you might be able to handle on your own,' Sergeant Skelton said.

'It seems to me that this is the sort of job that would be best done by a WPC. I don't understand why I should be assigned to play childminder when WPC Harkness is on shift,' Constable Drummond said.

Out of the corner of his eye Peter saw WPC Harkness making her way along the corridor towards the front desk. He tried to will her to slow her pace so she would not overhear Constable Drummond's insults, but she was too intent on heading off to question Melvin Hayes to heed his expression.

'See, there she is right now.' Constable Drummond pointed at WPC Harkness and Peter did not like the look on the other man's face.

'I think you'll find that I still hand out the assignments here, Constable Drummond. And yours takes you to room three. Considering her prowess as an investigator, hers takes her off to question a suspect,' Sergeant Skelton said.

He pointed his broad hand down the hallway past WPC Harkness's shoulder. WPC Harkness remained rooted to the spot as Constable Drummond took Mrs Hayes by the elbow.

She flinched ever so slightly as Constable Drummond passed closely enough to brush against her, but she hurried towards him as if nothing had happened.

'Does this mean we're cleared to question Melvin Hayes?' she asked.

'What else would it mean? Go see if you can close this case.' Sergeant Skelton turned his back on them without another word.

'We'd like to speak with Melvin Hayes if he's here today,' Peter said to the young woman sitting behind the reception desk in the lobby of City Hall.

She reminded Peter remarkably of a young woman he had taken out for several months before she had joined the WAVs and had been sent to another city for training. She gave him a warm smile and made quick work of locating where they might find Melvin Hayes that afternoon. In less than two minutes, he and WPC Harkness stood in a large room filled with both men and women bent over typewriters and speaking into telephones. He had no idea that there were so many clerks employed by the city council, but he supposed with all of the forms that were required for this, that and the other thing since war broke out, they would need a veritable army to process all of them.

A man with gray-streaked hair and a quality suit rose to greet them and pointed out Melvin Hayes as a young man bent over a ledger at a desk near the back of the room. Melvin looked up as the pair of constables approached him and Peter thought he saw fear in the other man's eyes. He had to give Melvin credit though, he did not betray any nerves as WPC Harkness introduced herself and informed him that they had a few questions for him.

'I can't imagine what you'd want to speak with me about, Constables,' he said, attempting a feeble smile.

'Perhaps it will make more sense to you if you allow me to introduce my colleague,' WPC Harkness said. She turned towards Peter. 'This is Constable Peter Upton. You know, the man whose badge you just happened to have in a box hidden away in your wardrobe at 153 Polk Street.'

More quickly than Peter would have thought possible, Melvin Hayes was on his feet, his chair knocked over behind him in his haste. He bolted around the side of his desk and made straight for the door. WPC Harkness neatly extended her leg and Melvin Hayes went sprawling headlong across the floor. Peter half expected her to drop on to his back and clip her pair of handcuffs around his wrists as she had done to a purse snatcher the very first time he had walked a beat with her. Instead, she stood back and allowed Peter to do the honors.

She bent close to his ear as he leaned forward to reach for Melvin's wrist. 'I think it's the least you can do considering he stole your badge,' WPC Harkness said.

The other office workers looked on agape as Peter hauled Melvin Hayes to his feet and frogmarched him past his colleagues. One of the women seated behind the desk closest to the door burst into tears and called out after Melvin. A trickle of blood ran from the suspect's nose, and it was starting to swell by the time they reached the ground floor of City Hall.

Peter thought it likely that he had broken it in the fall, but he was not going to challenge any rumors that might start about WPC Harkness being the one to have broken it for him. He thought it wouldn't be a bad thing for her to develop a reputation as someone who could handle herself in a physical altercation.

He was, however, glad that the station was so close to City Hall. It was one thing for fellow constables to consider WPC Harkness as someone capable of roughing a suspect up. It was quite another for the public to have that impression. He knew that they still had two spots to fill with WPCs on the force and he was not sure that process would be made any easier if something so violent was attributed to one of the female officers.

He wondered what Mrs Hayes would make of her son attempting to flee from the officers' questions. Surely that could not be considered a sign of his innocence. And to have done so in front of such a large group of credible witnesses would only serve to hurt his case further.

THIRTY-TWO

Melvin Hayes truly looked a pathetic sight as he held a damp rag to his swollen nose. Avis joined them in the interview room but seemed content for Billie and Peter to take the lead when it came to the questioning. Peter had retrieved the box of blank national registry cards Billie had found in Melvin's wardrobe and it sat on the table between them like a silent accusation.

Billie wished that Avis had not joined them. After all the effort they had gone to to keep anyone from knowing that Peter's badge was missing, it would be impossible to link Melvin Hayes to the murder without using it as the final bit of evidence. As much as she wished it would have been possible to simply give it back to him and keep silent about the whole matter, justice could not be served that way.

'Mr Hayes, how would you explain the presence of these national registry cards tucked under a woolen jumper in your bedroom wardrobe?' Billie asked.

'Someone must've put them there. Maybe even you two,' he said looking from Billie to Peter, then back again.

'We happen to have a statement attested to by your very own mother that she was with us when we discovered these cards hidden in your bedroom. Are you saying that your mother would perjure herself to incriminate you on such a serious charge as this?' Billie asked.

'My mother knows about this?' Melvin asked as he lowered the damp rag from his face and slumped back further in his chair.

'I'm afraid she does. You didn't really expect that it wouldn't all come out in the end, did you? And once it did, your mother would of course know about it,' Billie said.

'What if I told you I simply forgot that I had those cards

with me when I left City Hall? That would explain it, wouldn't it?' Melvin said.

'Do you have authorization to remove any official documentation from City Hall, let alone something as valuable on the black market as blank national registry cards?' Peter asked.

Melvin looked at the table as if it might give him a plausible excuse. 'It's not as bad as it looks,' Melvin said. 'It all started on such a small scale that I couldn't see the harm in it.'

'Why don't you walk us through exactly what happened. It will be far better for us to hear your side of the story than to simply draw our own conclusions,' Avis said from the side of the room. Melvin glanced over at her as if he had forgotten that the older woman was even there.

'The national registry sends blank cards to their local offices in order to have them easily on hand when people inevitably lose theirs or when someone enters the country legally, like a refugee from the continent, or in the case of a birth,' Melvin said.

'The blank cards come through City Hall in some way,' Peter said.

Melvin nodded. 'The office of the national registry is housed at City Hall. The same mailroom that serves the entire building provides them with the cards. I happened to be in the mailroom for some other business when one of the women who works at the national registry branch came in to collect their post.'

'How did you find out that the cards had arrived?' Billie asked.

'She didn't tell me, if that's what you're asking. The shape and size of the box was just about what one would expect if it contained the cards and there were only so many things that made sense. I made a point of chatting her up a bit and asking her about her lunchtime plans. She thought I was interested in a date, and she fobbed me off with an excuse saying she had a prior engagement with her sweetheart.'

'So, what did you do, break into her office while she was gone?' Peter asked.

'There was no need to break in since the door wasn't locked. And it was an easy enough thing to sift through her office and locate the box,' Melvin said.

'Did you take the entire box? Wouldn't that have raised the alarm?' Billie asked.

'I only swiped two of them, at least at first,' Melvin said. 'I really thought that would be the end of it.'

'Why did you take them? Was it for the money?' Billie asked.

'No, it was nothing like that. I have a friend from when I was a kid who turned up on my doorstep unexpectedly a couple months ago. He'd been home on leave and completely lost his nerve. He told me he just couldn't go back and had deserted. The poor guy was living rough and had been reduced to stealing food because he couldn't buy any using his legal ration card. He would've been found out straightaway,' Melvin said.

'So, you want us to believe that you stole a blank card to help your friend?' Billie asked.

'That's exactly what I did. I took two of them. In case he made a mess of the first one when he filled it out, I had a spare to give him,' Melvin said. 'I made my friend swear he would never say where he got it from if he were ever found out.'

'How does that lead to you taking an entire box of the blank cards? The ones we found in your room held a whole lot more than two,' Peter said.

Melvin fixed his gaze on the box in the center of the table. 'My friend told me he knew of a number of other men in his same position and asked me if I could help. Since I didn't know any of them, I didn't think that I had to stick my neck out from the goodness of my heart. There had to be some compensation for the risk I was taking. After all, I was sure that eventually someone was going to notice the missing cards,' he said.

'By compensation, do you mean you sold them?' Avis asked.

'I did. I feel so ashamed of it now, but at the time the lure of easy money seemed too hard to resist and I really couldn't see the harm in it. Those guys had deserted already, and it didn't do anybody any good for them to starve,' he said. 'But by the time I had sold a couple dozen of them I knew I was pushing my luck and decided to put a stop to the whole thing.'

Billie tapped the box. 'There's a lot more than a couple dozen cards in this box. You really expect us to believe that you decided to stop taking any chances?'

'Believe me or not, I had decided not to risk any more thefts. But sometimes things don't go the way you planned,' he said.

'You know that you're not the only person we've dealt with lately concerning national registry cards. They're not the hardest thing in the world to get a hold of, apparently, but I do wonder at how many sources for such things there might be in just the one city,' Billie said.

Melvin raised the rag back up to his nose and Billie wondered if he was doing so in part to shield his face from betraying any expression.

'I can't speak to what anybody else might have done,' Melvin said.

'The thing is your mother has already identified the man we found in possession of several falsified national identity cards as someone of your acquaintance. In fact, she reported him as someone who had swindled you out of quite a bit of money,' Billie said.

'My mother is always quick to try to protect me. I suppose it's one of the dangers of being an only child,' Melvin said.

'Are you denying that you had dealings with a man calling himself Donald Sumner?' Billie asked.

'I can't say as I recall knowing a man of that name,' Melvin said. 'But if I did sell him a national registry card, he could've filled it in with any name he wished. There's no reason why I should have been told it. As a matter of fact I preferred that my buyers kept such knowledge to themselves. It helped to protect us both.'

'If this is not someone you had ever met, how is it that you sent a telegram in his name, priority delivery, to your own mother asking for money to put him up overnight in London while he looked for a job for you?' Billie asked.

Melvin's posture stiffened and his knuckles of the hand clutching the rag turned white. She had to give him credit. His voice never faltered. 'I live with my mother. Why would

I send her a telegram, especially one sent priority? That sounds utterly preposterous,' he said.

'It makes sense if you are trying to wring some money out of your own mother without telling her the real reason why. It didn't hurt that it made it seem as though the man she saw you talking with couldn't possibly be the same person lying dead in an air-raid shelter right here in town if he were sending telegrams to her from London,' Billie said.

'You can't prove I sent a telegram to my mother. How would I know that this Donald someone was dead?' Melvin asked.

'Because you're the one who killed him,' Billie said.

'There's a big difference between stealing blank registry cards and murdering someone,' Melvin said.

'That may be, but your greed tripped you up in the end,' Billie said. 'The registry cards weren't the only thing we found in the box.'

Billie lifted the lid of the metal container and using a handkerchief plucked Peter's badge from inside it. 'We might never have been able to make the connection beyond a shadow of a doubt if you hadn't decided to take this off of the victim's body. That bit of greed is what's really going to cost you,' Billie said.

This time Melvin's voice cracked as he spoke. 'You can't connect me with any of it. Besides, who is Dennis Partridge?' Melvin said.

'That's Donald Sumner's real name, at least as far as we can tell,' Billie said. 'But he did use an awful lot of aliases. Not only did he pretend to work for the gasworks like you told your mother, but he also presented himself as an air-raid shelter inspector and an RAF billeting officer. It was when he was pretending to be a billeting officer that he helped himself to that police badge along with a lot of other items from the same boardinghouse. The rest of the items stolen from that boardinghouse were found among his possessions by his land-lady after he died. The only thing taken from that house that was still missing turned up in your wardrobe,' Billie said tapping on the badge once more.

Melvin slumped even further into his chair, a picture of defeat. 'When he turned up at our place with the story that he was from the gas company and needed to inspect the house, my mother was fool enough to let him in. She must not have given any thought to allowing a complete stranger to have the run of the place. He found the cards in my room and made some enquiries of my mother as to when I would return, feeding her some sort of nonsense about helping me find a better job in London. She always wants for me to improve myself, so she lapped it right up,' Melvin said.

'The money you gave him wasn't actually to go to London, was it?' Peter asked.

'No. He just made that up when she caught me giving him some money to keep his mouth shut. He had returned the next day and told me if I wanted him to keep silent, I was going to have to pay up. She came in and found me handing him the money I had on hand,' Melvin said.

'But he didn't stop there, did he?' Billie asked. 'Blackmailers always want more.'

'He demanded what amounted to a month's wages. I told him I didn't have it. It's not as if my job is a high-paying one after all, and my mother counts on me to contribute to the household expenses. He told me if I didn't have the money I'd have to get him more cards,' Melvin said.

'Is that how you came to steal this entire box?' Billie asked.

'I got lucky there. Somehow, they had ended up with extras because of some incendiary bombs taking out one of the other local offices. It is harder to keep track of so much inventory and I was able to sneak off with an entire box.'

'But you decided not to give it to him, didn't you?' Peter said.

'That's the thing, I did take it to give to him. He suggested that we meet at an air-raid shelter that he just happened to have the keys to. I didn't ask him how that came about, but since he said he would provide us a quiet place to talk, I agreed.'

'What made you decide to kill him?' Peter asked.

'I handed over the box and he looked through it. Then he said it made a nice start and that he expected me to bring him another one the following week. I just snapped. I knew there was no way that I was going to be able to keep up with his demands. Someone had strung up a clothesline in the shelter, probably for hanging up a blanket to provide a bit of privacy and before I knew what I was doing I yanked it off the wall, looped it around his neck and pulled it until he stopped struggling,' Melvin said.

'What did you do next?' Billie asked.

'I searched his pockets looking for any of the money he had taken from me. All he had was a bit of loose change and a policeman's badge. I figured that it might be worth something, so I pocketed it. I checked to make sure no one was looking before I slipped out of the shelter.'

Avis stood up. 'I think we've heard enough. You will be held until this goes to trial, however that is handled.'

'What do you mean by "however this is handled"?' Melvin asked, pushing his chair back as if to huddle in the corner.

'I'm not entirely sure that this matter will be handled through the regular courts. It won't be good for morale for the general public to realize that it's possible for criminals to profit by the fraudulent use of national registry cards. They very well may try you in camera on treachery charges.'

Avis walked to the door and stepped into the hallway beyond. A moment later she returned followed by Constable Thompson. From the scowl on his face Billie suspected there might be trouble with him once they left the interview room.

'Please take Mr Hayes straight to the cells. I don't want his mother to have to see him in cuffs. It will be hard enough if she sees him in court later without them,' Avis said.

She closed the door behind them, then turned to Billie and Peter.

'So how long was your badge missing, Constable,' Avis asked as soon as Constable Thompson had led Melvin out of the interview room and out of earshot.

'I noticed that it was gone the day WPC Harkness and I found Dennis Partridge's body,' Peter said.

Avis crossed her arms over her chest and scowled up at him. 'And your partner didn't mention it to anyone, at least not that I've heard. I can only assume she's covered for you ever since.'

'She didn't know it was missing for most of that time.'

'How is that possible? Didn't you realize your partner didn't have his badge with him when you went out on patrol together?' Avis raised an eyebrow as she glanced at Billie.

Before she could decide how to respond, Peter spoke up. 'I told her to show her badge anytime we needed with the excuse that I wanted her to have the chance to take the lead a bit more than usual.'

Avis's other eyebrow shot skyward. 'You lied to your partner to cover this up? Why didn't you just come forward about it?'

'I didn't want anyone to think less of me because of it,' Peter said. 'I felt like a damned fool and couldn't imagine how I could have allowed it to happen. And I didn't want to lose my job.'

Avis uncrossed her arms. 'If WPC Harkness did not choose to report you for this I will not do so either. But it will be part of the evidence in the case so it may come to the sergeant's attention regardless of your efforts.' Avis turned on her heel and strode out the door.

THIRTY-THREE

Peter stared after her retreating back and then turned to face Billie.

'It wasn't your fault, Peter. You had every right to expect your badge to be safe where you left it. If the case is tried in camera, I bet that Skelton won't even hear about it.'

He shook his head. 'I don't want to be the kind of man who lies and keeps secrets. I'm going to tell the sergeant. If he sacks me, I'll find a different way to volunteer in my free time.'

Billie took a step towards him. 'I'll go with you when you do. After all, I knew about it and didn't say anything either.'

'You know, if Drummond or Thompson had been in your shoes, the pair of them would have been off like a shot to report it to the sergeant to try to make me look bad,' he said.

'Do you really think so little of them?' Billie asked.

'Let's put it this way, considering how the sergeant has been taking them both to task lately for poor performance, I think they'd do anything they thought would improve their own standing in the department. They wouldn't be likely to keep a secret that did me any favors.'

Billie felt as if all the murkiness around her own situation had just cleared away. Wasn't that exactly what keeping silent was doing? She was doing Constable Drummond an enormous favor by not letting his true character be known. If she was going to have the kind of career in the constabulary that Avis imagined might be possible, she wanted it to be built on teamwork and trust, not fear and lies. She also had no interest in allowing officers to behave no better than the criminals they apprehended.

Besides, she really did want to encourage other women to serve as constables. She was becoming better and better at her job and there was no reason to expect other women might not excel at it too. But in order to feel confident about speaking in front of the council about increasing the number of women on the job, she needed to know there were male officers who would value their presence. The one officer who mattered most to her was the best place to start.

She looked up at Peter. 'Do you remember how you said we shouldn't have any secrets on the day you told me about your badge?' she asked.

'I do. And I meant it. Is there something you want to tell me?'

She drew in a deep breath and let it out slowly. 'I suspect that you may have heard a rumor that Constable Drummond and I are romantically involved.'

Peter's eyes widened, then he gave the briefest of nods. 'I may have heard something of the sort.'

'It isn't true. The sergeant found us in the kitchenette in what looked like a compromising position, but it wasn't consensual, at least not on my part.' She forced herself to meet Peter's gaze, unsure of what she would see there.

'Are you saying he put his hands on you without your permission?' Peter's voice dropped lower and Billie felt a shiver of fear shimmy up her back.

'He did.' She had gone this far, so she might as well tell the whole truth. 'He also followed me after work the other evening and threatened me with something worse than just being groped.'

His eyes narrowed and a vein in his forehead throbbed as if he had been running full tilt.

'Did he assault you?'

'He grabbed me by the arm, but before he could do anything else I blew my whistle in his ear and ran off.'

Peter shook his head slowly. 'Of course you did. I expect you are completely capable of landing on your feet whatever the circumstances. That said, you shouldn't have to sort this out on your own. I'll have a word with him.'

'I didn't tell you in the hope that you would speak with him. I just wanted you to know the rumors weren't true.'

'I didn't tell you I was going to confess about my badge to Skelton so that you'd offer to accompany me. We're partners.

Some of what we do calls for the skills you are best at and some of it requires mine.' Peter handed her his uniform cap. He strode towards the door and then turned. 'Just so that you know, I never really believed the rumors.'

Special Constable Upton's Police Notebook

He found Constable Drummond in the lot behind the station taking a final drag on a cigarette. He tossed the butt on the brick pavement and ground it out below his uniform boot.

'I heard you caught the guy responsible for the air-raid shelter murder,' he said.

'WPC Harkness and I worked the case together, but she should get most of the credit. She put some pieces together that none of the rest of us did.'

'You sure are eager to make her look good. It doesn't take a detective to figure out how she's getting you to sing her praises, now does it? I think I'll head in and make an offer to do the same and see what it gets me.' Constable Drummond moved towards the door.

Peter stepped in his way to stop him. 'You're not going to do that. Not now or any time in the future.'

'I don't take orders from you. You're not even on the payroll.' Drummond raised his fist and hurtled it towards Peter's jaw.

Peter raised his arm to deflect the blow with his left and landed a punch of his own with his right. Drummond staggered back but came towards him again swinging. Peter struck the side of Drummond's head with his full force and followed up with a jab to his stomach. He felt Drummond's gut clench and watched as he staggered backward and collapsed to the ground.

Peter stood over him with his fists clenched. His blood pounded in his ears so loudly it drowned out the sounds of the city around him.

'If I hear you say another lewd word about WPC Harkness, or I have the slightest suspicion that you have putting your hands on her or threatening her in any way, you will regret it.'

'Who says she didn't ask for it?' Drummond asked, wiping a stream of blood from his cheek.

Peter forced himself not to haul Drummond to his feet just for the pleasure of knocking him to the ground once more.

'She does.'

'Are you really going to side with a WPC rather than a real constable?'

'As far as I'm concerned, between the two of you, she is the only real constable. If you give her any more grief, you will wake up bound and gagged in a crate in the belly of a ship headed for somewhere even the merchant navy is afraid to sail.' Peter pivoted on his heel and walked back into the station. He found WPC Harkness seated at her desk gripping the crown of his uniform cap. As he drew closer, she looked up.

'What happened?' she asked.

'Nothing that you need worry about anymore,' Peter said.